ALSO BY KATIE RUGGLE

Fish Out of Water

ROCKY MOUNTAIN SEARCH & RESCUE
Hold Your Breath
Fan the Flames
Gone Too Deep
In Safe Hands

ROCKY MOUNTAIN K9 UNIT
Run to Ground
On the Chase
Survive the Night
Through the Fire

ROCKY MOUNTAIN COWBOYS
Rocky Mountain Cowboy Christmas

ROCKY MOUNTAIN BOUNTY HUNTERS
In Her Sights
Risk It All

BENEATH THE WILD SKY
The Scenic Route
Crossing Paths

Take a Hike

KATIE RUGGLE

sourcebooks
casablanca

Copyright © 2025 by Katie Ruggle
Cover and internal design © 2025 by Sourcebooks
Cover illustration © Carina Guevara
Map art © Travis Hasenour/Sourcebooks

Published by Sourcebooks Casablanca, an imprint of Sourcebooks
1935 Brookdale RD, Naperville, IL 60563-2773
(630) 961-3900
sourcebooks.com

Cataloging-in-Publication Data is on file with the Library of Congress.

Printed and bound in the United States of America.
KP 10 9 8 7 6 5 4 3 2 1

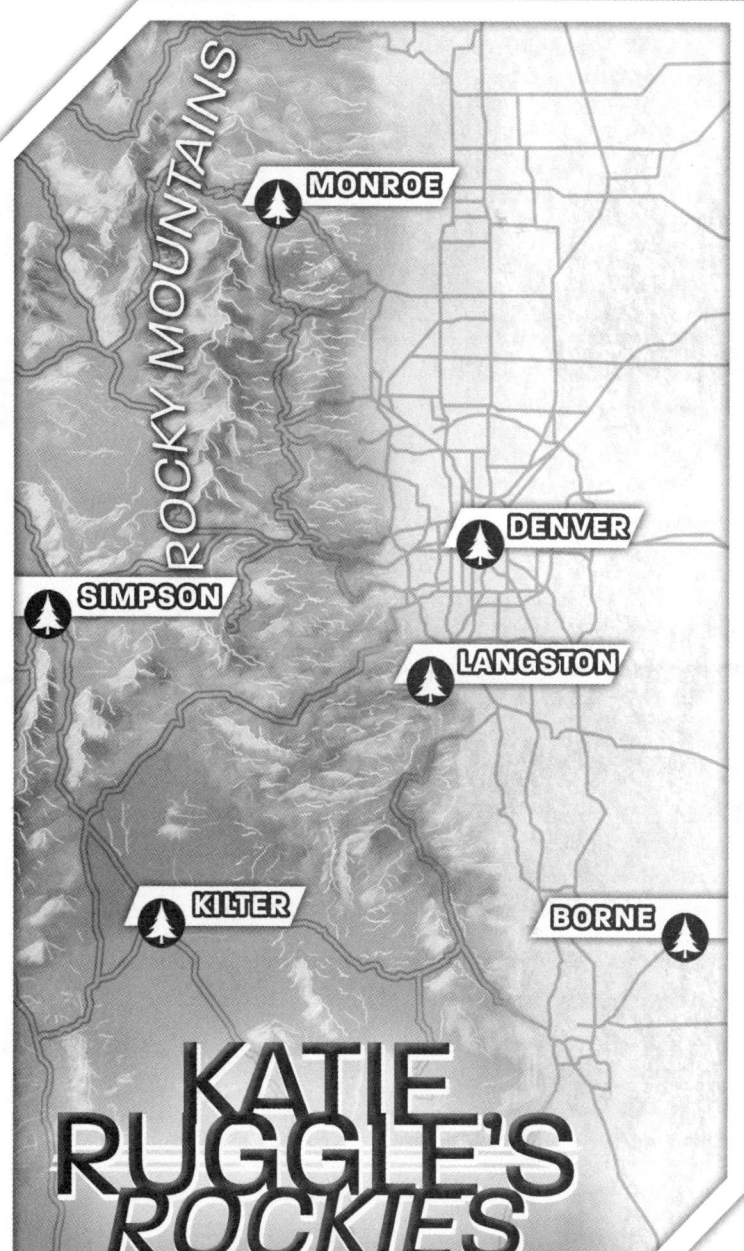

MONROE

ROCKY MOUNTAINS

DENVER

SIMPSON

LANGSTON

KILTER

BORNE

KATIE RUGGLE'S ROCKIES

MEET THE CHARACTERS

Take a Hike is the third book in Katie Ruggle's latest series, Beneath the Wild Sky…but along the way, we get the chance to see some familiar faces. If this is your first time dipping into Ruggle's extended quirky-yet-uniquely-action-packed universe, here's a handy run-through of everyone you'll meet:

LOU & CALLUM FROM *HOLD YOUR BREATH*

Lou, a chatty East Coast transplant determined to make her own way in the Rockies at any cost.

Callum, a taciturn (and charmingly uptight) dive rescue instructor who doesn't know whether he wants to strangle her or kiss her. (Spoiler: He wants to kiss her.)

These opposites attract when Lou stumbles across a headless dead body and begins a mystery that will lead to hijinks, danger, drama, and the formation of a certain murder club.

RORY & IAN FROM *FAN THE FLAMES*

Rory, a highly competent, no-nonsense gun shop owner. Raised by mountain doomsday preppers, Rory knows how to do just about anything but deal with people.

Ian, an almost impossibly hot firefighter struggling to reconcile his criminal background with where he wants to be in life. He's been head over heels in love with Rory since they were children.

These childhood sweethearts have their hands full when the local MC comes calling and strange arsons begin spreading out of control.

ELLIE & GEORGE FROM *GONE TOO DEEP*

Ellie, a sweet city girl with zero survival skills but enough grit to have her going toe-to-toe with the most grizzled survivalist.

George, a towering mountain of a man with a reputation for being something of a gruff hermit…until he falls in love at first sight.

This virgin lumberjack of a hero will do anything to help his heroine survive a trek through the Rockies in search for her father: even if he has to wrestle a bear to protect her.

DAISY & CHRIS FROM *IN SAFE HANDS*

Daisy, a kindhearted woman struggling with agoraphobia who witnesses a crime nobody will believe.

Chris, the devoted best friend who will stand by her side no matter who turns against them as a result.

When Daisy witnesses a leader of the community committing a shocking crime, only her best friend is willing to believe her. But the secret that has kept their mutual spark from truly igniting for years may be enough to end their story before it can ever begin.

MOLLY & JOHN FROM *IN HER SIGHTS*

Molly, the oldest of five sisters, is a bounty hunter by both necessity and choice, keeping her family afloat despite the way people whisper about them.

John, a rival bounty hunter and the biggest pain in her rear. He's always underfoot and getting beneath her skin with that obnoxiously handsome grin and cheeky wink.

When her criminal mother puts up the family home as collateral for her latest legal trouble—and then immediately skips bail *with* the stolen jewels in tow—Molly and her sisters vow to track her down and save the lives they worked so hard for. Too bad Molly's archnemesis is determined to stick by her side every step of the way.

CARA & HENRY FROM *RISK IT ALL*

Cara, one of five bounty hunter sisters, always dreamed of becoming a kindergarten teacher. But if she can bring in a target with a high payout, maybe she can retire from the family business guilt-free.

Henry, the man Cara is determined to bring to justice, is innocent. If only he could convince the beautiful bounty hunter on his trail of that…

When Cara goes after a high-level criminal, she never anticipated him to be so gentle…or so protective of her when the true villains came back for revenge.

FELICITY & BENNETT FROM *THE SCENIC ROUTE*

Felicity, the most driven on her sisters, determined to save her family by finding their criminal mother at all costs.

Bennett, a PI hired to find Felicity's mother, pulled against his will into the sisters' orbit…and under the thrall of the beautiful bounty hunter he's been tailing.

When Felicity Pax realizes a PI is on her tail, she says goodbye to her sisters and leads him on a merry chase up into the Rocky Mountains in a desperate bid to keep him from digging up any dangerous dirt. But when things take a turn for the deadly, Felicity and Bennett find themselves on the same side…and closer than either is willing to admit.

NORAH & DASH FROM *CROSSING PATHS*

Norah, the quietest and most vulnerable of the sisters, is determined to stop playing the victim and learn how to protect those she loves.

Dash, a frightening-looking MMA expert with a secret heart of gold will stop at nothing to protect her.

Tired of watching her sisters face danger while she waits safely behind a computer, Norah seeks out the toughest, gruffest MMA expert she can find to help train her in self-defense… only to realize that as big and scary as Dash seems, he has no defense against her.

PREVIOUSLY...

CHARLIE PAX AND HER FOUR sisters run a bounty-hunting business out of their family home in Langston, Colorado. Business is booming, and all is well until…

Jane Pax, their mom, steals a priceless necklace and skips town…

But not before Jane uses their beloved family home as collateral for her bail bond.

Now, shady bondsman Barney Thompson holds the title to their house, and he's willing to use it to coerce Charlie and her sisters into chasing after dangerous skips for him…

And all the thieves and treasure hunters in town—including Jane's crooked friends—think the necklace is hidden in the sisters' house…

Charlie has been chasing her mom for over a month, but Jane keeps slipping out of her grasp. Now it's just a few days before her first hearing, and if she doesn't show up, Charlie and her sisters are going to lose their home.

Charlie's determined that's not going to happen. She's sick of chasing Jane. Now that she has something her mom wants, the rules of the game have changed.

It's time for Jane to come to Charlie.

PROLOGUE

EVEN THOUGH CHARLIE WAS FINALLY lying in her own bed after spending the majority of the last five weeks fruitlessly chasing after their mom, she couldn't sleep. She frowned at the glow-in-the-dark stars on the ceiling Molly had given her and Cara on their tenth birthday. On her twin's side of the room, the stars were placed neatly, spaced so evenly it was obvious Cara had used a ruler. On her side, Charlie had stuck them on haphazardly, so there were bunches separated by long stretches of plain ceiling.

"It's more astronomically accurate," Charlie muttered out loud. "Nature loves chaos." There was no chance of her words waking Cara, since her sister was spending the night at Henry's. Charlie was happy for her, and she already adored her sister's boyfriend, but after a lifetime of sharing a room with one sister and a house with four, it was just…different.

And the difference made it hard to sleep.

With a huff, Charlie gave up on getting any rest. Flinging

her covers to the side, she slid out of bed. Once in the hallway, she stopped abruptly, realizing she didn't know where she was headed. She wasn't hungry or thirsty, so the kitchen was out. She didn't want to sit in the dark, silent living room either, alone with her thoughts. She was bored.

She eyed the closed door to what had been her mom's room. Now, Fifi and her new husband, Bennett, were using it. A few weeks earlier, their mom had broken in, and Fifi had caught her searching for something in her closet. Norah and Cara had turned the closet inside out after their mom had run again, but they hadn't found anything. Even though she trusted her sisters and knew they were more methodical than Charlie was, she was still tempted to try her luck.

The only problem was that the bedroom was occupied.

Charlie paused, debating whether she should risk going in or if she should play it safe and go back to bed to stare at the ceiling, bored out of her mind.

The answer was easy—Charlie had never played it safe in her life.

Pressing her ear to the door, she heard her sister's deep breathing that meant she was sleeping. Bennett wasn't making a peep, so he was either snoozing uncharacteristically quietly or was awake. Satisfied they weren't in the middle of sexy times— Charlie had interrupted those a few times when the three of them had been on the road, and one time was too many—she eased the door open and peeked inside.

Bennett was indeed awake, watching her with a cocked eyebrow as he held her sleeping sister tenderly against him.

Although Charlie couldn't read his expressions as well as Fifi could, she did know that look—wary curiosity with a touch of humor.

Charlie pointed to the closet, as if that explained her presence—and crept through the shadowed room to the goal. Without moving anything except his eyes, Bennett kept his gaze on her. Easing the door open, she slipped into the closet and closed the door behind her. Once she was shut into the tiny space, she turned on the light.

She knew Norah and Cara had gone over all the walls, ceiling, and floor with a fine-tooth comb, searching for secret cubbies or hidden hiding spaces. Still, she did all of it again, tapping ever so lightly to check for hollow-sounding spots as she ran her fingers over the smooth, painted drywall. As expected, she didn't find anything. The closet was strictly what it was built to be—a small space to hold clothes.

Frowning, Charlie checked everything again. She even unscrewed the light fixture and examined the inside of the wooden door, but still found nothing. Her sisters had cleared out all their mom's clothes and shoes, so there wasn't anything else to search.

Hands on her hips, she glared at the white space. The only reason their mom would've taken the risk of breaking in would be if there was something she needed desperately. There was a slim—very slim—chance that Jane had managed to grab whatever it was between Zach Fridley knocking Fifi unconscious—Charlie silently snarled in fury at that memory—and the rest of the family returning to the house. But it was unlikely. There just wouldn't have been time for Jane to get whatever she needed and also make it over to Mr. Villaneau's *and* convince him to smuggle her out in that minute or two window of opportunity. Charlie was certain whatever it was her mom was after was still there.

Think, think, think. She checked for vents and outlets, but there weren't any. Just blank walls, ceiling, floor, door, rod to hang clothes on… Her gaze snagged on the thick wooden dowel that stretched the length of the closet, and a smile touched her lips. Examining the spot where the rod met the wall, her grin grew. The screws at the top of the mounting were tarnished and old, matching the age of the house…or were they? Charlie knew all of Jane's tricks, including how to make something new look like it'd always been there. She ran the edge of her nail over one of the screw heads. Sure enough, a flake of dull paint peeled off, revealing the shiny silver of a brand-new screw.

She reached for her pocket, but her fingers slid over silky, pocket-less material.

Right, she remembered. *Pajamas.*

Turning off the closet light, she waited a few seconds for her vision to adjust and then stuck her head out the door. Bennett's eyes were still open, so she whispered, "Flathead screwdriver?"

Carefully moving his arm off Fifi, he reached for the bedside table and pulled a multi-tool from the top drawer. In the same motion, he tossed it to Charlie and then immediately resumed cuddling his wife.

She grinned as she caught it. After spending time with Bennett chasing Jane, Charlie knew he was never far from his multi-tool—or an impressively wide array of weapons. Not only did he worship her sister, but he was also a very handy guy to chase skips with. "Thank you," she mouthed before retreating back into the closet.

After turning the light back on, she made quick work of unscrewing the brackets holding the clothes rod in place. It fell toward the floor, but Charlie caught it before it could land with a Fifi-waking clatter. Her heart thumping with excitement, she checked one end—solid—before flipping it around to look at the other side. At first, it looked just like the first end, and her breath left in a huff of disappointment. Upon closer inspection, however, the wood grain didn't quite line up about an inch from the end.

Her triumphant grin returned as she pulled off the cap over the end, revealing a hole drilled into the rod. The opening was a good inch and a half in diameter and two inches deep, the hiding spot just deep enough for the key placed inside.

Feeling like the winner of a treasure hunt, Charlie fished out the key and held it up. It didn't have any identifying marks on it, meaning it could fit in any lock in any building in any town in the country, but she was still optimistic. Their mom had risked coming back to the house, even though she knew her daughters were searching for her. That meant this key was important.

"I'm sick of chasing you, Mom," Charlie whispered, closing her fingers over the very ordinary, yet extremely precious key. "Your turn to come to us."

Anticipation bubbled inside her, and she knew she couldn't keep it to herself. Holding back an excited giggle, she slipped out of the closet. Bennett's eyes narrowed immediately, and he gave her a warning glare promising death if she woke up Fifi.

Giving him her most innocent look, she moved toward the door, reversing at the last second and sprinting toward the bed.

"Charlotte Calamity Pax!" he whisper-yelled, but she just grinned as she pounced, landing on the bed next to her sister.

"Wha?" Fifi's eyes flew open, and she tried to sit up, but Bennett's hold kept her in place long enough for her to realize Charlie had woken her. Relaxing back against him, Fifi gave her sister a glare that matched the one Bennett was giving her. "Charlie, what are you doing? It's the middle of the night! This better be good, or you're going to be doing twice as many burpees as everyone else."

"It's good," Charlie promised, holding up the key.

Fifi tried sitting up again. This time, she managed as Bennett reluctantly released her. "A key? What's it for?"

"That what you were looking for in the closet?" Bennett rumbled, still looking peeved at Charlie for waking his wife.

"I wasn't sure *what* I was looking for, but this was hidden in the clothes rod, so I'm thinking it was what *Mom* was searching for." She dropped the key into Fifi's outstretched hand. "Think she wants it bad enough to come get it?"

Fifi looked up from the key and met Charlie's gaze. "Bait the trap?" she asked, starting to smile.

"Yep." Charlie grinned back at her, feeling a bone-deep satisfaction at the idea of finally, *finally* bringing in their mom. "Let's catch our skip."

ONE

"WHY ARE WE IN THE middle of nowhere again?" Charlie asked, sucking in a breath of thin, chilly air. She was used to living at a high altitude, but this seemed *excessively* high. Ridiculously high. Higher than any town with actual residents should be.

"I'm sick of Mom having the advantage," Felicity said in the overly patient tone she tended to use while explaining the same thing over and over. "She has too many friends in Langston."

Charlie knew she was being annoying. She'd first asked that very question before they'd left home, and then again while they were going over the first pass and her phone lost service. As she peered around the odd little mountain town—and the suspicious-looking residents glared back—she was just having a hard time seeing how being *here* gave them any advantage.

Fifi must've seen her skeptical expression because she gave a secretive little smile. "Just wait until you meet the murder ladies."

"Okay, I am excited about that," Charlie admitted.

Fifi and Bennett had spent some time here recently, and four local women had helped them chase a skip—and investigate the murder of Cobra Jones, a local militia leader. Apparently, the women had done some amateur sleuthing before—enough to dub themselves the Simpson Murder Club. Charlie found it intriguing that such a small town had enough killings to support an actual *murder club*.

She saw a sign for the Black Bear Inn. "Is that the place that kicked you out?"

Felicity was already headed for the coffee shop door, but Bennett gave a short nod.

"Want to burn it down later?" Charlie asked conversationally as she followed her sister into The Coffee Spot.

The corner of Bennett's mouth twitched up in a tiny smile that Charlie took as a definite yes. This was why she liked her new brother-in-law. He understood that no one who hurt Fifi—or any of her sisters—should be allowed to go unpunished. She doubted he was actually down for some arson, but she bet she could talk him into some minor graffiti, possibly an egging. It was also nice to have him in her back pocket as someone who'd help her get rid of a body without giving her a sisterly lecture, if the need arose. Between that and his ever-present multi-tool, he was a handy guy to have around.

Bennett proved his usefulness yet again by holding the door open for her. Charlie gave him an absent nod of thanks as she took in the occupants of the busy shop. There were four acting shifty that she was going to keep her eye on, plus one woman at the counter who looked a little *too* sweet to be authentic. The innocent-looking ones always caused the most trouble when it came down to a tussle.

"Fifi!" The barista's voice filled the coffee shop. "My favorite best friend!"

"I'm sitting *right* here, Lou," the too-innocent-looking woman complained, although she couldn't completely contain a laugh.

"Oops." The barista—who was apparently the famous Lou that Fifi had told them about—attempted to look contrite, but a smile was tugging at the corners of her mouth. "You're my *equally* favorite best friend, Daisy."

"Uh-huh. Nice save." Daisy was having as hard a time holding her mock-offended expression as Lou was. Turning to Felicity, Daisy smiled. "Good to see you again, Fifi." Her gaze moved to Bennett, who'd taken a seat at the counter right next to his wife. "You too, Fifi's stalker-husband."

Charlie laughed. "That's our nickname for him too!" Surging forward, she grabbed the seat between Daisy and Bennett. "I'm Fifi's sister—her *favorite* sister—Charlie."

"Charlotte," Bennett muttered under his breath, making her poke him.

"Char-*lie*." She emphasized the second syllable as Bennett and Fifi snickered, their heads together.

"Don't worry," Lou said as she washed her hands. "I get it. I'm a Louise on all my legal documents."

Charlie gave her a grateful nod before shooting her sister and new brother-in-law a death glare.

Bennett was undeterred. "Charlotte *Calamity*."

Scowling, Charlie said, "I liked it better when you didn't talk."

"Your middle name's Calamity?" Daisy asked. "That's amazing."

"Mom named her perfectly," Fifi agreed.

"Except for the Charlotte part." Charlie made a face. Her full name sounded so proper and not-her.

"I'll help you kneecap anyone who calls you Charlotte," Lou promised.

Sending a sideways smirk toward Bennett, who'd suddenly sobered, Charlie gave Lou a grateful nod. "I knew I'd like you."

"Ditto." Lou extended her fist, and Charlie bumped it.

"Okay, down to business," Fifi said, and Lou and Daisy leaned closer, their eyes alight with interest.

"Yes, tell us everything." Lou leaned on her forearms, close enough to Fifi that she could keep her voice low. "You were *extremely* and unhelpfully vague on the phone. Who's your latest skip? How can we help?"

"Our mom," Fifi said.

Before she could elaborate, Lou jumped in again. "Your mom? She's here?"

"Not yet." Charlie grinned, pulling out the key she'd found in her mom's closet. "But she will be."

The door jangled as a customer entered. Charlie glanced over automatically at the sound, closing her fingers protectively around the key, but then she did a double take. The man striding toward them was out-of-this-world gorgeous—all muscles and bad attitude, wrapped in a black "Field County

Fire Department" T-shirt. His thickly lashed blue eyes stood out dramatically against his tan skin and black-as-night hair, his gaze spitting fire and ill-temper at everyone in the shop.

"Holy moly," Charlie muttered, resisting the urge to fan herself.

"You're not kidding," Lou said just as quietly. "Here comes trouble." Straightening, she put on a customer-service smile. "Hey, Kieran. What can I get you?"

In response, he thrust a sheet of paper at her. Lou stared at the list with such a horrified expression that Charlie was intrigued.

"What is it?" She craned her neck, trying to read what was on the paper. "A robbery note?"

Kieran snapped his head to the side so he could pin her with the full force of his glare. Unfortunately for him, she wasn't easily pinned—especially when she was curious. Popping up onto the counter, she pivoted around on her butt so she could swing her legs over and hop down next to Lou, who stared at her with envy.

"You made that look so easy," Lou complained, the note forgotten in her hand. "I've attempted jumping over the counter during customer lulls, and it's always ended in tears and/or broken things."

"I'll coach you," Charlie promised, tugging the paper out of Lou's grip. Running her gaze over the scribbles, she frowned. "This is just a coffee order."

"A *big* coffee order," Lou corrected, a note of tragedy entering her voice. "A *humungous* coffee order. What is this?" Glaring at Kieran, she pinched the paper, pulling it from Charlie's grip and holding it away from her like it smelled.

"Coffee maker at the station broke." Kieran's voice sounded like he gargled with whisky and broken glass every morning, and the baritone rasp sent a funny little shiver down Charlie's spine. Cocking her head, she eyed the firefighter curiously, trying to figure out why the grumpy, muscly guy had caught her attention. She was used to hanging out with cranky, hot guys since her sisters—except for Molly—seemed to share a type. Despite this, Kieran was…intriguing.

He met her gaze and dialed his glare up to eleven, and Charlie started to grin. He was so cranky and delicious—who knew that the mountains held such a delight? His scowl shifted to bafflement as their stare-off continued, and he seemed almost relieved when he turned his attention to a wilting Lou.

"This is going to take *hours*," Lou warned. "Am I going to have a horde of caffeine-deprived, ill-tempered firefighters descending on me in fifteen minutes, demanding their beverage of choice? Because listening to those drama queens whine is not going to work for me."

Kieran gave an audible huff and yanked out his phone, stabbing at the screen like it was the cause of all his woes. Charlie realized that she was leaning closer to where he stood on the other side of the counter. There was something about the guy that made her want to push all his buttons.

"They won't come here," he barked in that raspy voice before meeting Charlie's gaze again. "What?" His glare was a challenge, one she was all too happy to meet.

"You're mesmerizing," she said, unable to stop smiling at him. She hadn't expected to be so entertained in this tiny town, and finding someone new who reacted so dramatically to her teasing delighted her. Her sisters—and most everyone who knew her, honestly—had learned to ignore the more outrageous things that came out of her mouth, but here was a gorgeous firefighter whose temper flared higher with each of her quips. It was *exhilarating*.

He managed to hold on to his scowl, but Charlie could tell it was an effort, which only made her grin widen. She knew her dimples were in full effect, giving her an innocent, sweet appearance that her twin Cara deserved but Charlie absolutely did not.

"Tell me you're featured front and center in the local fire-fighter calendar."

"Nope," Lou said absently, already organizing empty cups in an assembly-line fashion. "He refuses. There was even a petition with eighty-seven signatures demanding that he participate, but nope. He wasn't swayed by community pressure—and that sort of petition doesn't have any legal weight, unfortunately."

"Hmm…" Charlie hummed, her eyes on his torso, making it obvious she was mentally peeling off his shirt. From that five-o'clock shadow, she was guessing he had a nicely furred, werewolf-esque chest.

"Was that a murder-club petition?" Fifi asked, hiding her laughter very poorly. Even Bennett was snickering.

"Of course not." Daisy looked a bit offended. "We don't bother with non-death issues like that."

"Only what the local militia is called." Fifi gave her a pointed look.

"Right." Daisy didn't seem at all bothered by the reminder. "That's a matter of local pride. A name like Freedom Survivors reflects poorly on the whole town." For some reason, she gave a startled little jump and shot Kieran a look that seemed almost… guilty? Charlie tucked it away in the mental file she'd just created on the grumpy firefighter. Since she was still focused on Kieran, she saw his expression shift from a flash of pain back to his usual scowl.

"It does," Fifi said, "but it's also a matter of local pride to have the objectively hottest firefighters in the calendar." Bennett gave a wordless, displeased grumble, and Fifi patted his arm. "If you were a firefighter, I'd campaign to have you be Mr. June." He flushed a little but couldn't hide his pleasure at that.

"Very true—about the local pride thing, not the stalker-husband-as-Mr.-June thing," Lou said as she steamed milk. "I have no opinion on the latter, so don't choke me out, Fifi. Plus the more calendars that sell, the more money Fire gets. It's a civic-improvement issue."

Charlie was loving the play of confused emotions passing over Kieran's face. She saw the point where he decided he was definitely finished with the conversation.

"I'll wait in my truck," he growled at Lou, turning on his heel and blasting out of the shop before anyone could respond. Everyone left at the counter exchanged glances before breaking into laughter.

"What's his deal?" Charlie asked, keeping her question

vague in the hope that Lou and Daisy would tell her absolutely everything about this angry and extra-handsome firefighter. She was already hoping she'd run into him again so she could poke the bear some more. He seemed like the best bet to keeping herself entertained while they were stuck in this tiny, sleepy town.

To her surprise, Fifi spoke first. "Well, his dad was one of the Freedom Survivors."

"Oops!" If Lou hadn't had lids in her hands, Charlie had a feeling she would've been covering her mouth as she tried to take back words she'd already said. "I completely forgot about the militia connection. In retrospect, that was kind of an awkward topic of conversation, wasn't it?"

Daisy let her head drop to the counter, connecting with a gentle *thud*. "Sooo awkward. I have retroactive embarrassment."

Charlie started to laugh. "No wonder he looked so taken aback. I figured it was just the firefighter centerfold thing."

"No, it was that his dad tried to kidnap me," Fifi said, and Charlie immediately sobered. When her sister and Bennett had last been in Simpson chasing a skip who'd holed up with the local militia, they'd gotten on the bad side of Clint, the Freedom Survivors' new leader, and Finn, a firefighter who'd secretly also been a militia member and, apparently, Kieran's dad. When Fifi and Bennett had started investigating Cobra's murder—with Clint as their main suspect—Finn and Clint had gone so far as to kidnap Fifi. They'd soon regretted that decision, thanks to the ass-kicking Fifi and Bennett had handed out before the two militia members were arrested.

"Was Kieran involved in all that?" she asked, tensing, even

as she tried to figure out why she cared so much. He was a stranger—an extremely hot, very cranky stranger. She might've enjoyed teasing him, but it was no skin off her nose if he was a militia weirdo. If he'd been involved in Fifi's kidnapping though…it didn't matter how hot or entertaining the guy was. Charlie would get her revenge. Her stomach squeezed at the thought, though, as she waited for their answer.

The only problem was that they weren't answering. Instead, the two Simpson residents and even Fifi and Bennett were exchanging looks that Charlie translated to mean that they weren't sure how much to share. Charlie hated not having information—especially when other people had it—especially, *especially* when her sisters knew and she didn't. "*Well?*" she prompted.

"No idea," Lou was the one who answered. "He says he wasn't involved—didn't even know that his dad was. Apparently the cops believe him—or don't have enough evidence to prove he's lying—because he hasn't been arrested or even been forced out of his job with Fire."

"Is he local?" Charlie asked, pocketing the key and washing her hands. Once they were clean and dry, she started putting lids and sleeves on the coffees Lou had finished.

"Thank you," Lou said gratefully. "Watch out, because I might kiss you on the mouth for helping with this monstrous order. The Byrnes have lived here for a while at least, but I'm not a local. Daisy?"

She looked thoughtful. "I vaguely remember Kieran in school—he was several years older than me—but other than that…" She shrugged.

"Daisy was a homebody," Lou explained, making Daisy give a crack of laughter.

"Home*bound*," Daisy corrected, although she looked amused by Lou's downplaying. "I'm agoraphobic. I've just been leaving the house again for a couple of years."

"Really?" Charlie was distracted from their Kieran discussion. "So you stayed home your whole life until just a few years ago?"

Daisy shook her head. "It didn't get bad until I was sixteen," she explained. Tension had crept into her words and expression, so Charlie changed the subject.

"Back to Kieran—what's the gossip? Is he married? Kids? Do you believe him that he didn't know about his dad's involvement?" Charlie asked. She wasn't sure why she wanted to know more about the man, but she'd never been good at suppressing her curiosity. "Could he be one of the Freedom Survivors?"

"No wife, kids, girlfriend, or boyfriend that I know of," Lou said easily, although she slid Charlie a sideways glance. "Hot, isn't he?"

"Objectively, yes." Even as the word left her mouth, Charlie knew she wasn't fooling anyone. When the other women burst into laughter, it just confirmed it. She gave them all a mock glare. "Fine. He's *subjectively* hot as well—as long as he didn't help kidnap Fifi. Grumpy, but hot."

"It's a type," Daisy said, lifting her eyebrows meaningfully at Lou, who grinned at her over the drink she was making.

"It is a type," Lou agreed. "A very, very, *very* attractive type."

"Oh." Charlie's stomach took a disappointed dive down to

her toes. It'd feel strange to continue to poke at him if he were Lou's. "You and he…?"

Lou actually put down the milk she was steaming so she could raise her hands, palms out, as if stopping traffic. "Oh no. I have my own hot-but-surly specimen, and one high-maintenance, protective grump is plenty. Kieran is all yours." Giving Charlie a magnanimous smile, she picked up the milk again.

"So Charlie…" Fifi's tone was smug. "Remember all the stalker-husband jokes you made?"

"What jokes?" Charlie asked innocently, trying to channel her angelic twin as she applied herself to capping and sleeving the cups Lou had filled. "He was a stalker—self-professed, I might add—and now he's your husband. Voilà—stalker-husband. It's less of an insult and more of a recap of your relationship."

Fifi snorted, but Lou interrupted before she could argue. "As fascinating as this is, I want to know more about that key. What does it unlock, and why does your mom want it so badly?" After a short pause, she continued, "I guess the answer to the first one will also be the answer to the second, so answer the first one first."

Charlie blinked at her.

"Sorry." Lou thrust a mocha with whip at her. "Huge orders stress me out, and that makes me less coherent than normal."

Making an understanding sound, Charlie accepted the drink and added a cap and a sleeve. "We don't know the answer to either question, actually. All we know is that this key is important to Mom, and she was willing to risk going back to jail to get her hands on it."

"Oh," Lou said. "That's…not the thrilling tale I expected."

Charlie shrugged as well as she could with her hands full.

"How will she know you have the key—or that you're here?" Daisy asked.

Grinning, Charlie pointed a coffee stirrer at her. "That was the fun part."

"Fun for you, maybe," Fifi complained. "I hate Dutch's—and so does everyone else except for you."

"It's always exciting there," Charlie said with a warm glow starting in her stomach as she thought about the brawls and deals that'd gone down at Dutch's. "Fights, bets, skips galore—what's not to love?"

"Dutch's," chorused Fifi and Bennett—the latter who'd been in the bar a grand total of *one* time.

"Who is Dutch, and what does he have to do with your mom knowing the key is here?" Lou asked, making a latte without even looking down at it. Instead, her fascinated gaze was fixed on Charlie and Fifi.

"Wellllll," Charlie drew out suspense, wanting to laugh at the way the others leaned closer, as if she were a snake charmer and they were her mesmerized serpents. "We all went to Dutch's—which is a dive bar, by the way—last night and—"

"We *all* did?" Fifi rested her chin on her fist, a smile quivering at the corners of her mouth.

Charlie gave a hoot of laughter. "That's right! I almost forgot the best part. Norah wasn't allowed in—*Norah*!" She laughed again at the memory before noticing that everyone who wasn't related to her was looking puzzled. "Sorry, Norah's our most rule-abiding, cautious sister. I still can't believe she got banned from Dutch's. Even *Molly* didn't get banned, and she got the place blown up."

"I need to hear that story immediately," Lou breathed.

"Watch that coffee—you're about to have very hot toes."

Lou glanced down at what her hands were doing and readjusted so the coffee went into the cup rather than on her feet. "Oops—thanks. Now tell me about your sister blowing up a bar."

"Nope," Daisy interrupted. "We need to stay on track. Tell us about last night."

"Way to focus, Daisy," Charlie said approvingly as she mentally switched gears. "After Norah was banned…" She couldn't contain another chuckle. "Norah was banned" was not a phrase Charlie ever thought she'd say, unless it was from an Extroverts Anonymous meeting or something. "Sorry, I just can't get over that. Anyway, the rest of us non-banned Paxes and Pax accessories"—she gestured toward Bennett, who tipped his chin in acceptance of the term—"got a booth at Dutch's and proceeded to talk very loudly about the key we found. Both Dane Sanders *and* Eddie Cord were there, so they're sure to have texted Jane that bit of info."

"Who are they?" Daisy asked.

"Zach Fridley's minions." When Lou and Daisy continued looking blank, Charlie elaborated. "Zach's in prison now, but up until recently, he was Jane's literal partner in crime."

"Ooh," Lou and Daisy chorused.

"But how will your mom know to come to Simpson to find you?" Lou asked.

"We had no less than five tails on our drive from Langston to Simpson," Fifi said, and then patted Bennett's arm. "B did a fantastic job of driving, so we didn't lose even one of them." Bennett accepted his wife's praise with a tiny, pleased smile and a kiss on Fifi's temple.

"He did great," Charlie added, knowing there would've been no way she could've driven that slow the entire way up the mountain. Plan or no plan, she would've left the tails in her dust by the time they'd reached the outskirts of Langston. Bennett turned that small smile on her but left off the temple kiss, to Charlie's relief. As much as she liked her new brother-in-law, she barely hugged her own sisters. Physical affection made her feel squirmy.

Lou paused putting all the firefighters' drinks in carriers and rushed to look out the window. "Where are your tails hiding?" she asked.

With a shrug, Charlie took over readying the cups for travel. "Who knows? Four of the five aren't too bright, so you'll probably see them around town, peeking out from behind rocks and trees and road signs. The one to watch out for is Rhys Erie."

Fifi straightened from her spot cuddled against Bennett's side, worry creasing the skin between her eyebrows. "You spotted Rhys following us? He must be slipping."

"Yep, I saw his green Jeep with the crooked license plate. Barely a glimpse though, so just a minor slip-up."

"Ugh." Fifi gave a full-body shudder. "Jeeps."

Charlie tilted her head, eyeing her sister as Bennett wrapped an arm around Fifi, as if he was going to protect her from her hatred of a random car brand. "You know that's a really strange aversion to have, right?"

Fifi just shuddered again as she waved off Charlie's comment. "Rhys will bear watching."

"On it," chorused everyone in the coffee shop except for Fifi.

With a laugh, Charlie moved the now-full drink carriers to the counter. Giving up looking for the treasure hunters, Lou grabbed a couple and headed for the door. Without discussing it, Daisy, Fifi, and Bennett all picked up two each and followed Lou out to the parking lot.

Charlie frowned when she saw all the drinks were gone before grabbing a handful of napkins. If there wasn't an actual reason for her to go out to Kieran's car, she'd make one up. Sliding over the counter, she charged through the door after the others. She wasn't about to give up the opportunity to poke at Kieran as he scowled at her. Just the thought made her grin as she stepped out into the fall sunshine.

Kieran was already backing his truck out of the parking spot, and Charlie hurled herself toward the passenger window, managing to wedge her upper body inside before he could escape. He slammed on the brakes and—she waited for it, almost trembling with anticipation—scowled.

"There it is!" Laughing triumphantly, she tucked her handful of excuse-napkins between a few of the drinks.

"Get. Off. My. Truck." It sounded as if each word was forced between gritted teeth.

"Answer a question for me first."

"No."

Charlie gave him her best innocent puppy-dog eyes, a look she'd learned from Cara but that Fifi had helped her perfect. "Please? Just one?"

He turned his frown up to the ferocious setting, but it just made her smile wider. When she didn't move, they stared at each other for what felt like an eternity. His black-fringed eyes were as light and cold as ice, and she wanted to stare at him forever. The thought jolted her, and she ducked her head, dropping his gaze. Kicking herself for losing their stare-down, she was about to remove herself from his truck when he spoke—well, more like snarled. "Fine."

Her gaze shot back to his, surprised hope flaring inside her. "Really?"

When he growled, she beamed at him.

"Which one of these coffee orders is yours?" She gestured at the sea of cups covering almost every surface in his truck.

He actually looked surprised at her choice of question, but then his scowl returned. His fingers tightened on the steering wheel, his knuckles turning pale, and Charlie had a feeling he was about to drive away with her hanging halfway in and halfway out the window. Instead, he grumbled, "Mocha, extra whip. Now get off."

"Good chat. Let's do it again soon." A deal was a deal, so she jumped down, despite wishing she could go on staring at that hewn-from-rock face of his. "See you around!"

She was pretty sure he muttered, "Not if I see you first. Back up."

Charlie glanced down at herself, noting that she was already well clear of his truck. He wasn't moving, though, so she shrugged and took a giant step back. His scowl didn't lighten, but he gave a tiny, tight nod before his truck's engine roared and he shot backward, shifted into drive, and then peeled out onto the road.

He immediately braked hard again, stopping abruptly in the middle of the road. Charlie craned her neck to see why he'd stopped so suddenly and saw a red squirrel scurry into the road, pausing right in front of Kieran's truck to flick its tail before continuing across. Kieran waited until the squirrel had reached the safety of a scrubby evergreen before the truck rolled forward again.

"Oh, he's fun," Charlie said, beaming as she watched the back of the pickup grow smaller. *And sweet*, her brain added, touched by how careful he'd been not to hit the squirrel. He'd been cautious with her too, making sure she wasn't anywhere near his truck before he'd backed out of his parking space. Apparently, Kieran liked her almost as much as he liked a random squirrel. The thought wasn't as lowering as she would've expected.

Fifi snorted. "And you say I'm weird."

"I've never said you're weird." Charlie faced her sister once Kieran turned the corner and disappeared from sight. "I said your random hatred of a certain vehicle is weird. Otherwise, you're almost disturbingly normal." She saw a flicker of movement in her periphery and glanced over her shoulder. "Hey, Dave! How's the treasure-hunting business going?"

"Good?" a sheepish voice came from behind the coffee shop's dumpster.

"Glad to hear it." Turning back to Fifi and Bennett, she asked, "Ready to go check into our honeymoon suite?"

"Murder club meeting at seven tonight," Lou called over her shoulder as she opened the coffee shop door.

"At the gym?" Fifi asked.

"Nope, here." Lou gestured at the building as if it were a game-show prize. "I told the owner my civic improvement group needed a place to meet, and she said we could use it."

"Civic improvement?" Daisy repeated.

"Where's the lie?" Lou asked, and the others looked at each other and shrugged.

A car pulled into the lot, and everyone stared suspiciously as it rolled into a parking spot, making Lou laugh. "Guys, guys—it's a customer."

"Oh," Charlie said, easing up on her deadly-laser glare. "Oops."

"Off you go," Lou ordered. "Don't want you scaring off the customers."

"Since when?" Fifi asked. "I seem to remember—"

"La-la-la, can't hear you!" Lou turned toward the woman who was warily approaching the door that Lou still blocked. "Hi, Mavis. Sorry about all the weird looks we were giving you. We're uh…practicing for a play."

"Oh!" The woman sounded much too interested. "A play? Can anyone audition?"

Giving them a *help me* look over Mavis's head, Lou continued improvising. "It's already cast, sorry. I can sign you up on the Simpson Drama Club email list if you like though."

The door swung closed behind Lou and Mavis.

"Lou's going to have to start a drama club *and* put on a play now, isn't she?" Charlie asked, torn between amusement and horror at all the work in Lou's future.

"Yep," Fifi said matter-of-factly.

They were all quiet for a moment of sympathy before shaking it off.

"Need a ride?" Charlie asked Daisy.

"No thanks." Daisy headed for the coffee shop door. "I still have forty-five minutes before I need to be at the gym, and I'm going to use every one of them watching Lou dig her drama-club-sized hole even bigger."

Charlie laughed. "Enjoy." Turning to Bennett and Fifi, she asked, "Honeymoon-suite time?"

"You do know you're not actually going to be staying in the honeymoon suite with us, right?" Fifi asked, looking amused.

"I'm not?" Charlie put on her best shocked face. "Why not? Bennett knew when he married you that we were a package deal."

"No, I didn't."

At Bennett's interjection, Charlie turned to him. "Well, you should've assumed it. Fifi and I go *everywhere* together—trashy motels, dark back alleys, *honeymoon suites...*" She gave him a meaningful look, but he just sent his best deadpan stare in response.

"He called you 'Charlotte' up until after we were married. I doubt he had any idea what he was getting himself into," Fifi said, heading for the left front seat. "You don't mind if I drive, do you, honey? You know I love these curvy mountain roads." Her smile—and his return one—were full of secret meaning.

"Hmm…" Charlie frowned at Bennett in mock concern. "You're going to have to step up your game when it comes to background checks on the women you stalk."

"Woman," Bennett said, finally tearing his gaze from his wife.

"What? And shotgun." Charlie quickly slid into the front seat before Bennett could take it.

"I don't stalk 'women.' Just one woman." Leaning into Fifi's open window, he kissed her before getting into the back seat without complaint.

Charlie twisted around so she could eye him doubtfully. "Isn't your job basically stalking people? So approximately fifty percent of the time, you're stalking women professionally."

"*Investigating*," Bennett corrected her. "I *investigate* people, and it's more like seventy-two percent men."

"Makes sense." Turning back around, Charlie looked around with interest as Fifi drove through town. "Guys do tend to do shady things more often."

His grunt could've been agreement or disagreement, but Charlie decided to believe he supported her theory. They'd already reached the edge of Simpson, and the road curved up and to the left. Eyeing it, Charlie started to smile.

"So, Fifi," she said without taking her gaze off the rocky cliff rising next to the right side of the road. "Let's see why you like driving these mountain roads so much."

Giving Charlie a grin, Fifi took off like a shot.

"Woo-hoo!" Charlie yelled, excitement thrumming in her chest. Looking over her shoulder, she saw that even Bennett was grinning. "Your wife knows how to have a good time."

"I know," he said proudly.

TWO

"Now I know how a goldfish feels," Charlie muttered, looking at the coffee shop glass door and window. Even though it was only seven o'clock, it was pitch-dark outside. "Don't you have any blinds or shades?"

"Isn't the darkness unsettling?" Lou pushed a table against another, adding to the four she'd already mashed into one big table. "Just imagining someone out there, watching us, running their fingers over a freshly sharpened machete…"

Charlie stared at her. "That just made the creepiness seventeen times worse."

With a laugh, Lou walked to the door and pulled down the shade. "I convinced the owner to install these after my house was burned down. She's kind of cheap, so I used my tragedy strategically."

"Your house was burned down?" Charlie asked with interest as she walked over to the window and pulled down the shade, unable to stand even a few more seconds of being so exposed. "Vindictive ex-husband?"

Lou cocked her head as she studied Charlie. "Despite the statistics that say it's always the husband, I actually wasn't married at any time to the arsonist—although I *did* have a vindictive ex-sort-of-boyfriend who tried to kill me and Callum. Different attempted murder though—he wasn't the one who burned down my cabin."

"You live a very interesting life."

"That's not always a good thing." Lou grimaced at a memory, but a knock on the now-covered door snapped her out of her reflections.

As she bounced over to unlock it, Charlie frowned. "Now that the shade's down, we can't see who's at the door. It's like the Catch-22 of window coverings."

Although Lou laughed, she did pull the shade over enough so she could see outside. "George, Ellie, and the little peanut. We're safe—for now."

Lou unlocked the door, allowing a dark-haired woman and a yeti-sized man carrying a toddler into the empty coffee shop.

"Charlie, this is Ellie, George, and the most adorable baby ever, Mila." Lou held her hands out to the little girl, who lunged for her. As she scooped up Mila, Lou said over her shoulder, "I have to take advantage of all the snuggle time I can get before Callum arrives."

"Callum?" Mila said hopefully, looking around.

"See?" Lou laughed. "I can't even blame her for it. Callum's the best."

"That's up for debate," Ellie said, with an adoring glance at her super-sized husband, who gave her a tiny secret smile back. "I think George's been awarded the title already."

"I have a feeling no one's going to win this argument," Charlie interrupted before Lou could counter. She resigned herself to being around even more lovey-dovey people—as if all the Fifi and Bennett mushiness wasn't enough. "I'm Charlie, Fifi's sister."

"Nice to meet you," Ellie said with a sincere smile. "Where are Fifi and Bennett?"

"I've learned while traveling with the two of them that letting them have lots of couple time really cuts down on the PDA." She made a gagging face but couldn't hold it without laughing. "They should be here soon—unless they decide to never leave the honeymoon suite, and then it's up to us to pull this off."

Daisy arrived with her sheriff deputy husband, Chris, followed by a serious-faced woman and objectively hot man both wearing T-shirts matching the one sexy Kieran had on earlier. The two were introduced as Rory and Ian, and Charlie immediately pounced.

"Did the fire station get your coffee maker fixed?" she asked.

"No." Rory frowned. "Everyone at the station is really cranky."

"What about all the coffees I made?" Lou protested.

Ian gave her a level look. "I don't think you understand how much coffee the average firefighter drinks."

Unable to think of an unsuspicious segue, Charlie just jumped right in with the question she was dying to ask. If he'd just been another hot and grumpy guy, she could've easily dismissed him from her mind, but the way he'd been so careful not to harm her or that squirrel kept replaying in her brain. "Kieran Byrne—what's up with him?"

Rory blinked at her, looking confused, but Ian smirked. The expression immediately elevated him to supermodel-hotness levels.

"Your husband is really hot," she told Rory honestly.

"I know."

"Just objectively hot," Charlie quickly amended, even though Rory hadn't seemed at all offended or jealous at her statement. "I don't find him subjectively hot at all."

"Really?" Rory gave Charlie a doubtful look before studying her husband. "How can you not find him subjectively hot?"

Grinning at his wife, Ian gave her a smoldering look that promised Rory even more hotness later before turning back to Charlie. "Do you find Kieran subjectively hot?"

"Of course." She didn't see any reason to lie about it. "Don't you?"

Before Ian could answer, Fifi and Bennett arrived, so Lou immediately called the murder club meeting to order.

"I have a question," Charlie said as soon as everyone was settled in chairs around the amalgam of tables. "Is the murder club an actual thing here? Do you meet regularly to solve murders? And, if so, why are there so many people getting killed? I mean, the town's not that big. A pretty significant portion of the population has to be getting axed for you to have a steady supply of murders for your club."

Lou laughed. "We've only had what—two murders? At least since I've moved here. So no to the regular meetings."

"Three," Daisy corrected. "My dead body, remember?"

"Right! Thanks, Dais."

Charlie met Fifi's eyes and raised an eyebrow. Answers from the murder club seemed to lead to more questions. "Um…you had your own personal dead body, Daisy?"

"Oh no." She waved a hand, as if Charlie had given her credit for something Daisy hadn't actually accomplished. "I just saw the dead body being moved. It wasn't really mine."

"We've had quite a few *attempted* murders though," Ellie said, and everyone made agreeing sounds—except for George and Bennett. They were, apparently, having a competition to see whose face was the poker-iest.

"This area does have an unusually high crime rate," Chris said. "And these four"—he pointed at Lou, Daisy, Rory, and Ellie—"always seem to end up in the middle of whatever investigation's going on. Not sure when they formed an official murder club though."

"Oookay." Charlie drew out the word, intensely curious about so many things they'd said, but also knowing she had to focus on the topic at hand. "Putting aside all the dead bodies, arson, attempted murder—am I missing anything?"

"Assault."

"Burglary."

"Theft."

"Stalking."

"Improper use of the 911 system."

"Dog theft." That last one led to a round of laughter, which Charlie thought was a touch sociopathic.

"Oh no, it's not like that." Ellie must've seen her and Fifi's expressions, because she hurried to reassure them. "*We* stole the dogs. Puppies, actually. They weren't being cared for properly, but now they're all fat and happy and spoiled."

At the explanation, Charlie relaxed a little. "Good. Okay, so speaking of an exorbitant amount of crime-ing, should we talk about our mom?"

Fifi was the only one who laughed at that, but Charlie didn't mind. She was used to people not getting her jokes. The others nodded in agreement, though, so she held up the key she had been carrying on her at all times since she'd pulled it out of her mom's closet rod.

"Our mom, Jane Pax, wants this key. We've made sure she'll hear that we've found it, plus we led five treasure hunters to your little town, so word'll get out about where we are too."

Chris cleared his throat. "Five treasure hunters? I counted four."

"Behind the dumpster, under the southeast evergreen, inside the VW Fox parked in front of the bank, and next to the taxidermy shop/liquor store's propane tank," Callum reeled off, and Chris gave a nod as he held up four fingers.

"You'll have to look harder for Rhys," Charlie said, feeling a little guilty for bringing the treasure hunters to Simpson. Because of that twinge, she offered them a tip. "He likes height. Check trees and rooftops."

"Sorry for leading those guys here," Fifi said, as if she'd read

Charlie's mind. "They likely won't cause any trouble and should clear out as soon as we do."

"Don't worry about it," Lou said. "It's like a live-action *Where's Waldo*."

"What's the timeline on this?" Callum asked, apparently not as entertained as his wife by the sudden influx of criminals.

Charlie met Fifi's gaze again and had a short, silent conversation via expressions. "Two days, if we're lucky," she finally answered. "If it takes five, we're pretty much screwed. Mom's first court date is in four days."

"So what do you need from us?" Ellie asked, and Charlie grinned at her before looking over at her sister.

"I'm starting to get why you like this town," she said. "Where else would we find such a helpful murder club?"

————

The meeting lasted an hour, and people gradually left until just Lou, Charlie, Fifi, and Bennett remained in the coffee shop. Ian and Rory headed out with a fresh supply of coffee for the night-shift firefighters, and Callum mentioned needing to stop by the station quickly.

"He's just going to search for that last treasure hunter," Lou said after her husband had left. "I know that was driving him crazy."

"He shouldn't feel bad." Charlie carefully zipped the key into her pocket. "Rhys is the stealthiest of that bunch."

"Thanks for hosting, Lou," Fifi said, standing up and stretching.

"No problem. I would've had us meet at our place, but Callum's having the kitchen remodeled, so everything is everywhere. I'm tempted to join you guys in the honeymoon suite."

"Even *I'm* not allowed in the honeymoon suite," Charlie mock-complained, tossing a balled-up Post-it note at her sister. Bennett caught the paper before it could hit its target and then launched it into the recycling bin across the room. When the paper ball dropped into the bin, Charlie gave her brother-in-law an approving nod. "Smooth."

Bennett grinned, looking disarmingly pleased for a second before his usual stoic mask dropped into place.

"Feel free to take off," Lou said, starting to pull one of the tables back to its original spot.

"We'll help you clean up." Fifi grabbed the other side of the table, and the two women moved it across the room to its original spot. Bennett lifted a table by himself, being a burly strongman type, and Charlie followed him with two chairs. Once the shop was back to how it looked earlier in the day before the murder club meeting, the room felt silent…well, *almost* silent.

"What's that buzzing?" Charlie asked. She'd watched a video about murder hornets a few nights earlier when she couldn't sleep, and her brain instantly went into killer-insect mode.

The other three stood still and listened for a moment.

"Drill," Bennett stated.

"Phew," Charlie said. "I thought murder hornets at first— wait…why is someone drilling right now?"

"And *what* are they drilling?" Fifi asked.

"It sounds like they're right outside." Lou's eyes went wide.

With an audible inhale, she lunged for the locked door, the other three close behind her. Lou fumbled with her keys for a second before shoving it into the lock.

"Wait!" Fifi and Bennett chorused.

For once not taking the opportunity to make a joke about the way her sister and her new husband acted more like twins than she and Cara—her *actual* twin—did, Charlie eased the shade to the side so she could peer out into the darkness. The buzzing had stopped, but there was something across the front of the door that hadn't been there an hour earlier—or even ten minutes earlier, when Callum had left.

"What is that?" she asked, peering around again, looking for whoever had been making the noise.

"What's what?" Lou wedged her face next to Charlie's so she could see outside. "Oh, that's what. That doesn't look good."

"What doesn't?" Fifi asked, trying to get a glimpse through the gap Charlie had made.

With an irritated grumble, Bennett reached past their heads and snapped up the shade so the entire door was revealed. Halfway up, a two-by-six board was now spanning the width of the door.

"Is that…?" Lou unlocked the door and tried to shove it open. The door didn't budge, the board holding it shut. "I guess it is. Why would someone bar the door?"

Only very bad reasons to block the door immediately struck Charlie.

"Back door," she said, turning to see that Fifi and Bennett were already charging toward the counter and the employees-only hallway behind it. Rather than go around, Bennett, Fifi, and Charlie all vaulted over the counter.

"Can *everyone* except me do that?" Lou grumbled as she ran for the opening instead. Charlie waited for her to catch up before chasing after Fifi. By the time she reached the back door, Bennett was already slamming his body against it. The door shook in its frame, but it didn't open.

"This one too?" Lou asked, her attention on her phone.

"Looks like," Fifi said grimly. "Are you calling 911?"

Lou shook her head, her fingers flying over her phone screen. "Texting Callum. He has tools in his truck, a radio, and a quicker response time."

A familiar smell drifted to Charlie. "Tell him to hurry—and to give his firefighter buddies a shout."

"Is this really the time to finagle another meeting with your crush?" Fifi asked, obviously trying to keep her voice calm and light. As soon as the words were out, she paled, and Charlie knew her sister had caught a whiff of what Charlie had just smelled. "Oh no."

"Is that…?" Lou inhaled. "Yep, that's smoke."

Even as she spoke, the air around them got hazy, and Charlie felt heat radiating from the outside wall. Reaching out, she touched it and then immediately pulled her hand back, shaking away the sting. "The wall's hot."

Fifi reached toward the painted surface, stopping a foot away, and gave her a scolding look. "Why would you touch that? I can feel the heat radiating from here."

She shrugged, turning to head back to the front of the coffee shop. "I've always had to touch the hot stove, just to see for myself. Any openable windows?" The last question was directed at Lou, who shook her head.

"I mean, there are, but the one behind the counter isn't big enough for any of us to fit through, and the big picture window is basically unbreakable."

"How do you know that?" Charlie asked curiously as she stepped into the area behind the counter. "Have you tried to break it?"

"The owner got a little freaked out after everything with the headless dead guy a few years ago, and she had this monster installed." Lou coughed, and Charlie felt her heart rate speed up. The smoke was thickening, and it looked like they were trapped in the burning building. She still managed to make a mental note to ask Lou about the *headless dead guy* once things were a little less life-threatening. "That's why the doors are reinforced." Lou's tone was apologetic as she looked at Bennett.

"Okay, doors are blocked," Fifi said in her too-reasonable voice that she only used when she was three seconds away from freaking out. "Windows are out. Any suggestions?"

Bennett reached into his pocket. "See if I can take the door off the hinges." He pulled out his multi-tool.

"Figured you'd start with a grenade or something," Charlie joked, but she could hear the underlying hint of panic in her voice. "Blast us out of here."

"Plan B." He headed over to the door.

"Stay low!" Fifi called after him and then began coughing.

Taking her own advice, she crouched. Charlie followed her lead, and Lou did as well.

"Any word from Callum?" Charlie asked.

Lou checked her phone. "He's on his way, and Fire's right behind him."

"ETA?" Fifi's voice was tight.

"Seventeen minutes."

The women studied each other as the simmering dread low in Charlie's belly grew even heavier. "Why so long?"

"Well, it's Simpson," Lou said huskily, her words ending in a cough. A rasp built in Charlie's throat, but she ignored it, knowing that if she started coughing, it'd just make her throat feel worse. "Everything's pretty spread out up here, so response times can be long. Plus, there was a rockslide blocking Highway 34. They have to go around."

Losing the battle to hold in her cough, Charlie hacked for an endless moment as her brain spun, trying to come up with solutions. "Can we go through the ceiling?" she asked once she'd stopped coughing and caught her breath.

Lou and Fifi looked up doubtfully. "Maybe, but how would that help us get out?"

"Through an air intake?" Charlie raised her hands in a shrug. Her knowledge of commercial HVAC systems was pretty much nil, but she hated her current helplessness. At least Bennett was doing something to possibly get them out. She didn't want to sit around doing nothing while the smoke thickened and the flames blazed around them. "You have a flathead screwdriver around here?"

Staying low, Lou shuffled closer to the counter and rummaged in a compact tool kit. The screwdriver she handed Charlie was small, but it'd have to do.

"Thanks," Charlie said, waving toward the hallway. "I'm going to work on the back door's hinges."

"Be careful," Fifi warned before turning to Lou. "Got a hammer in that kit?"

When Lou held up the tool, Fifi offered her a shaky smile.

"Let's see if we can enlarge this window." She gestured toward the small square of glass set in the wall behind the counter.

"Oh, I picked the wrong tool," Charlie said, trying to hide her anxiety when her voice came out rusty from the smoke. "I want to smash."

"Go on." Fifi waved her toward the doorway, giving her a sympathetic smile that told Charlie her sister knew exactly what she was really feeling. "We smash. You screw—well, unscrew."

She hurried down the short hallway to the back door, noticing it was definitely hotter and smokier now. Charlie wasn't at all tempted to touch the wall this time. In fact, she carefully stayed in the middle of the hallway, as if playing a real-life version of The Walls are Lava.

The smoke made it tough to see, and she blinked tears from her eyes just in time to stop before she ran into the door. Crouching, she felt for the hinge, which was painted the same color—dark green—as the door. She set the screwdriver in place, although she wasn't very hopeful with the paint slathered over the screws. There was little chance she could get the screws out.

With both hands, she cranked the screwdriver to the left, holding her breath as she strained.

"Come on, come on, come on." When she started coughing again, she quit her muttered mantra and just put all her effort into trying to turn the screwdriver. When she heard a *crack*, she jumped with delight, sure that the sound meant the screw had broken loose of its paint prison.

Then the majority of her borrowed screwdriver fell into her lap.

Her stomach dropped, and she fumbled to grab the remains of her tool. A roaring sound distracted her from her fruitless task, and she looked up, just in time to see the ceiling burst into an upside-down sea of flames.

Unable to look away, Charlie breathed, "Well…shoot."

THREE

Forcing herself to tear her gaze away from the rippling flames covering the ceiling, she turned her back on the not-going-anywhere hinges. Charlie figured it'd be best to rejoin the others in the main coffee shop, where hopefully the fire wasn't as well-developed. If it was, she'd suggest to Bennett that it might be time for his Plan B—B for Blow a hole in the wall big enough for them to escape through. Crouched as low as she could go and still walk, she took one step.

With a crash, a flaming chunk of ceiling fell to the floor. Flames shot up in front of her, and she leapt backward away from it, her back hitting the door. She turned her face away, throwing her arms up in front of her as embers stung any exposed skin.

Peeking through her upraised arms, she groaned. "You're in a pickle now, Charlie."

The ceiling and entire wall on her right was on fire, and black smoke filled the air, making it hard to see anything except the too-bright flames. The smoldering pile of ceiling tiles on the floor created the impression of a ring of fire in front of her, especially as the flames on the ceiling started to lick down the left wall, as well.

"Okay, so what do you do with a ring of fire?" she muttered to herself, her voice raspy. Pressing back against the door, she took as deep a breath as she could without setting off a coughing fit and then sprinted forward. The heat was intense, growing hotter the closer she drew to the fiery ring, but she pushed on, launching herself forward and up, sailing over the remains of the ceiling and landing on the other side—right on another pile of flaming debris.

"Ouch, ow, ow!" she yelped, hopping to another spot on the floor that was still hot, but at least wasn't actively on fire.

"What are you *doing*?"

Charlie froze. Those growled words definitely didn't come from inside her head. Before she could figure out who was in the smoke-darkened hallway with her, she was swept off her feet and deposited none-too-gently over a pair of broad shoulders.

"What?" she squawked—or tried to, at least. All she managed was a hoarse rasp.

"What're you doing, jumping into a fire?" The owner of the shoulders demanded.

"I wasn't jumping *into* a fire," she managed to croak in her defense. "I jumped *through* the ring of fire. Like Evel Knievel."

He snorted. "More like a badly trained circus poodle."

Suddenly, the shoulders, the voice, the crankiness, and the bunker coat her cheek was currently mashed against all came together in a light-bulb moment of recognition. "Kieran? What are you doing in here?"

"Saving your ass."

"*I* already saved my ass," she corrected him, wanting to push herself up and insist that she walk, but by the way her legs were trembling, she was a little worried that she wouldn't be able to stand on her own, so she kept quiet—about that at least.

His only answer was another snort, which she distinctly heard despite it being muffled by his SCBA gear. He charged through the front room, and she peered through the smoke.

"Are Fifi, Bennett, and Lou already out?"

"Right after we got the door open. *They* didn't jump into fires and make things difficult."

"I didn't—" The rest of her indignant response was lost in a flurry of coughing, and Kieran picked up the pace, running through the door and not slowing down once they were outside.

Hands reached for her to help her off her undignified perch, but Kieran's snarled "I've got her" made the hands withdraw.

They're worried he might bite them. If she hadn't still been coughing, she would've laughed at that thought.

"Charlie!" Fifi's voice rose above the babble of other people and loud thrum of the fire engine.

Kieran placed her on her feet and then helped her sit on the extended bumper of the fire truck. Fifi, her face pale, rushed over to her with Bennett close behind. His poker face was ruined by the worried wrinkles between his eyebrows, and Charlie made a mental note to tease him later.

For now, she knew they needed reassurance. "I'm— *mmmph.*" Unfortunately, her "I'm fine" was interrupted by the oxygen mask that was jammed over her face.

When she turned a glare to Kieran—the holder of said oxygen mask—he just raised an imperious eyebrow and growled, "Breathe."

"Oh, Charlie! Are you burned? Smoke inhalation? Of course you inhaled smoke. Why would you be getting oxygen if you didn't? I'm so sorry! We should've stayed together in the front." Fifi's eyes were wide and watery, and the sign of impending tears made Charlie up the scowl she'd fixed on the man who was keeping her from reassuring her worried sister. Since talking was out for her at the moment, Charlie gave Kieran's arm a punch.

Instead of reacting, he just continued giving her a flat stare with just the hint of a snarl. His lack of a flinch was extra infuriating, since her punching hand hurt now.

"I don't think you should be punching the arm that saved you," Fifi said, her eyebrows high and startled as she looked back and forth between Charlie and Kieran. "I mean, the man carried you out of a burning building and is currently giving you first aid. Maybe wait a few minutes before beating him up?"

To Charlie's relief, her sister at least no longer looked like she was about to cry, so she was grateful to the ass in front of her for that. Now he just needed to take off her oxygen mask so she could tell her sister that she'd been in the middle of saving herself when her unrequested—and *unnecessary*—rescue took place.

From his scowl, he wasn't about to let her tell him off anytime soon, so she settled back against the cool metal of the truck and plotted her revenge. If the stories were right, it was best served cold anyway—not that she'd know, since she was always too impatient to wait. Right now, she just needed to find out if Lou was okay, so she gave her sister a questioning look.

Fifi settled on the bumper next to her. "Lou's fine too."

Charlie was grateful that her sister was a fair hand at reading her mind.

"Callum hugged her for a solid five minutes and is currently making her sit still so the paramedics can check her out." Fifi nodded toward the ambulance, where Lou—a long-suffering look of strained patience on her face—was indeed being examined while Callum hovered.

Still muted by the mask, Charlie gave a thumbs-up to express her relief that no one had been hurt. Pointing toward the still-flaming building, she then lifted her hands in an exaggerated shrug, hoping Fifi's charades skills were still on point.

"They don't know yet," Fifi answered her unspoken question. "Either that, or they're not telling. The sheriff was trying to get a statement from me and B, but we were too worried about you to pay much attention to her questions. She'll be back around, I'm sure." Fifi turned her head as she examined the growing crowd, and then finally gestured toward a woman in a sheriff department uniform striding toward them. "Incoming, in fact."

Charlie hated law enforcement interviews. She was suddenly grateful for Kieran's overzealous application of first aid.

"Charlotte Pax?" the sheriff asked, focusing on her with a laser intensity that made Charlie feel instantly and undeservedly guilty. "Sheriff Summers. I have some questions for you."

Trying to look as pitiful as possible, Charlie gestured toward the oxygen mask, giving the sheriff huge I-wish-I-could-help-but-I'm-incapacitated-after-nearly-dying eyes.

Kieran, that contrary beast, started to pull the oxygen mask away.

Grabbing his hand, Charlie jerked the mask back against her face, sending him a threatening glare.

His eyebrow and the corner of his mouth quirked up in a smirk, but he kept the oxygen mask in place. "Later, Sheriff," he grumbled. "I'm treating her for smoke inhalation."

The sheriff eyed them flatly, making Charlie fairly certain that Summers had caught the interplay, but she continued giving her best innocent-and-dumb expression until the sheriff turned to her sister. "Felicity Pax. Tell me why we're lucky enough to have you visiting again so soon?"

Fifi hopped off the bumper and stood next to Bennett, leaning against him. Charlie appreciated her sister's effort to get the sheriff's attention off her. Batting her eyelashes at her new husband, who looked as amused as a boulder-made-human could look, Fifi said sweetly, "We never got a honeymoon. What better place to spend it than Simpson, where we fell in love?"

Summers gave the couple a sour look. "You brought your sister with you on your honeymoon?"

Fifi didn't miss a beat. "He knew when he married me that my sister and I are a package deal."

The sheriff's eyebrows shot up, and even Kieran gave Charlie a startled glance.

"Um...not a second-wife type of package deal," Fifi quickly corrected, sending Bennett a panicked look. When he just smirked at her, she turned her flustered gaze on Charlie, who shrugged helplessly, grateful for the oxygen mask for the second time in as many minutes. "I just...really like spending time with my sister."

"On your honeymoon." Summers's voice was flat.

"Well...sure." Fifi was looking positively desperate for a save now. "All this free time...what better way to use it than for Bennett to get to know a member of his new family?" Her voice rose in the end, making it even more obvious that she knew exactly how ridiculous her explanation was.

Kieran's grunt sounded like it might actually be related to a laugh—not a sibling, but maybe a cousin? Or a laugh's second cousin? With him holding the mask on her face, Charlie couldn't turn her head, so she rolled her eyes toward him instead, wanting to see what a laughing Kieran looked like. His scowl was still in place, however, so apparently slightly amused Kieran was indistinguishable from cranky Kieran.

"Right." The sheriff turned to Charlie. "Ms. Pax, I want to talk to you as soon as that oxygen mask comes off."

Rebooting her innocent expression, Charlie gave a small wave of assent. She avoided nodding, since she wanted plausible deniability that she'd never *actually* agreed to the interview later. After a silent, steady glare at all four of them, the sheriff stalked away.

Once she was out of earshot, Charlie let out a long breath that was echoed by her sister. Rolling her eyes toward Kieran, she gestured for him to remove the mask. When he continued to frown at her, she turned her gaze pleading. He only lasted three-and-a-quarter seconds before folding.

"Fine," he grumbled. "But if your cough gets worse, or you develop a headache or any other symptoms, go to the hospital." He waited until she nodded before removing the mask.

"Thanks," she said. Turning to Fifi and Bennett, she resisted the urge to clear her throat, since Kieran looked ready to jam the mask back on at the first sign of a cough. "First, I didn't need rescuing. I'd just saved myself when he showed up." She jerked a thumb at Kieran.

"You jumped into a fire."

"Yes." Charlie had to give Kieran that point. "But then I immediately jumped *out* of that tiny fire, without your help. When you snatched me up, I was standing on a section of floor that was very clearly *not* burning, thank you very much."

"You're welcome." He turned and started putting equipment away.

"I didn't...grr." His grumpiness wasn't *quite* as fun as it had been earlier—more like infuriating. She snuck a glance at his profile. He was still incredibly hot though. Tearing her gaze away from him, she refocused on her sister. "Second, you know better than to try to lie, Fifi."

"Right?" Fifi sighed. "As soon as the words were out, I knew I shouldn't have jumped off that verbal cliff."

"It's okay." Charlie couldn't stand to see her usually cheerful sister so down on herself. "If I had to have a sister-wife, I'd definitely pick you."

Another amused grunt came from Kieran as Bennett looked slightly alarmed at the direction of the conversation.

"Don't worry, B." She gave her brother-in-law a pat on the

arm. "I don't think it'll come to that. It's too bad a certain over-zealous firefighter didn't have another oxygen mask he could've used on you, Fifi, rather than just leave you scrambling to answer the sheriff."

"That *would've* been handy." The subtle note of accusation in Fifi's voice made Charlie hide a grin as Kieran glanced up, frowning.

Under their censorious gazes, he huffed, grumbled something unintelligible, and stomped away, looking ridiculously hot during the whole process.

"Charlie. Charlie. *Charlie!*"

"Hmm?" Charlie hummed, reluctantly turning away from her most excellent view of Kieran's backside.

Fifi tried to glare, but her stern expression collapsed into a laugh. "Focus, sister-wife. Someone tried to kill us. We need to figure out who trapped us inside and set the coffee shop on fire."

"Right." Charlie shook her hands by her sides, bringing her brain back in line. "Attempted murder beats lust. There'll be time to discuss the whole Kieran Byrne subject after we bring in Mom."

Bennett suddenly looked very uncomfortable, making Charlie laugh and slap him on the shoulder.

"It's okay, big guy," she reassured him. "You don't have to contribute to that conversation. But you have to admit that it's better than having me as your second wife, right?"

"Yes," he said, a little too quickly to do much for her ego, but Charlie just laughed again.

"C'mon," she said, making her way toward the ambulance

while keeping a wary eye out for the sheriff. "Let's go talk to the president of the murder club. See if we can narrow down a suspect list."

Fifi skipped a step to catch up. "Isn't this place the best? I mean…a *murder* club."

Rolling her eyes toward her sister, Charlie gave an amused snort. "We were almost just murdered by fire."

Fifi grimaced. "I didn't say Simpson was perfect."

Bursting into laughter that changed to a coughing fit, Charlie gave her sister a flat look through watery eyes. She only lasted a few seconds before admitting, "Yeah, this place is the best."

———

"I've lived a fairly enemy-free life for the past couple of years, so I'm thinking one of you—or all of you—were the target." Lou gave the EMT a smile as he unwrapped the blood pressure cuff. "Am I good to go?"

"Sure, unless you want to have them check you out at the hospital," the medic said with an answering grin. "I can give you a ride."

"Nope." She ignored Callum's "Yes," giving the EMT a wave as she moved away from the ambulance. Callum made unhappy grumbly noises but followed close behind his wife, joining their group with a bigger frown than usual.

"Probably," Charlie agreed with Lou's assessment. "We do tend to rack up the enemies."

"Around here though?" Fifi sounded skeptical. "Bennett and

I were only in Simpson what—a week?—and Charlie just got here. We couldn't have made *that* many people want to kill us during that time."

"What about the militia with the stupid name?" Charlie asked, a little offended at how Fifi was underestimating their ability to drive people to murder.

"The Freedom Survivors?" Fifi asked. "We did put three of their members—including their leader—in jail," Fifi admitted. "I mean, I suppose one or two might be holding a grudge?"

"So the militia members are all going in the suspect column on the…oh." Lou sounded sad.

"What's wrong?" Callum asked immediately, as if he had an internal alarm that activated every time his wife's mood dropped.

"I just realized the whiteboard burned up."

Charlie stared at the forlorn woman, confused. "Um…I think you can get a new one at Target for about twenty bucks?"

"Sorry." Although Lou waved off everyone's baffled concern with a weak laugh, she still looked suspiciously teary-eyed. "I know it was just a whiteboard, but I was fond of it. Silly, I know. I hadn't even named it or anything. I need to stop getting so attached to my murder boards."

"Um…sorry for your loss?" Fifi offered, shooting Charlie a look.

Charlie just shrugged. Different people got attached to different things. Whenever Charlie killed an electronic device— something she did with unfortunate regularity—Norah always looked as if she was about to cry. "Who else can go in the suspect column?"

"Hey, guys?" Fifi stared into the crowd. "The sheriff's heading this way. Hang on, some woman just grabbed her and is talking her ear off."

"That's my boss—the owner of the coffee shop. I don't have the energy to deal with her, much less the sheriff. Let's head back to our cars and plan to meet at the honeymoon suite in thirty?" Lou suggested, but Callum shook his head.

"No more murder meetings tonight." When Lou frowned at him, his stoic expression slipped, and a flash of exhausted worry was visible before his poker face returned.

Lou must've spotted that glimpse of Callum's emotions too, since she didn't argue but took his arm instead. "We'll chat tomorrow," she said. "I think we need some time to mourn the murder board and for Cal to realize I didn't die this time."

He let out a low grunt, as if punched in the stomach.

"Sorry." Lou grimaced and patted the arm she held. "Of course I didn't die. Just a little fire…*another* fire, where I work, and the murder board didn't make it out." By the end, Lou was sounding a little weepy, and it was Callum's turn to pat her.

"That's fine," Charlie hurried to reassure her, not wanting Lou to break down into full-on sobs. She was terrible at consoling sad people. Angry people, she could handle, but the sad ones made Charlie want to run away. "Get some sleep, and we'll regroup in the morning. I have some treasure-hunter ass to kick anyway. What's the use of being stalked if your stalker doesn't save you from being barricaded in a coffee shop and burned alive?"

"Why'd you look at me?" Bennett asked, looking as offended as a man made out of a boulder could look.

"You were a stalker." Charlie gestured toward him. "Don't you know the stalker code of conduct?"

His eyes narrowed as he glared at her. "There's not a club with rules."

"Maybe you should think about starting one." When he continued glowering at her, she shrugged. "I'm just saying that being a stalker comes with some expectations, like not allowing your stalkee to be killed by someone else."

Callum, who'd flinched at the "burned alive" part and then even harder at the "killed by someone else," was being led away by Lou. "See you tomorrow," she called over her shoulder.

"Bye!" Fifi called back.

Preoccupied with a thought that just occurred to her, Charlie gave them an absent wave before asking Bennett and Fifi, "Maybe one of the treasure hunters saw the person who barricaded us in and set the building on fire."

"I don't know." Fifi looked around them, frowning. "I don't see any of them around. They're always in everyone's business, so they'd be watching the show if they could."

"You don't think the arsonist hurt them, do you?" Charlie peered around the crowd, the faces easy to make out, thanks to the firefighters' floodlights. She didn't even see Dave, who was the worst hider of the lot of them. Even Bones's VW Fox was missing from her parking spot in front of the bank. A guilty twinge awoke in her middle. She and her sister had lured the treasure hunters here. If they'd gotten hurt, Charlie would feel responsible. "Hang on, there's Tassie."

She headed toward the treasure hunter hovering by the

edge of the onlookers. When Tassie spotted Charlie making her way toward her, she didn't run or even try to fade into the crowd. Instead, she waved her arms as if to attract Charlie's attention.

"Yes, I see you," Charlie muttered under her breath, confused by this un-treasure-hunter-like behavior. She was used to the five of them lurking around, at least attempting to be covert and ninja-like. This time, however, Tassie met her halfway.

"It wasn't us," Tassie blurted out before Charlie could even say hello.

"What wasn't us?"

"We didn't burn down the coffee shop." There was a gleam of desperation in Tassie's eyes. "We weren't even here. I swear it."

Charlie blinked, taken off guard by her words. The idea that the treasure hunters had tried to kill them hadn't even occurred to her, but she stopped herself before assuring Tassie of that. Here was some free leverage, and Charlie wasn't going to throw that away. "Hmm...so you say. Why don't we let the sheriff decide who's guilty?" She half turned, starting to raise her arm as if to flag down the sheriff.

Tassie grabbed her arm. "Wait! No! We were having dinner at Levi's."

Charlie cocked her head, confused. Tassie was just as much a newcomer to Simpson as Charlie was. How did she know the locals already?

"Levi's—the barbecue joint?" Tassie must've seen the blank look on Charlie's face. "We figured you'd be meeting in the coffee shop for a few hours, so we grabbed some dinner."

"All five of you?"

Tassie nodded.

"Even Rhys?" Suspicion was heavy in Charlie's voice.

"Yes." Tassie smirked a little. "He's had a crush on Bones for, like, forever."

"Really?" Charlie caught herself before she could dive deeper into this fascinating piece of information. "So I'm supposed to believe all of you just bailed for a few hours? It hasn't even been a full day! What if we'd taken a field trip to the necklace? Or, you know, someone tried to *kill* us?" She couldn't help but glare at Tassie, who shrank into herself.

"Sorry! It's just been a long time since we'd gotten together and caught up. I didn't even know that Dave had another kid."

"What time did you leave?" Charlie asked, again resisting the urge to ask for more details.

Tassie shrugged. "Not sure what time exactly, but your sister and her stalker had just arrived. We all know how much you Paxes like to talk and talk and talk…" She trailed off under Charlie's stern gaze and started again. "Anyway, since we didn't have the coffee shop bugged yet, we figured there was no sense in sitting around in the cold, waiting for you. It was Lachlan's idea," she finished defensively.

Charlie knew it'd be no use taking Tassie to task for intending to bug the coffee shop, but she did make a mental note to warn the others about the potential for eavesdroppers. "Bennett's her stalker-husband now," she corrected mildly instead. "Did you see anything before you left? Anyone lurking, looking shifty—besides the five of you, I mean."

"Nah." Tassie looked relieved at being off the hook. "It was dead quiet. That's why we decided to go eat."

"What are you still doing here?" The snarled question made Tassie jump as her eyes went wide. Charlie's heart leapt, but it was more from an inappropriate excitement rather than from being startled.

She raised an eyebrow at Kieran as he came to join them. "Why shouldn't I be here?"

"You should be in bed. You almost died."

"Not really." A tiny, doubtful chorus in her mind tried to replay scenes from earlier, when the fire roared all around her, but she threw a mental bucket of water on her inner voices. "We were in the process of getting ourselves out when you arrived. Firefighters became our plan C or even D when we heard your response time was *seventeen* minutes." She tsked.

The tips of his ears turned red, and it was strangely adorable. "It only took us nine minutes, and it's a big county. Seventeen minutes is a good response time up here. Under ten is almost unheard of and—wait. Why am I arguing with you?"

"Because I'm irresistible, debate-wise at least?"

Now the cherry edges of his cheekbones matched the tops of his ears. "You—"

"Hang on," Charlie interrupted, looking around at the dwindling crowd. "Where'd Tassie go?"

"Who's Tassie?"

"The fortune hunter who was standing right here a second ago." Charlie pointed at the ground in front of her, which was now unfortunately Tassie-free.

"There." Kieran pointed at the back of Tassie's green jacket, which was currently climbing into the back seat of a VW Fox. The driver gave Charlie a wave—evidently, Bones figured that Tassie had erased any suspicion of the fortune hunters' guilt. In the front passenger seat sat another familiar face.

"Is that Rhys?" Charlie asked as the Fox did a U-turn and drove away.

"Who's Rhys?"

"Another fortune hunter, the slippery one Callum was annoyed he couldn't spot," Charlie explained absently. "Apparently, he is also the fortune hunter who has a huge crush on Bones. I knew I should've asked for more details about that. Now the curiosity's going to kill me."

"Seems like a popular occupation," Kieran muttered.

Charlie wondered if she'd missed part of their conversation. "What is?"

"Murdering you."

His flat delivery made her laugh. "You have no idea."

FOUR

CHARLIE KNEW IT WAS A risk, but she'd never been afraid of taking a chance...especially when the stakes were so high. Raising her clenched fist, she knocked on the door. She heard the angry thud of each footfall as someone closed in on the door. When it was ripped open, she had to keep herself from outwardly flinching.

"You are *not* going to be my other wife," Bennett growled, and Charlie swallowed a snicker.

"Of course not." She used his height to her advantage, waltzing under his arm and into the honeymoon suite. "I already have my husband picked out, and I'm sorry to tell you that you weren't even in the running."

"Really?" Fifi said, emerging from the bathroom in her pajamas. "Who's your husband-to-be? And were you really running around the hotel dressed like that?"

"Cranky firefighter Kieran, of course." Charlie plopped down on the bed and made herself comfortable. "He's hot, fun to wind up, and he has a soft spot for small animals…i.e., the perfect potential husband. What's wrong with my llama jams?" Her sleepwear actually covered quite a lot, plus she had on fuzzy socks. She wasn't sure what her sister's objection could be.

"Does Kieran know?" Charlie was glad to see that her brother-in-law's irritation was quickly shifting to amusement.

"Of course not." Charlie waved her hand, dismissing the idea that his lack of knowledge could be a problem. "We're only in the introductory stages. He'll find out before we're actually married, though, don't worry."

"Was that a dig about our wedding?" Fifi asked, sitting next to Charlie and tugging the covers over her lap.

"Of course not." Charlie patted her sister's leg through the bedding. "Maybe your wedding wouldn't make the cover of *Bride Magazine*, but you made it work for you, and I'm very happy with the result." She gave Bennett an approving nod. "Now we have a multi-tool around whenever we need it."

His eyes narrowed, but he didn't ask if "tool" was referring to the one he carried or the man himself.

Taking pity on him, and because she really did like Bennett, Charlie assured him that she was being literal. "It's very handy to have access to your multi-tool."

"I'll get you one for Christmas," he promised.

Although she tried to appear pleased, she must've wrinkled her nose, because he gave her a frowning head tilt. "That's great and all, but it works a lot better when the tool is connected to a set of burly muscles." She gestured at Bennett, who looked pleased, flexing a little while shooting Fifi a sideways glance.

His wife rolled her eyes—although she very obviously checked out her husband's muscly display—and made a get-on-with-it gesture at Charlie. "Since you've invaded our honeymoon suite *again*, you must want to talk about something. Let's discuss so you can go to your very beautiful, very functional room that—most importantly—isn't this one."

"I do want to talk," Charlie agreed, "since, you know, someone tried to *murder* us tonight. Again."

"We do seem to come off as rather murderable," Fifi said as Bennett scooted in behind her so that she was leaning against his chest.

"I don't know." Charlie grabbed a pillow to squeeze, since she didn't have a living teddy bear of her own like her sister did. "Apparently, attempted murder is pretty common around here."

Bennett gave an agreeing grunt.

"There has to be a reason though," Fifi said. "People don't barricade us inside coffee shops and burn them down without a good reason." When Charlie gave her a look, she amended that. "Without *a* reason."

"Who'd you annoy the most when you were here before?" Charlie asked. "The militia?"

"Bennett did run down one of their members with a golf cart," Fifi said thoughtfully. At Bennett's grunt, she shrugged. "Humiliation makes people—especially men—feel rather murder-y."

"True." Charlie was quiet for a few moments while she thought. "Lou could've been the intended target too."

Bennett made a skeptical sound.

"Yeah, B's right," Felicity translated her husband's grunt-speak. "It's been years since someone attempted to kill Lou. Seems coincidental, especially since someone tries to kill a member of our family…what? Once a week?" Bennett grumbled unhappily, and his wife gave his arm a reassuring pat.

With a nod, Charlie said, "So it sounds like we were the attempted victims, likely by the militia?"

"Could Jane have done it?"

The question startled Charlie—the thought hadn't crossed her mind.

From Fifi's expression, it hadn't crossed hers either.

Charlie wasn't sure why the suggestion took her by surprise. Jane would definitely toss every single one of her daughters under the bus if it benefited her. There was a flaw to that logic though. "She needs the key."

Relief flashed across Fifi's face. "Right. She never would've killed us like that if she wanted the key back. Arson scenes are notoriously messy."

Charlie's laugh came out of her in a dizzying rush. "Can you imagine her wearing a pencil skirt and stilettos, hair in a French twist, digging through the ash and soot like a bougie Cinderella?"

Fifi's giggle was real, although with a high-pitched edge, but Bennett's arms wrapped around her as his expression tightened into rock-hard lines. Charlie realized that, in her imagined scenario, Jane would've been digging through their cremated remains, and her laugh ended abruptly.

"So…militia," she rushed out, trying to change the subject so quickly that she stumbled over it.

Fifi must've translated her expression correctly—or she felt the tension in the death grip Bennett had around her—because she glanced up at her husband and then said, "I think we need sleep. We'll meet up with Lou tomorrow and maybe talk to Chris—Daisy's husband. He might've heard something around the sheriff department about the Freedom Survivors being all up in their emotions about the golf-cart incident—or the whole jailing-their-buddies thing."

Eager to escape the tension in the room, Charlie quickly agreed, relinquishing her pillow and hopping off the bed. "Sleep tight, you two." She bit back a joke about surviving until morning, since she was pretty sure Bennett wasn't in a place where he could appreciate black humor at the moment. Instead, she gave them both a wave and slipped out into the corridor.

An older couple gave her startled stares as she hurried past them on her way to the stairwell. Once the fire door banged closed behind her, Charlie muttered, "Maybe Fifi had a point about the llamas." Still, she smirked as she glanced down at her flannel sleepwear while skipping down the flight of stairs to her floor.

Habit had her pausing before she pushed open the door, peering through the narrow window to check for danger before leaving the stairwell. Her palms flattened against the release bar, but she froze before she shoved it down, peering more closely at the alcove hiding her room door.

Is that a foot?

A boot, to be precise—well, two of them, sticking out of the alcove as if someone was leaning against her door with one foot casually kicked over the other. It seemed awfully laid back for an assassin in the middle of a job, but she knew better than to assume the boots belonged to a friend. As relaxed as the person appeared—at least by the position of their boots—they were planning to ambush her at her hotel room door.

Easing the stairwell door open, she slipped into the hall, her eyes on the protruding toes. She held on to the door as it closed, but she couldn't prevent the click of the latch engaging. The boots disappeared as the person straightened, and Charlie winced. So much for the element of surprise. Her hands slipped over her hip where a pocket should be, and she mentally vowed to sew pockets into all her pajamas and fill each and every one with weapons. Surely Bennett could be persuaded to give up a few from his personal arsenal.

She briefly considered going back up to bring Fifi and Bennett with her, but now her curiosity was eating at her, and she worried that the person would disappear. Instead, she silenced her phone and sent a quick text to Fifi.

Someone's standing in front of my room door.

It was only a few seconds before a response came through.

On our way. Who?
Not sure. Can only see boots.
Wait for us in a secure spot.

Charlie held back a snort. That last one must've been dictated by Bennett, because Fifi knew her better than that. Emboldened by the knowledge that help was on the way, she crept closer to the door of her room, keeping tight to the wall, mentally swearing at the hotel's design that tucked each of its doors into a private alcove, one just big enough to hide the person waiting for her to return.

She made it all the way to the doorway next to hers before the person waiting made a sound. Once she heard that already-familiar growl, she huffed out an exasperated breath.

"Cranky firefighter," she said as she rushed past the final section of wall and turned in front of her door. "Is that you?"

It was indeed Kieran Byrne, still smudgy and rumpled from the smoke and gear. To Charlie's annoyance, it was a good look for him.

"What on earth are you doing here?" Before he could answer, she held up her phone. "Hang on." After she typed out an It's just Kieran text to her sister, she looked back at his scowling face. "Okay, go ahead."

"Go ahead with what?"

"Explain why your boots are acting all menacing." When his eyebrows crashed together in apparent confusion, Charlie realized that hadn't made much sense to someone who hadn't been inside her head with her for the last few minutes. She revised her question to something a little more universally understood. "Why are you here?"

"You left this." He held out his closed fist, and Charlie automatically reached out to take whatever it was he was offering.

She stared down at the charred remains in her palm for a solid ten seconds before asking, "Uh…what is it?"

"Your screwdriver."

"My screwdriver." She poked at a metal bit with her free hand. "I guess I can see how it could've once been a screwdriver, but mine?"

"You dropped it in the fire."

"Wait—is this the screwdriver I used to try to take off the back door of the coffee shop?"

His scowl deepened as he glared at the remains on her palm. "It was much too small for that."

"Yeah, it broke." She looked meaningfully at the pieces he'd just given to her. "Plus it's Lou's broken screwdriver. Why are you really here?"

A door across from them opened, and a man with a sour expression stuck his head out into the hall. "Can you keep it down?"

"Probably not." Charlie had never been very good at maintaining a proper inside voice. When the man continued to glare at her—but not in a hot-Kieran-type way—she rolled her eyes and pulled her key card out of her sock. "C'mon." The light by the door flashed green, so she grabbed Kieran's sleeve and tugged him behind her into her room. Not even waiting for the door to fully shut behind them, she slapped the light switch on and turned to face him. "Now, why are you really here?"

He scowled at her so hard, looking completely offended by her presence, that she almost felt like she should leave the room—but then she remembered that it was *her* room and that he'd come to her for some reason. It was just that his resting-crank face was so severe that it was constantly in a state of get-off-his-lawn-edness.

She made a get-on-with-it gesture. "You're very hot and entertaining to stare at, but it's been a *day*, so say what you came to say and then let me collapse on that *extremely* comfortable-looking bed."

That entertaining, baffled look entered his eyes, softening the edge of his glare, and the tips of his ears turned red again, possibly in response to her comment about his hotness. Just when she thought she was going to have to kick out his silent butt, he spoke. "Your sister found Cobra."

It took a long moment to process that statement. Even though it was only four simple words, she had to pick it apart to figure out the meaning of each one. Finally, the light bulb in her brain flickered to life. "Oh! Fifi's dead body!" She grimaced. "Now I'm sounding like Daisy—not that there's anything wrong with that. Daisy's adorable. Okay, now I'm sounding like Lou. Let me start over." Clearing her throat, she organized her thoughts into a straight line. "Fifi did indeed find the remains of Cobra Jones, the previous leader of the militia formerly known as the Freedom Survivors."

Kieran blinked only once, which was fairly impressive. Charlie often reduced people to silent stupefaction, blinking so rapidly that it looked like they were trying to send a message using Morse code. "Formerly known?"

"Really? That's the part you got stuck on?" Charlie shrugged. "Apparently there's a petition out to change the local militia's name. Not sure where in the name-change process the murder club is, so that might be premature, but I have a feeling it's inevitable."

"What's inevitable?"

She gave him a consoling pat on the arm. Even if he wasn't involved in the militia—and she really hoped he wasn't—his dad had been, so there might be some nostalgia connected to the old name. "The murder club *really* hates Freedom Survivors—the name, not the actual militia." Her head cocked slightly. "Possibly the militia too, which is understandable, since they do seem to be rather murder-y. Sorry."

His glare took on an intensity that she hadn't seen from him yet. "Do you *ever* make sense?"

She opened her mouth to tell him that she was making perfect sense, and that his listening skills must be the problem, when a heavy-handed knock on the door made her jump.

"Either that's some sort of law enforcement officer or I have more than one brother-in-law with a cop knock." Charlie took a step toward the door, but Kieran blocked her with his body as he peered through the peephole. For just a raw second, she wondered if she was stupid to have let this possible militia member into her hotel room, and whether she was about to be held hostage by said militia member, but then Kieran opened the door.

Peeking around his rather massive body, she saw the pair in the doorway.

"Ah," she said. "Just a family of cop knockers then. Everyone come in and shut the door before the crabby guy yells at us again." Glancing at Kieran, she gave him a reassuring flap of her hand. "Not you—the guy across the hall."

By the way his eyebrows squashed into an even more angry line, he wasn't soothed by that.

Fifi maneuvered past the guys and sat in one of the two chairs by the window. Charlie grabbed the other before one of the guys could take it, although they seemed content to lean against opposite walls, flexing and watching each other suspiciously.

"So why are you here?" Charlie asked her sister with more curiosity than annoyance. "I told you it was just Kieran."

"We weren't sure 'just Kieran' was *just* Kieran, if you know what I mean," Fifi said, making faces filled with hidden messages. The problem was that Charlie wasn't having any luck translating.

"Not really," Charlie admitted. "Because of his possible ties to the militia formerly known as the Freedom Survivors?"

"Exactly," Fifi said, even as Kieran sighed impatiently.

"I'm not in the militia."

Charlie was inclined to believe him, but she still studied him critically. She couldn't let a pretty face blind her to his possibly nefarious motives. Instead of giving any other denials besides that first flat statement, he just glared back at her until she shrugged, accepting his word. If more information came at a later point that proved him to be a liar, she'd reevaluate, but until then, she was going to go with her gut. "He was asking about your dead body, Fifi."

Bennett growled as he seemed to swell several coat sizes.

"Settle down, Hulk," Charlie told him fondly. It was nice

having someone else around who liked her sister as much as Charlie did. "Not *her* dead body, but the dead body she discovered. Cobra's dead body, if you want to be literal about it."

"I do," Bennett said swiftly, the remains of a growl still lingering in his voice. "I want to be literal when discussing dead bodies, especially when my *wife* is involved."

Fifi rolled her eyes, but she also gave her ridiculous husband a loving look, softening the first gesture. "Why were you asking about Cobra's remains, Kieran?"

His glare turned to Fifi, but Charlie noticed that it was a lot less intense than when his scowl was focused on her. She found this to be more interesting than offensive. "Clint's been cleared," Kieran said.

Charlie made eye contact with Fifi and Bennett as her mind quickly flipped through the significance of that. The most important one made her heart beat faster. "He hasn't been released, has he?"

"No," Kieran answered, and air left Charlie's lungs in a sigh of relief. "Just the murder charge has been dropped."

"Why?" Fifi asked, leaning forward in her chair, her face alight with interest.

"Alibied."

"Ohhh…" Charlie and Fifi said in unison, their gazes meeting. This wasn't helping them get their hands on their mom, but it was still extremely interesting, like an unsolved mystery. Plus, Fifi had to feel some possessiveness about the remains she found. If Charlie had stumbled over her own body, she knew she'd feel extra invested in finding the killer.

"Cops like you for it?" Bennett asked Kieran flat out. The complete lack of tact was so Bennett-like that Charlie could barely hold back her laugh. Despite her amusement, she was extremely interested in Kieran's answer.

"Yes." It was as bare and unvarnished as Bennett's question had been, and Charlie loved her future husband even more for it.

"Did you kill him?" Fifi asked, joining in the no-holds-barred question-and-answer session.

"No."

"Why do the cops think you did?" Charlie asked with more curiosity than suspicion.

He just shrugged—a tight, angry twitch of his shoulders. "My source wasn't sure."

Charlie considered the oddly worded answer before asking, "Why do *you* think they want to talk to you about it?"

His glare pinpointed her, but it wasn't like he was trying to intimidate her. It was more…searching. Just when she thought he'd refuse to answer, that he'd judged her and found her wanting, he spoke. "I'm not popular right now."

At that, her laughter escaped. "Sorry," she said once she'd gotten her amusement under control. "But you have to agree that the idea of you being a popular, student-council-president of a guy is hilarious." When his glare didn't waver, she snickered again. "Please. You're the bad boy lurking under the bleachers."

Fifi, God love her, nodded solemnly. "Totally the angry bad boy."

"Flicking your lighter like you're mad at life."

At Bennett's contribution, the room went silent, and then Charlie lost it, laughing so hard her belly hurt. Fifi was snort-laughing next to her, which just set Charlie off again.

When they finally recovered enough to speak, Charlie let out a quivery, "Oh man…" She refused to mentally replay the image of a surly teenage Kieran, because it was guaranteed to set her off again. "Back to the dead body and your supposed involvement… Your popularity, or lack thereof, seems like a shaky basis for a murder accusation."

"Agreed," Fifi said, wiping residual tears of laughter from under her eyes. "They have to have *something* else. Motive? Eyewitness? Forensic evidence?"

Charlie watched Kieran's face as her sister listed off the possibilities, but Kieran's expression stayed impassive. "Why'd you come here tonight?" Charlie asked.

Kieran's lips pressed tight. "To see if you knew anything. About Cobra's death."

"You think we did it?" The idea was so ridiculous that Charlie almost laughed. "I hate to tell you this, but Simpson doesn't need to import its killers. You seem to have more than your share of homegrown ones."

With a sharp, negative shake of his head, Kieran said, "Because you found him, not because you did it."

"Why?" Fifi asked. "So we can tell you what the cops know?"

He looked as close as he'd ever come to rolling his eyes. "I already know what the cops know, and it's basically nothing. If they had something, they wouldn't be coming after me."

Maybe it was his ridiculous hotness level, or the way he spat his words out so angrily, but Charlie was inclined, once again, to believe him. "Who do you think killed Cobra?"

"Clint." The answer was swift, but also confusing.

"I thought he was cleared?" The reminder brought up another question. "And how did he alibi out? Forensic science is an amazing thing, but there were just a few bones left. There's no way they narrowed his time of death down to hours or even a specific day."

"Cobra drove him to jail six months ago, where Clint served almost five months on a weapons charge," Kieran said. "Caught Cobra on the security footage arriving and leaving—all while breathing."

Glancing at Fifi, Charlie nodded. "That'll do it." Just because Clint didn't actually pull the trigger—or swing the tire iron—didn't mean he didn't order it done, however.

"Lots of people seem eager to do Clint's bidding," Bennett said, echoing Charlie's thoughts. "Could've been a hit. He had a motive, since he took Cobra's spot as the Freedom Survivors' leader."

"And got his pickup," Fifi added. When everyone looked at her, she shrugged. "People have murdered for less than a nice truck."

Charlie nodded in agreement before she considered Kieran once again. "So were you ever involved in the militia? You know, like a father-son bonding activity?"

"Never." The way he spat out the word like a vow was extremely convincing.

"You have an inside source of information though," Fifi said reasonably.

Kieran stared at the ceiling for a long moment, as if asking for patience. When he eventually met Fifi's even gaze, however, he didn't appear to have gained any. "I'm a firefighter."

Charlie met Fifi's eyes, but her sister looked just as confused by the apparent non sequitur, so Charlie asked Kieran directly, "Very noble and all, but what does that have to do with anything?"

He gave a deep sigh as he switched his focus from Fifi to Charlie. "*They're* my source."

"The firefighters? They're all militia?" Charlie frowned. This was seriously the weirdest, most crime-ridden town she'd ever visited.

"Of course not." He stared at her like she was an idiot. "They're just in everyone's business."

"Oh." Charlie took a second to process the roller coaster of conflicting information. The idea of firefighters not being dangerous militia members but rather a bunch of nosy Nellies was a relief and also a bit adorable. "So not militia members, just gossipy hens?"

His nod was short, although his mouth twitched up slightly when she called the firefighters hens.

"Okay, so what did you need from us?" Charlie felt like the whole point of the conversation had been lost—plus her fascination with this particular gossipy hen didn't help.

"I want you to investigate Cobra's death."

She met Fifi and Bennett's eyes, reading their reluctance to get involved, but also seeing that same spark of curiosity that she felt. How could they ignore a mystery when it just flopped down at their feet, begging to be solved? It'd be a bonus if Clint was involved, since he'd been the one to organize Fifi's kidnapping attempt.

"Between trying to trap Mom and burning down the Black Bear Inn, things are getting busy," she said thoughtfully, trying to keep from blurting out immediately that *of course* they would investigate Cobra's murder.

"Don't burn it down," Kieran snapped.

"Sorry, that'd be more work for you, wouldn't it?" Charlie frowned. "How about blowing it up? Do you have enough explosives, B?"

Bennett nodded, but Kieran sliced his hand through the air, as if decapitating that idea. "Who do you think would respond to an explosion?"

"Right." Now that he'd said something, it seemed obvious that the fire department would be called to an explosion too. "Maybe we could excavate underneath it, so it just kind of dropped into a ho—"

"If I get the health department to do a surprise inspection of the motel, will you let this go?" Kieran grumbled.

After considering the idea—while not being able to come up with a revenge plan that wouldn't create more work for the firefighters—Charlie huffed out a breath. "Fine. *Several* surprise inspections. And you'll need to give us a day's head start, so we can release the rats and cockroaches. But if we investigate Cobra's death, you're going to have to help us with Operation: Catch Mom."

Fifi made a skeptical sound as Kieran stared at Charlie,

apparently finally shocked out of his normal cranky mood. "What?" the other three said at the same time.

It had been an impulsive ask, but the more Charlie thought about it, the more she liked the idea. Not only would her fascinating future fiancé be within ogling view, but she had a feeling he'd be a handy guy to have around, like a second Bennett, but with fewer explosives. "He could be our muscle. If someone who likes lighting coffee shops on fire is after us, it'd be good to have a firefighter in our back pocket, right? Also, the gossipy hen part is useful too."

"I'm not—" Kieran started to say, but whatever he wasn't was drowned out by Bennett and Fifi's protests.

"Let's talk about this first, Charlie," Fifi said, just as Bennett made general concerned grumbly noises.

"Fine." Charlie interrupted the rest of what she was going to say with a wide yawn. "Let's meet tomorrow after we pick Daisy's deputy's brain."

"I'll go with you to talk to Chris," Kieran stated, as if it were a done deal.

Charlie laughed. "Yeah…no. He's probably not going to give us anything good, but he's guaranteed not to tell us anything if you're tagging along. Let's meet at ten at the coffee… shoot." She pulled a face. "Where's a good place to meet that isn't a blackened shell of a building?"

"Fire department."

Charlie met Fifi's gaze, and they exchanged smirks.

"Okay," Fifi said. "That way we'll have some eye candy with our discussion. Good idea."

Both Kieran and Bennett looked a bit grumpy at that.

"Now get out," Charlie ordered on another yawn. "I need sleep if we're going to accomplish world domination tomorrow."

"World domination?" Fifi repeated, sounding amused as she pushed to her feet.

"Well, we'll be solving a murder, bringing in our skip, and saving our home, so pretty close."

Bennett stepped back so that Kieran could leave first. With a final scowl directed at Charlie—which she chose to take as a polite goodbye—he left the room.

"Hey, B," Charlie said before her brother-in-law could follow Kieran out. When Bennett stopped and raised an eyebrow at her, she put on her best entreating face. "You wouldn't happen to have a sewing kit on you, do you?"

"Sewing kit?" Fifi asked.

"Need to make some alterations to my pajamas." *Like adding useful pockets.*

Bennett, bless him, pulled out a small, flat box and tossed it to her.

"Thanks, B," she said as she caught it. "How about a hand grenade?"

Before she could snicker at her joke, something came flying at her. She managed to drop the kit into her lap and catch it before it made contact with her face.

"Private Investigator Bennett Green," Fifi growled. "Did you just throw a *grenade* at my *sister*?"

Turning the object Bennett had just tossed to her in her

hands, Charlie noted that it was indeed a grenade as she requested. "Nice."

"She needed one." Bennett spread his hands wide in a what-could-he-do gesture. "Besides, it's just a stun grenade."

Charlie felt a bit disappointed, but the down-ranking of the weapon in her hand didn't seem to appease Fifi. "It doesn't matter. Don't throw grenades at my sisters."

"I really did ask for it," Charlie said, feeling a bit bad for getting Bennett in trouble. Besides, she hadn't been lying about how tired she was. "Can you take your marital spat and the inevitable making up to your honeymoon suite please? That room is specifically designed for both of those things."

"I don't think it's designed for marital spats." Fifi frowned at her, distracted from her displeasure about the grenade tossing.

"It's definitely designed for the making up part, though, so shoo." Charlie waved her hands at them. "I love you both, but now I'm tired. Good night, and text me if you need backup."

Although Fifi looked like she wanted to keep arguing—about either the grenade or the intended use of the honeymoon suite—Bennett caught her gently by the hand and towed her out the door.

"Good night!" Fifi called over her shoulder as they disappeared into the hall.

Charlie got up to lock the door behind them. For all the times she teased them about moving into their suite, she was glad to have the quiet stillness of her own room. Then the silence settled over her, the nagging need to talk about the wild day they'd had, and she felt the familiar tug of loneliness.

Mentally shoving it away, she turned the dead bolt with extra force and tried very hard not to think of a certain firefighter.

FIVE

"You know I can't tell you anything about the case," Deputy Chris Jennings said for the third—maybe fourth—time in less than thirty minutes. "*Either* case."

"Everyone who tried to kidnap Fifi is still in jail, right? At least tell us that." Charlie eyed his desk, hoping to catch a glimpse of something useful, but except for his laptop, a blank block of sticky notes, and a framed picture of Daisy, the desktop was empty.

"Yes," Chris said, his smile softening slightly from the professional mask he'd worn the whole time since they'd trooped inside the sheriff's department. "All four are being held without bail, due to their militia connections."

"Buuuut, Clint was cleared of all charges in Cobra's murder, right? So he's just being held for the explosion and kidnapping and all that malarkey?"

That tiny bit of softening dried up, replaced by exasperation. "Charlie, stop. I'm not telling you anything."

"Not even whether Kieran Byrne is your top suspect in Cobra's murder, now that Clint's been cleared?" She eyed his face closely, monitoring his micro-expressions, hoping to at least get confirmation of what Kieran had told them the previous night. Unfortunately, all she could read in his expression was that he found her extremely aggravating.

"Charlotte Pax—" he started, only to have her interrupt.

"Calamity."

He paused, eyeing her. "What?"

"My middle name," she said helpfully. "Calamity. From the sound of it, you were about to launch into a well-meaning lecture, which is more effective if you can triple-name the recipient."

His annoyance was fighting with amusement now, she could tell, which was a good sign. Often at this point, people's exasperation would turn to rage, and Charlie would rather face laughter. Occasionally, angry interviewees would spill information, but throwing punches was more typical.

"Charlotte Calamity Pax," he corrected himself, although he didn't sound nearly as lecture-y as a few moments earlier. "You need—"

"Oh good." A woman's voice interrupted Chris, and everyone in his office looked over at the doorway where the words had come from. Of course it was Sheriff Summers. Charlie held in a sigh. This was not panning out to be the most productive morning. "You came in to give your statement. Come with me." The sheriff turned and walked away from the open doorway, not even waiting to see if they were going to follow.

Charlie decided to take advantage of that. "I'll go," she mouthed to her sister. "You two…" She made her fingers into pretend legs and ran them over her palm. There was no reason all three of them should be trapped with the sheriff for possibly hours when they could be out looking for Jane or looking into Cobra's murder.

Fifi gave a quiet snort but nodded, which was good, because Bennett was staring at Charlie as if she'd just spoken in Japanese. She forgave him for not understanding her charades yet. After all, Fifi still had to interpret his grunt language for her.

"Ms. Pax," the sheriff called, and Charlie sighed heavily, pushing herself to her feet and giving Chris—who definitely looked amused now—a thank-you wave. Outside the office, Charlie turned left to follow the sheriff, while Fifi tugged Bennett to the right toward the exit.

At the end of the hall, the sheriff opened a door to what Charlie assumed was an interview room. It had a table and four straight-back chairs, a camera mounted close to the ceiling, and that was about it.

Summers gestured toward one of the chairs before settling on the opposite side of the table. With a silent sigh, Charlie settled into the seat and gave a small wave to the lens on the video camera.

"Let's start with why you're in Simpson," the sheriff said.

This is going to take a while. Mentally bracing for a several-hour interrogation, Charlie wished Kieran was there to jam an oxygen mask over her mouth. At least Fifi and Bennett got away, so the entire day wouldn't be wasted. She was disappointed she wouldn't get to meet with Kieran though. *Rein it in, Ms. Lustypants*, she told herself. It wasn't like she was missing a date with her fireman. It was a murder investigation. Somehow, though, missing out on both seeing Kieran again as well as not getting to look into Cobra's death was even worse than missing a plain old date would be.

At a knock on the door, the sheriff rose and opened it a crack.

"Gabrielle Jones wants to talk to you," an unfamiliar deputy—i.e., not Chris—said in a low voice. It was a good thing that Charlie had bat-like ears.

Jones…as in related to Cobra Jones?

"Where is she?"

"Lobby."

Summers turned to look at Charlie, who immediately put on her best innocent expression. "Wait here."

Charlie smiled, as if in agreement, intentionally not nodding. Why would she agree to wait in the tiny, boring room, when she could potentially find out information about the case?

With a final, suspicious glare, the sheriff left the room. The door had barely shut behind her before Charlie was on her feet. Slipping out of the little room, she headed for the lobby, staying far enough back from the sheriff that a squeak of her boot soles wouldn't give her away.

The sheriff shoved through the security door into the lobby, and Charlie flew down the hallway, catching the door right before it relocked. Crouching so she couldn't be seen through the small rectangular window set in the top half of the door, she held it open a crack with her shoulder, hoping that the sheriff and Cobra's—widow? daughter? mother?—whoever Gabrielle was to him would hold their conversation close to her hiding spot.

"Gabrielle," the sheriff greeted the woman in a carrying voice, and Charlie grinned. *The acoustics are perfect.*

"Sheriff." The husky, feminine voice wasn't as clear as Summers's, but Charlie could hear it if she strained her ears. "Thank you for talking with me."

"Of course." The sheriff sounded slightly stiff, making Charlie wonder if Summers was more comfortable doing interrogations than soothing victims and their relatives. "I don't have much new to tell you, unfortunately."

Gabrielle gave a soft sob. "I heard that Clint was cleared. Is that true? Is the killer still running around free? What if he comes after me next?" Her voice quickly gained in volume, echoing through the high-ceilinged lobby. "I need protection!"

"How did you…? Never mind." The sheriff sounded irritated, probably at how everyone and their dog knew all the details of her case. "We're just starting the investigation, Gabby. We'll be talking to a lot of people, but we'll find out who did this. Are you still out at the compound?"

"Yes." Her voice quavered, but a note of defensiveness crept in. "It's my home."

"I understand that, but it won't do any good for us to post a deputy outside," the sheriff explained with strained patience. "What about your brother? Can you stay with him?"

"Ugh. No." The transition from weepy to disgusted was

so fast that Charlie dared push the door open enough that she could peek around it, wanting to see what Gabrielle looked like. "His wife is an enormous bitch."

Relieved to see that Summers had her back to her hiding spot, Charlie got an almost straight-on look at Gabrielle. Even with her forehead wrinkled and her full lips puckered in an expression of distaste, Gabrielle was beautiful. Tall and willowy, she had big eyes and strawberry-blond hair that tumbled over her shoulders in shiny fat curls. Curiosity satisfied, Charlie retreated, allowing the door to close until it was barely cracked open.

"I just don't think the compound is the safest place for you right now," the sheriff continued. "You're surrounded by people of interest in your husband's murder. Until we clear them and find who's responsible for his death, your brother's place or even a motel room would be a safer choice."

"I need to be around family right now," Gabrielle said, the weepy shake back in her voice. "*Real* family. That's what the Freedom Survivors are to me."

"Things are going to get tense," the sheriff warned. "We're just starting interviews, and I know the militia members don't take well to questions from law enforcement."

The door swung away, almost sending Charlie sprawling. She jumped up and back several steps as Chris—the door opener—eyed her with amusement.

"Should you be here?" he asked.

"Ah…just checking how long the sheriff was going to be." Even though it was probably too late, she widened her eyes in her best innocent look. "I have a meeting at ten, so I'm in a bit of a time crunch."

"A meeting." He eyed her suspiciously. "Would that be with the murder club, by chance?"

"No." She didn't mention that some of the murder club ladies *might* be attending. "It's with a potential source."

"Mm-hmm." He packed a *lot* of skepticism in that wordless sound. "Who's your source?"

She snorted. "You want me to rat out my source before I even get any information? What kind of…source-haver do you think I am?"

His heavy sigh was a familiar sound. Charlie made quite a few people sigh like that, as if it came from their very weary soul. After a quick glance over his shoulder, he gestured for her to move down the hallway. "Sheriff's almost done. You might want to get back to the interview room and put on your innocent face again."

Charlie grinned. "It's like you know me, Deputy Daisy's Husband." Turning on her heel, she hurried back to the tiny room and took a seat. In just a handful of seconds, the sheriff joined her, eyeing her with suspicion.

I get that look a lot, Charlie thought, following Chris's advice and imitating her twin's angelic expression.

The sheriff's frown deepened, but she didn't call out Charlie for eavesdropping, so Chris might've kept his mouth shut. "Why are you in Simpson?" Summers asked, picking up where they'd left off before Gabrielle's interruption.

"Why would you even ask that? Look at this place!" Charlie

spread her hands, intending to indicate the beauty of the town and surrounding area, but only managing to wave at the tiny interview room, which made her comment come off as sarcastic. "The whole mountain thing, I mean."

As the sheriff's frown deepened, Charlie heaved a sigh. This was going to take *hours*.

————

"You made it," Fifi called across the sheriff department parking lot before turning to Bennett in the seat next to her. "I won the bet."

"Love your confidence in me, Feef." She'd only accomplished it because the sheriff had been called away to help with a multicar accident a half hour into the attempted interrogation, but Charlie smiled and took the credit anyway as she trotted over to the car and climbed into the back seat. "What'd Bennett bet?"

"That you'd be arrested for mouthiness."

After considering that for a moment, Charlie gave her brother-in-law an approving nod. "Fairly safe bet, but I don't think mouthiness is an official crime."

"If anyone could be arrested for mouthiness, it'd be you." Fifi pulled out of the parking lot. She must've already entered the fire station's address into the GPS, because a robotic female voice told her to turn left.

"Awe, thanks, Fifi." Charlie settled back against the seat. "So I got a glimpse of Cobra's widow."

"Yeah?" Fifi glanced at her in the rearview mirror, and Bennett turned to look at her, interest clear on both of their faces.

"She came in to talk to the sheriff. I just *happened* to be in a place where I could overhear a bit of their conversation." She ignored Fifi's amused snort. "So, interesting thing—Gabrielle Jones is staying at the compound."

"Weird." Fifi frowned as she made another prompted turn. "She's living with her dead husband's murderer?"

"Probably." Charlie didn't want to assume, but when a militia leader was offed, it seemed likely that one of the other militia folks was involved, especially the brand-new leader. "She was surprised Clint was cleared, and she'd been living there with him. Even when the sheriff told her it'd be safer to move to her brother's house for now, Gabrielle refused. Apparently, her sister-in-law is a bitch." Charlie nudged the back of Bennett's seat with her knee. "You lucked out, B. Think of the nightmare family you could've married into."

"I did, yeah." Bennett's words and sweet smile surprised her. Charlie had been teasing, so she'd expected an eye roll, and his sincerity threw her off her game.

"Uh...anyway." Clearing her throat awkwardly, she returned to the subject at hand as Fifi snickered. "The sheriff didn't tell her much. Not sure if they don't really have anything, or if she's just tight-lipped."

"Speaking of lips," Fifi said, "are we going tight or loose?"

"With Kieran?"

"Yeah." Fifi shot her a warning look. "I know he's your future fiancé, so think with your brain, not your lady bits."

Charlie opened her mouth to answer but then shut it again. Her sister knew her too well. "You two better decide then. My lady bits are bossy and won't be denied."

Bennett and Fifi had a silent conversation, which Charlie felt was quite the accomplishment since Fifi was driving and could only spare a few brief speaking glances at her husband. Finally, he shrugged in an affirmative way, and Fifi gave him a tight nod. "Okay."

"Okay?" Charlie repeated. "What does that mean? I don't speak Finnett. Or Bifi." She snorted at the latter name amalgam. "Beefy. Heh."

"Okay, we're going with loose lips—*limited* loose."

"Excellent." Charlie grinned. It would've been hard to deny Kieran information when his glower was so adorable.

The fire station was small compared to the Langston one, but it was bustling. Busy looking around, Charlie almost crashed into a firefighter.

"Sorry," she said, giving him an apologetic grin. "I was distracted by all the eye candy around here."

He just scowled as he skirted around her.

"Oops," Charlie said to Fifi. "Was that creepy of me to say? Should I go after him to apologize for being harass-y?"

"Nah." It was Rory's objectively handsome husband who replied as he joined their small group. "It's nothing personal. Dane's just caffeine deprived—we all are." Ian frowned.

"Haven't you gotten a new coffee maker yet?" Charlie asked.

"No." The word came out with a bit of a snap. "Everything's back-ordered—supply chain issues."

"Just have people bring their little ones from home," she suggested.

"Tried that." Somehow, he even managed to look even

grumpier. Apparently, all the firefighters had joined Kieran in the cranky club today. "This building's old. That many coffee makers overloaded the circuit and melted the insulation on the wiring. Almost started a fire. So until the electrician can update all our wiring, we're hooked up to the emergency generator just for lights and basic power."

"A fire…at the fire station?" Charlie bit her lip to hold back an inappropriate snicker and very carefully avoided meeting Fifi's gaze. Ian's glare told her he wasn't in the right mood to appreciate the irony. "At least you have all the fire-putting-out equipment here. Save on diesel, and all that." One glance at Ian's face told her that he wasn't ready to look on the bright side of things, so she scrambled for something inoffensive to say. "Sorry for your coffeemaker loss."

"And with the coffee shop burned down…" Fifi trailed off with a sympathetic grimace.

"We're stuck with *instant*." Ian's voice was heavy with gloom as Charlie gagged vicariously at the thought.

"Ian!" One of the other firefighters roared. "Get over here and help me with this."

"Be a miracle if we manage to get through this without murdering each other." Clamping his jaw tightly, Ian stomped off toward his glaring coworker.

"Is it wrong that I find all these surly firemen even more attractive than happy, smiling ones?" Charlie mused, looking around.

"Yes," Bennett and Fifi chorused.

"Bah." Charlie waved off their judgment. "What do you

two know? You save all your googly eyes for each other. You're completely biased."

She spotted Kieran walking toward them, and her breath caught. Here was in-person proof that the grumpiest guys were the hottest.

He jerked his head, gesturing them toward a small office in the corner.

"Check that out," Fifi murmured quietly. Charlie eyed Kieran as he weaved through his coworkers. He didn't really have to weave, however, since the other firefighters drew away from him, leaving a wide path open in front of him.

"They're acting like he stinks," Charlie said under her breath. "And I know for a fact that the man smells like the mountains in winter." As if they'd choreographed it, Bennett and Fifi glanced at her out of the corners of their eye before meeting each other's gaze. "You know what I mean—cold, unpolluted, delicious air with just a hint of woodsmoke. And, oddly enough, hints of new-car smell."

Fifi and Bennett did the same side-eye-then-silent-conversation look again—something Charlie was discovering married people did with annoying frequency. Heaving a heavy sigh and shoving away that little niggle of loneliness that she always felt when her lack of coupledom was tossed in her face, Charlie strode toward the office door, where Kieran was impatiently waiting.

"So what's up with that?" Charlie gestured toward where Kieran had just been. His coworkers were still eyeing him—or maybe both of them—with obvious distrust.

"What?" he snapped.

"Why are they treating you like Leper Larry?"

The corners of his mouth pinched in the way she was beginning to learn meant he was holding back a smile—or at least a less-intense frown. "Leper Larry?"

"Smelly Stanley?" One of these days, she'd score an actual grin from him.

Not today, though, since his scowl settled more heavily into place as his gaze settled on Bennett and Fifi behind her. Instead of answering, he jerked open the office door and ushered them into the small space.

"Whose office is this?" Charlie asked, immediately prowling around. Despite the boxlike dimensions of the space, someone had managed to cram in an impressive amount of clutter.

"Chief's." He closed the door and leaned against the wall next to it, crossing his arms over his chest. The office's contents couldn't hold her attention when she had Kieran's bulging biceps to ogle instead.

"We met Chief Early last time we were in Simpson," Fifi said, settling onto one of the two guest chairs in front of the paper-strewn desk. Bennett stood behind her, like he was her bodyguard. "He was with you and your…" She cleared her throat, looking uncomfortable as Kieran's face turned even more granite-y than usual. "Your…erm…dad." She did manage to get the words out, although they sounded a bit strangled.

Wanting to break the stiff, frozen silence that'd settled over the office at the mention of the militia-loving kidnapper Finn

Byrne, Charlie sprawled in the second chair next to her sister. "So any word on who set the coffee shop on fire?"

Kieran narrowed his eyes at her, but his shoulders relaxed an infinitesimal amount, so Charlie considered that a win. "Why are you asking me?"

Waving a hand at the office walls surrounding them, she said, "Because the fire thing is sort of your whole deal?"

He stiffened again. "You think I had something to do with—"

"Stop. Don't get all porcupine-y on me," Charlie cut him off, unable to hold back an eye roll. The man truly was a prickly beast. "Of course you didn't leave the fire station, barricade us inside the coffee shop, set it on fire, return to the fire station, go out on the call, help tear down the barricades, and perform an unnecessary rescue. You're one of the few on our 'Absolutely Could Not Have Participated in This Particular Arson' list."

Although he made some token grumbly noises, especially about the "unnecessary" bit, Charlie was pretty sure he was appeased by her reassurance that they didn't suspect him—for the fire, at least. "So? Did the sheriff or fire chief pinpoint any people of interest?"

"Even if they did, how would I hear about it?" he asked. "Besides, aren't you here looking for your mom? Why are you looking into the arson?"

"I heard you firefighters were the best at information-passing in the county." Charlie answered his first question. "Maybe even the state. Case in point, how you already know the whole deal with my mom. Right now, we're waiting for her to show up, and I need a distraction so I don't create my own entertainment."

"That never ends well," Fifi interjected, and Bennett nodded.

Charlie couldn't really argue with something that true, so she settled on giving the peanut gallery a chilly glance before turning back to Kieran. "Speaking of, don't you have a whole 'nother distraction for us to look into?" When he just glowered at her, she clarified, "Tell us why the sheriff thinks you killed Cobra."

"I already told you," he grumped. "It's because I'm not popular right now."

Unable to hold back her amusement, Charlie laughed out loud. "If that's all it takes, I would've been arrested for murder every day in high school. There's got to be more than that. Sheriff Summers seems like a fact-loving person."

Kieran glowered at her, but eventually gave in and grudgingly admitted, "We might've been seen talking."

That was weirdly vague and didn't seem very motive-y to Charlie. "Talking?"

"Loudly."

Ah. "Arguing then. When?"

He scratched the line of his jaw, the rasp of stubble loud in the tiny office. "Right before he disappeared."

"So you fought, in public, the last time he was seen in a not-murdered state?" Charlie gave him a flat look. "Yeah, I'm sure the reason you're a suspect is because you're *unpopular*."

The faintest touch of red colored his cheekbones. "Well?" he demanded as she tried to not find his pouty look unbearably attractive. She was discovering all sorts of things about herself on this trip to Simpson. Who knew her type was moody, caffeine-deprived firefighters who might've murdered the local militia leader? Even as she thought it, she mentally shook her head—not at the thought that she found the crabby man attractive, because she definitely did, but at the idea that Kieran was a killer. *Mood*-killer, maybe, but unless he glared Cobra to death with his eyeball lasers, Charlie's instincts were telling her that Kieran wasn't the murderer.

It took a moment to get her brain back on track enough to answer him. "Well, what?"

"Who do you think killed him?"

"It's really too bad Clint has an alibi," Charlie said with a sigh. "He's the perfect suspect."

"A good alibi too." Fifi sounded a bit sour, which was understandable. Clint had tried to kidnap her, after all. "Hard to argue with 'he was in jail.'"

"Yeah." Charlie was quiet for a moment, mourning the loss of their perfect suspect. "Who else besides you hated Cobra?"

"I didn't hate him," Kieran grumbled.

"Then why'd you scream at him in the middle of Main Street?" Charlie asked.

Looking slightly offended, he corrected her assumption. "It wasn't in the middle of Main Street." When Charlie raised her eyebrows and just waited him out, he finally admitted, "It was in the grocery store."

"That's so much better." Her tone was dry enough to draw a snort of amusement from Fifi. "What was your fight about?"

"It wasn't a…" He must've noticed that Charlie was about three seconds away from leaping out of her chair and choking a straight answer out of him, because he cleared his throat and started again. "He was saying rude things to his wife. I told him to knock it off. He didn't appreciate it much."

"Gabrielle Jones?" Charlie asked, and Kieran lifted his chin in a tight nod. *Hmm…interesting.* "If he was abusive to her, that opens up the suspect pool—Gabrielle, her family, friends, any boyfriends or wannabe boyfriends…" She trailed off as an unwelcome thought occurred to her. "Were you one?"

"One what?"

"One of the hypothetical boyfriends?" When he frowned even harder in confusion, she clarified, "Were you involved with Gabrielle? As a friend, or…romantically?" The thought made her stomach feel squirmy for some reason, but she told herself it was just because Kieran was making himself look more and more like a viable suspect.

"No." His flat answer rang with honesty, and Charlie's shoulders dropped a few inches. "Barely know her. Don't have to be screwing her to step in when her husband's being an ass."

Charlie blinked as she absorbed his statement that was strangely honorable in a rough, angry way. "So, Cobra was being nasty to his wife at the grocery store, you stepped in, the two of you argued, and then…?" She rolled her hand in a please-continue gesture.

He shrugged. "Then nothing. They left. I shopped. Everyone else stared like brainless idiots."

"Not a big fan of humanity in general?" Charlie asked.

"No."

"Understandable." Except for her sisters—and recently, their respective men—Charlie wasn't wild about most people either. She'd always figured her antisocial bent was because the bounty-hunting thing tended to feature the more unpleasant side of humanity, but Kieran was a firefighter. He should be surrounded by other disproportionately attractive heroes and adoring groupies, so she wondered what skewed his worldview. Then she remembered who his dad was, and his crabbiness made more sense. She met his gaze, feeling a bone-deep curiosity to discover all of this man's secrets.

"What exactly did the sheriff say?" Fifi asked, bringing Charlie back to the point of this discussion. It was too easy to get distracted while Kieran was filling up all the space in the room.

Kieran's gaze lingered on Charlie's for an extra hundredth of a second before moving to Fifi. "What questions did she ask me?"

"Not unless they're something very different than what we've just asked you?" When Kieran gave a tight shake of his head, Fifi continued. "Then no. I'm wondering how she left it. Don't leave town? We'll be back later today with an arrest warrant? We'll be watching you from the shrubs outside your living room window tonight?"

Kieran flicked a look over at Charlie before his gaze returned to Fifi, and his almost-smile was back. "Sometimes the family resemblance is obvious."

Bennett gave a cough that sounded like he was disguising a laugh.

"She just told me she'd be questioning me again later." The hint of amusement was gone as if it'd never existed. "The don't-leave-town part was implied."

It was Charlie's turn to chuckle. "I know the sound of that."

"Any alibi?" Bennett asked, his deep voice a surprise after he'd been silent so long. Charlie didn't think she'd ever not be startled when he spoke.

Kieran didn't look fazed, however. "Work. Other than that, I was usually home. Alone."

"Ugh." Charlie made a face. "That's a terrible alibi. It just screams, 'I killed Cobra!' Too bad you don't live here. That'd be an excellent alibi to be constantly surrounded by all the cranky, caffeine-deprived hotties milling around out there." She gestured toward the door.

Kieran's frown had deepened at the word "hotties," and he opened his mouth to speak, only to snap it closed as the door swung open.

A ginger-haired firefighter filled the doorway. "What are you doing in here?" His accusing gaze instantly landed on Kieran. "You shouldn't be in here when the chief's gone."

Charlie waited for Kieran to explain that he had Early's permission, but of course he didn't. The contrary man just glared at the redhead for a solid ten seconds before turning his head as if he couldn't even be bothered to *look* at the other man anymore. It was so deliciously cold and cutting that Charlie could barely keep the gleeful grin off her face. Kieran was constantly, eternally furious, so the fact that he couldn't be bothered to waste any of his rage on his coworker was a rather glorious insult.

When the ginger's face turned an unhealthy shade of angry red-dish purple, however, she decided to smooth things over before his head exploded.

"It's all good," she said. "Early doesn't mind that we're in here."

Somehow, that seemed to enrage the man even more. "I'm texting him." He released the doorknob so he could tap at his phone more efficiently, and Kieran wasted no time. Reaching in front of the other man, he pulled the door closed with a solid thud and then turned the lock.

The sight of the redhead's startled, open-mouthed expression before he was shut out of the office struck Charlie as funny, and she muffled her chuckle with her hand. "Can't believe that some people never grew out of their ten-year-old petty-snitch stage."

Kieran focused his bitter-cold gaze on her, and those icy-blue eyes warmed to the flickering heat of a Bunsen burner flame. Suddenly, she lost her ability to speak.

SIX

"So!" Fifi slapped her hands together sharply, jerking Charlie out of the daze Kieran's hypnotic gaze had caused. "What's the plan?"

A pounding on the door interrupted before anyone could answer. Ignoring the knocking, Charlie turned back to Kieran. "How much longer until your shift's over?"

He glanced at his watch. "I was off an hour ago."

"Perfect." Fifi clapped her hands again. "Let's split up and tackle all the crimes."

Charlie wrinkled her nose, not liking her sister's newly acquired mannerism. "Is that going to be a thing?"

"What? Splitting up to investigate mysteries like the Scooby gang?"

"The clapping."

"Maybe. Why?" Fifi eyed her with a look Charlie didn't trust. "Don't you like it?"

"Maybe." Her tone was cautious. Once her sisters knew

her weaknesses, they could annoy her to their little hearts' content.

"You don't, do you?" Fifi was positively gleeful, and Charlie's heart sank.

"The clapping is going to be a thing, isn't it?"

"Now it is."

"Okay." Kieran was obviously having trouble holding his scowl, but Charlie appreciated the effort. "Are you two done?"

A booming voice from outside the office was easy to hear, despite the closed door. "Chase, why the hell are you still knocking? Don't you think I would've answered if I were in there?"

Kieran reached over and unlocked the door right before an older man—Chief Early, Charlie assumed—charged through it. He came to an abrupt stop at the sight of the four of them filling his office.

"I tried to tell you, Chief," the ginger's triumphant voice came from behind Early. "Byrne's been in there with the door closed for almost an hour. Who knows what files he's dug through—or what he's taken."

"Chase…" Chief Early somehow managed to both sigh and bellow at the same time. Charlie was impressed. "Byrne asked to use my office. He's allowed to be in here. Why don't you do something useful, like inventory the spare bunker gear?"

"But, Chief—"

"Go." Early's firm tone cut Chase off, and the ginger slunk away, presumably to start his inventory. Charlie couldn't hold back a smirk. That had been very satisfying to watch. Turning back to Kieran, the chief muttered, "We need to get caffeine into everyone. Maybe one of the medics can set it up on an IV drip. You get your meeting finished, or do you need my office for a while longer?"

"We're done." Even though he was talking to his boss, Kieran still sounded as cranky as ever, although he did add a grudging, "Thanks."

The chief just grinned. "At least you're always the same, coffee or no coffee. Enjoy your days off then." He greeted Fifi and Bennett before turning to Charlie. He gave her a friendly—albeit assessing—look as he held out his hand to shake. "You must be Felicity's sister—Charlie, is it?"

"It is." Once again, she was impressed by the efficiency of the small-town gossip pipeline. "And you must be Fire Chief Early, who very kindly let us have this satellite murder club meeting in your office."

Although he blinked at the murder club reference, he quickly recovered, grinning at her. "The very one. Let me know if I can be of any help."

"Will do." In fact, she could check his helpfulness levels right at this very moment. "Any idea who locked us in the coffee shop and turned it into an oversized smoker grill?"

"Nope," the chief said. "My part is to figure out the origins and causes of fires. The coffee shop was definitely arson—and an obvious one at that—so I left the rest of the investigation up to the sheriff. She's the one to ask."

"Yeahhh…" Charlie drew out the word as she headed for the door. "We'll consider asking the sheriff plan B—or maybe plan F or G. We're not her favorite people."

"She likes me just fine," Kieran said smugly.

Did he just make a joke? Charlie was struck silent for a whole three seconds before she huffed a laugh. "Well, sure she does," she said once she'd recovered. "She has eyeballs, doesn't she?"

"What does that mean?"

"Good to meet you, Chief," she said over her shoulder as they left his office. "If I ever need to know the origin and cause of a fire, you'll be the first one I'll come to."

"Thanks?"

As Fifi and Bennett said goodbye to Early, Charlie returned her attention Kieran, still slightly in shock that Kieran was actually joking around with her. It was a bit like bantering with a shark—she was well aware that at any moment, he could bite her head clean off—but that knowledge just gave the whole conversation an exhilarating edge. "It means that your face and body are extremely...likable."

Especially at this moment, when his scowl had lightened into something close to astonishment and he had a very adorable bit of side-eye happening, but Charlie wasn't about to say that part out loud. She was already calling him hot.

"Are you calling me hot?"

"See, your surprise at that just adds to your appeal," she said.

"But that's just illogical."

He'd managed to lose her, and Charlie didn't like that. She prided herself on her ability to banter with the best of them. "Your hotness is illogical?"

"No, that the sheriff likes me because of my...alleged hotness." He sounded like he choked a bit on the last two words.

"If that were true, she'd *really* like you, and from what I've seen, she can't stand you."

"Awe, Kiki." She stopped in the middle of the parking lot. Somehow, she hadn't noticed their walk through the hostile firefighters and out of the station. Kieran was apparently a master distractor. "Are you calling me hot?"

He winced at the nickname but didn't protest out loud, which was a bit disappointing. Charlie prided herself on choosing nicknames that people loathed. Instead, he snorted and gave her a look of disdain. "You know you're gorgeous."

"I do?" She had a twin, so she knew she was cute from staring at Cara's face her whole life, but she'd never considered that she fell into *gorgeous* territory. "I don't know if I'd go that far. *Adorable*, maybe, when my dimples are showing, but—"

"Stunning," he interrupted. When she stared at him, once again shocked into silence, his cheekbones reddened. "You're stunning when your..." He coughed, dropping her gaze as his scowl reemerged, and the rest of his words sounded like they came out through gritted teeth. "When your...dimples are showing."

She was straight flummoxed by that, so much that she couldn't think of anything to say. She'd always thought of herself as strong and smart and maybe a little too brave, but she'd never even considered the idea that anyone would find her *stunning* or *gorgeous*. After opening and closing her mouth soundlessly a couple of times, she was a little relieved when Fifi and Bennett caught up with them.

"What's going on?" Fifi asked, looking between Kieran and Charlie with her eyes alight with avid curiosity.

"Hmm?" Charlie non-answered before tearing her gaze away from Kieran's grumpy face, which looked impossibly more attractive when he blushed. "Oh, nothing much. Just discussing where to go from here."

From Fifi's narrowed eyes, she knew that for the lie it was, but Charlie held her innocent look until her sister gave an annoyed huff. "Fine. I'll get it out of you later. Right now, Bennett and I are going to meet Lou and the coroner at the Simpson Bar, see if she can tell us anything about Cobra's remains."

"Be careful," Charlie said.

"Of what?" Fifi raised an eyebrow. "Alcohol poisoning?"

"Well, last time you went to a bar, you ended up getting married, so that is a little concerning, but I was thinking more along the lines of someone lighting the place on fire while you're in there."

"Oh." Fifi frowned. "Maybe we'll sit on the patio."

"It'll get cold soon," Kieran warned, but Fifi just shrugged.

"Better cold than on fire."

"This town isn't a relaxing place to be," Bennett muttered.

Charlie grinned. "Isn't it great? Never a boring moment." Bennett didn't look like he agreed, but she charged on ahead. "What's the plan for me and Kiki here?"

"Kiki?" Fifi asked in a strangled voice.

"No," Kieran said flatly.

"Don't fight it," Bennett warned. "The more she knows you hate it, the more entrenched it'll become."

Charlie smiled at her brother-in-law approvingly. "You're such a quick learner, B."

"Thanks," he said dryly.

"You two are going to meet Rory at her store." Fifi quickly tapped at her phone screen as she spoke. "Just sent you the address. She's agreed to arrange an interview with one of the more…reasonable militia members, see what they know about Cobra's murder."

"Maybe we can sneak in a few questions about the coffee shop fire too." Charlie glanced at her phone and saw the text pop up on her screen. Turning to Kieran, she asked, "Okay if we take your car?"

He gave a short nod, and she gave him a beaming smile.

His eyes narrowed in suspicion. "Why are you so happy about that?"

"I just appreciate how you didn't argue or try to take over." Giving a wave to Fifi and Bennett, she started toward the line of cars that stretched across the back of the lot. All of the vehicles had been backed into the spaces, so they were parked facing out. "Most people take longer to give in to the inevitable after they first meet me. Is backing into a parking spot a firefighter thing?" She waved toward the orderly line of cars.

He opened his mouth, closed it, and then must've decided not to ask any questions about what was "inevitable" because he simply said, "Yeah. Well, first-responder thing."

"Interesting. I'm going to have to start doing that. I can see how it'd save time when the skip you're chasing down Maple Street jumps into his girlfriend's green Impala and takes off." She scanned the motley mix of vehicles before spotting the truck he'd brought to the coffee shop before it'd been burned. Making a beeline for the pickup, she decided to see how far she could press her luck.

"I'll drive."

He actually laughed. Well, it was more of a choked snort, but she was still going to put it in the laugh column. "No, you're not driving my truck. You don't even know where we're going."

"Shotgun then." She headed for the passenger side instead. "You've been to Rory's gun store?"

"Why'd you call shotgun?" He was getting that baffled note in his voice again, and Charlie hid a tiny grin. "No one else is riding with us. And yeah, I've been to Rory's."

"What'd you get?"

"Nothing." He beeped the unlock button on his remote and stomped over to the driver's door, his boots thumping hard against the ground as if the asphalt surface had done something to offend him. "I was working both times."

"She had a fire?"

"Explosions."

Charlie paused in the middle of boosting herself into the passenger seat. "Explosions? Plural?"

"Yeah."

"Huh." She finished getting inside and pulled the door closed. Reaching for her seat belt, she said, "The more I learn about this town, the more I like it."

She was rewarded with yet another laugh from him, this one slightly less choked than the last one. *I'll get a belly laugh out of him before we leave this crazy town*, she thought, but the thought brought her up short.

"What's wrong?" Kieran barked.

"Nothing." She shook off the sense of loss that'd settled over her at the thought of leaving Simpson in her rearview mirror—or, more accurately, the thought of leaving *Kieran* behind in just a few short days. "Just a weird thought."

"Please don't share it."

A laugh burst out of her, dissolving the last of her melancholy. "You know that just makes me want to share every random thought that passes through my very active brain, right?"

His mutter sounded something like, "Oh, sweet Jesus, no."

She let the quiet tick by for a solid eight seconds before saying, "My butt itches."

His agonized groan made her laugh out loud.

———

Since Rory had a customer when she and Kieran walked in, Charlie took the opportunity to explore the store. She wasn't a huge gun fan, but Rory had the place set up as a sort of mix between a store and museum, with all sorts of weapons, old and new, lining the glass cases.

"Come over here," Rory called from her stool behind the counter. "Kevin's the one."

"I'm the one? What one?" The customer—Kevin, apparently—asked suspiciously. He was a nondescript blond guy in his thirties. *Looks like a very Kevin-like Kevin.* Charlie made a mental note to share that random thought with Kieran later.

"You're efficient," Charlie said approvingly to Rory as she

crossed the store to stand in front of Kevin, who took a wary step back.

Kieran took up a position behind and a little to the side of her, and she felt a warm feeling spread through her middle. She'd expected that having someone else—other than her sisters—with her while investigating would feel claustrophobic and unnecessary, but it wasn't like that at all. In fact, if this was what it felt like to have a hot guy at her back, then no wonder her sisters had gone all gaga over their respective men. She could already tell that having Kieran around could be addictive.

That cozy glow in her middle made her smile extra wide, and Kevin turned an unhealthy shade of greenish pale. "Kevin! So good of you to help us out like this."

"I'm not..." His eyes darted toward the door, and in her peripheral vision, Charlie saw Kieran shift to block the other man's escape route. "I–I didn't... What?"

Ignoring his stammered mumbling, Charlie turned up the wattage on her grin. Surprisingly, Kevin didn't seem to be reassured. Instead, he looked positively hunted. "So tell us...what'd you think of Cobra?"

Kevin blinked. "Cobra?"

"The former militia leader?" Charlie prompted. "Was he a good guy? Did you like him?"

"Well...yeah, I guess? I mean, I didn't know him that well?" From the way all his statements were curling up at the end, turning them into questions, Kevin had been taken off guard by the direction her interrogation was going.

"Not that well?" Charlie repeated, keeping a close eye on

his sweating face. "Did you just recently join the Freedom Survivors?"

Rory let out a quiet sound that was close enough to a gag to make Charlie glance at her.

"Sorry," Rory said, looking a little shamefaced. "That name... Lou's been rubbing off on me."

"Don't worry—I'm sure the murder club will get it changed soon enough." Turning back to Kevin, who looked very confused by that sidebar, Charlie gave him an encouraging nod.

"Yeah, no. Not very recently, I mean. Maybe five years ago."

Cocking her head, Charlie allowed a small frown to draw her eyebrows together. "But you didn't know Cobra well? Is the militia that big?"

"We don't really call ourselves a militia."

Holding back an eye roll, Charlie limited herself to circling her hand in a let's-get-on-with-it gesture. "I'm trying to keep Rory from losing her lunch all over that sparkling-clean counter, so let's just go with 'militia,' but your objection is noted. Now, why didn't you know Cobra well?"

"We weren't... I mean, I wasn't really in the inner circle. I only lived out there for six months before I moved to Liverton, so I just saw Cobra at training sessions and potlucks, things like that."

"I love that the militia has potlucks," Charlie said, and Kieran cough-choked behind her, a sound she was beginning to recognize as a stifled laugh. "So from your limited encounters with Cobra—and living in the same compound as him for six months—did he seem like a likable guy?"

"I guess?"

Charlie held back a sigh. She appreciated Rory offering a militia witness up on a platter, but she wished Kevin was just a touch more voluble. "Did the other members like him?"

Kevin paused before saying, "Sure."

Eyeing how his shoulders were scrunched up by his ears as Kevin spat out that obvious lie as if it tasted bitter, Charlie stayed silent and waited him out.

"I mean, some people must've liked him, since he was in charge." His eyes widened at his own words.

"Did *you* like him?" Before he could say anything, she added, "What little you knew of him?"

"I guess?"

And we're back to that. Gathering the crumbs of her limited patience, she asked, "Really? Because you don't sound too enthusiastic about our friend Cobra. He's dead, you know. You can tell the truth, and it won't get back to him. Or if it does, he won't have a corporeal body, so you should be safe." She decided not to bring up the possibility of poltergeists being real, since that information probably wouldn't be helpful.

Kevin let out a harsh breath. "Fine. I thought he was an asshole and a bully."

Charlie perked up. *Now things are getting interesting.* "Give me some examples."

"He always punched down." The words flowed out of him in a rush, as if finally allowing them out was a relief. "Made fun of the new recruits, the weaker guys, even his wife."

"Anyone stand out in your mind as hating him especially hard?"

Kevin raised his shoulders and then let them drop. "Mostly I stayed out of it. I like the training and the friends I made, but the politics…" He shook his head. "Not my thing."

"So the inner circle you mentioned earlier, did they all behave like Cobra? Or did any of them stand up to him?" Maybe the murderer had thought he'd been doing a public service of sorts.

"Nah, they were all as bad as Cobra."

"What about Clint?" Charlie tried to keep her own feelings buttoned up tight, as hard as it was to not let them color her words. He'd kidnapped her sister after all, and Charlie knew how to nurture a solid grudge. "What was he like, before and after he took over?"

"He wasn't around much until about a year before Cobra took off—uh, disappeared," he corrected himself since, Charlie assumed, the remains Fifi and Bennett had found pretty much proved that Cobra hadn't driven himself out of town. "Even after, he's spent a lot of that time locked up."

Charlie chewed on that for a few seconds before asking, "How is he leading the militia if he's been in jail most of the time?"

"His buddies talk to him, get his orders."

Charlie met Kieran's gaze, pretty sure he was thinking the same thing. If Clint could run the militia from jail, why couldn't he arrange for Cobra's murder while behind bars, as well? "Who are some of his buddies?"

Although he'd been looking more relaxed the longer they talked, at this question, Kevin's gaze shifted back over to the door again. "I–I don't know if I should… I mean, if they hear I ratted them out, it won't go well for me."

"You're not ratting them out." Charlie tried her most soothing smile, but that just made him shuffle uncomfortably. "I'm not the cops, and I'd never reveal my source. Besides, it's not a secret who Clint's friends with. I bet I could ask any of the locals hanging out at the coffee shop, and they'd say exactly the same names as you're about to tell me." Too late, she caught her mistake and winced. "If the coffee shop wasn't a burned-out shell, that is."

The reminder of the arson didn't seem to settle Kevin's nerves at all. If anything, his sweating increased.

"Speaking of the coffee shop, any idea who set it on fire?" She purposefully left out the part about being locked inside, trying to make the question sound like idle curiosity. Kevin was already rattled enough.

"No." Surprisingly, the change of subject seemed to have calmed him down. "Word around town is that it was one of the city people who followed you here."

"It wasn't them," she said. "The five treasure hunters have been cleared, since they were all eating at Levi's when it happened."

"Six."

Turning so she could look at Rory straight on, she repeated, "Six? You sure?"

"Yeah. They're all outside." She gestured toward the laptop screen in front of her.

"Huh. Who's the late arrival, I wonder? Mind if I take a look?" Charlie gestured toward the space next to Rory, who shrugged affirmatively. Boosting herself onto the counter, she slid across the glass top and hopped down on the other side.

"If you don't need me anymore, I'll just…" Kevin started to sidle around Kieran to get a clear path to the door.

"No." Kieran stopped him with one word and a glare.

"Thanks, Kiki."

"Call me that again, and I'll let him leave."

Kevin looked hopeful.

"Sorry." She sucked in her cheeks to hold back a smile. "Thanks, *Kieran*."

His grunt was grumpy, but he didn't let Kevin leave, so apparently her apology was sufficient.

Ignoring the byplay, Rory was bringing up various camera angles until she paused and pointed at the screen. "There's one."

Peering at the figure trying to blend into the shadows between two pine trees, Charlie said, "That's Dave. He's hopeless at hiding. He'd really be better off as an accountant or something. Why does he have snow camo on? Does he think we're in Antarctica?"

"Two."

"Tassie."

"Three."

"Lachlan. He's not much better at this than Dave. There are a gazillion trees, guys. It shouldn't be that hard to stay invisible."

"Four and five." Rory pointed to two shapes up in the tree branches, fifteen feet off the ground.

"Rhys—he's always climbing things—and…" Charlie squinted. "Huh. That's Bones. Can't believe she got out of her car, much less is sitting up in a tree. Tassie was right. It must be love."

It took Rory another minute and several different camera views before she pointed to the screen again. "And six."

"Huh." Charlie crouched and squinted at the figure, barely visible despite the high quality of the security camera footage. "Can you zoom in?"

"Yes, but we'll lose resolution, so it doesn't help much with identification." Rory made the figure larger, but she was right—it didn't make it any easier to identify the sixth treasure hunter.

Charlie peered at the screen for another couple moments before looking up and meeting Kieran's gaze. "Want to go for a stroll in the woods?"

His eyes lit up as the corners of his mouth curled. Charlie felt her breath catch and was glad she was crouched close to the floor, because an excited Kieran was gorgeous enough to make her topple over. "Yes."

"I'll just…um, go then," Kevin mumbled.

"Do you have his cell number and address?" Charlie asked Rory, who gave a short nod. "You're good to go then. Thank you for all of your help. Just write up that list of Clint's friends and email it to Rory. If you don't have a chance to do that before tonight, that's fine—we'll just swing by your house later to pick it up, wave it around a bit, talking loudly about how you gave us a list of suspects in Cobra's murder. Thanks, Kevin! You've been a peach!" The last bit she called out as the door swung closed behind him. As soon as she'd told him he could leave, he was out of the store like a shot, pausing only to look sick when she mentioned stopping by his house later. She had a feeling Rory would be getting that email shortly.

Charlie slid over the counter again. "Thanks, Rory. Mind if we run around your property, chasing mystery treasure hunters?"

"Go out the door and turn right. Look northwest about twenty feet, and you'll see where this camera is mounted on a pole."

"You're the best," Charlie said over her shoulder as she hurried to the exit. Kieran held the door open for her, but Charlie leaned back into the store. "As soon as we solve all these crimes, I'm going to come back in and take my time looking around. You have a fantastic store."

Rory smiled, just a flash of a beautiful grin before it was gone and she'd settled back into her usual somber expression. "Thank you."

With a final wave, Charlie was out the door and turning right. Her gaze scanned the area. "Which way is northwest?"

Kieran pointed. "That way. There's the pole."

"And the camera is pointing…" She moved in the direction the lens was facing. "There are the trees we saw."

A flicker of movement caught her eye, and she ran toward it. "And there's the sixth treasure hunter."

SEVEN

CHARLIE ALWAYS APPRECIATED FIFI WHEN she had to run after a skip. Training was never fun, but she was almost always faster than the person she was chasing, so all the sprints and intervals and long-distance runs she'd had to suffer through were worth it in the end—although she'd never admit that to Fifi.

With Kieran easily keeping pace next to her, Charlie ran for the tree line, her eyes scanning the area for any more movement in the trees that might reveal her target. There was nothing out of place, though, so she stopped where she'd initially spotted the sixth treasure hunter and looked down.

Crouching down next to her, Kieran pointed at a spot on the ground. A few dead leaves were scattered across the rocky soil, and there was a crescent-shaped impression pressed into one that bore a strong resemblance to the back of a bootheel. Pulling out the sheriff's business card and her phone, Charlie snapped a few pictures of the boot print with the card next to it to provide scale.

Tucking the phone and card back in her pocket, Charlie listened, but the only sounds were leaves rustling in the breeze, a distant birdcall, and the clicking sound of someone who hadn't turned their phone keyboard sounds off. She glared across the gun shop's small parking lot to see Dave had given up any attempt to be stealthy and was texting away with both thumbs. Charlie was 97 percent sure that he was live texting her search for the sixth treasure hunter to the rest of the group.

"He could at the very least silence his phone. Remind me to break into Dave's room at the Black Bear Inn and put fire ants in his bed later," she whispered to Kieran in a voice so low she wasn't sure if he'd be able to hear it. "Send the health inspector in right after—two birds with one fire-ant-covered stone."

Kieran must've had ears like a bat, just like she did, because he gave his usual clipped nod. That almost made her laugh, since his serious expression gave her request an undeserved gravity, as if he was going to make an effort to remind her about her threat later, in case punishing Dave slipped her mind.

Her amusement slipped away as Kieran took the lead, moving deep into the trees as he followed the faint signs of the sixth treasure hunter's trail. Charlie narrowed her eyes at his back. Although she fell in behind him, she made a mental note to have a tracking competition later. She was fairly sure she'd wipe the floor with him.

For now, she restrained her competitive urges and followed, although she kept a close eye on the signs, just to make sure he wasn't leading them astray. She also kept her head on a swivel, watching for any possible dangers approaching. The trees were quiet, but it felt too quiet, as if the forest was holding its breath. Kieran moved soundlessly, tracking so quickly that Charlie felt a grudging respect, suddenly less sure who would be wiping the floor with whom in their future tracking competition.

They reached a tall fence and turned left along it. Kieran picked up the pace, and Charlie followed suit. Their target was heading back toward the shop drive with its open gate—and likely a waiting vehicle just outside the fence.

"There," Kieran said, his voice low but filled with keen satisfaction.

Peering around him, Charlie saw the back of a dark-clothed figure darting through the trees. A thrill coursed through her as she sped up, keeping pace with Kieran as they sprinted as fast as possible over the uneven forest floor, dodging roots and rocks and entire trees. They slowly narrowed the distance, and each time Charlie peered around Kieran's broad form, the runner in front of them was a little bit closer...and more familiar.

All she could see were glimpses of the person's back, but there was something about the way they moved that rang a bell. Dismissing the niggling feeling of familiarity, Charlie concentrated on running. She'd be able to get a great close-up front view as soon as she tackled the mystery runner.

Her phone vibrated against her leg, a short double pulse that meant a text. Although she was tempted to ignore it, Charlie pulled the phone from her pocket. Even in this rather urgent situation, she still needed to know if one of her sisters needed help.

A glimpse at the screen showed that it was from Rory and was a short, two-word, all-caps message.

GET DOWN

Her distraction cost her, and her toe caught on a ropy root that emerged from the soil several inches. She stumbled, almost face-planting before she caught her balance, pushing off the ground with one hand as her feet drove her forward. A sharp *crack* split the air, followed soon after by a meaty *thunk*.

Bits of bark peppered the side of her face and neck. Startled, she looked to the side to see a chunk missing from the papery trunk of the aspen tree a mere few feet from her vulnerable skull. Her legs worked on autopilot, propelling her forward even as her brain spun.

Rory's text, the fresh hole in the tree, the familiar bark of sound snapped together in a flash of sudden comprehension. Fear grabbed her lungs in a vicious bear hug as she focused on Kieran. Thanks to her almost-fall and distraction, he'd managed to get a couple of strides ahead of her. Lunging forward, Charlie launched into a dive, desperately hoping it would be enough, that she'd be able to reach him in time.

Time seemed to slow as she flew through the air, Kieran's body getting closer, but not soon enough. Her body was descending too early. She wasn't going to make it.

Stretching her arms out in front of her, she reached for him anyway, knowing it was probably a futile effort. Somehow, her hands managed to touch his calf, and she extended her arms another impossible few inches. Clamping her fingers around his ankle, she held tight, as if her life—or his—depended on it.

To her utter relief, her grip held, and his body began to fall forward.

There was another crack, and then another, the sound piling on top of each other until she couldn't distinguish one shot from the next. Kieran hit the ground with a *thump* and a low grunt, and the earth shook slightly beneath them, as if she'd just felled a redwood tree.

Now that he was on the ground, she didn't pause. Instead, she belly crawled from his feet, over his legs, until she could stretch herself over his back and head, covering all the most vulnerable, important parts, the ones that made Kieran who he was. Only then, when her body was protecting his vital organs, could she take a breath and wait for the next storm of bullets.

Instead, everything went silent.

It could've been ten seconds or ten thousand, but everything went still and quiet until a low, rough, unfairly attractive voice growled, "Did you just *tackle* me?"

The question made the world start turning again, all the clocks resumed ticking, and Charlie finally dared to raise her head. "Yes. It wasn't my best work, but it did the job."

"The job? Of bringing me down?" He seemed to be at the point where he was more befuddled than actively hostile, which was kind of a fun change. As much as she really, really liked cranky Kieran, bewildered Kieran was nice too. "*Why* did you tackle me? I almost had them!"

"So you wouldn't get shot." She looked up to see chunks

of bark had been knocked off the trees next to them, revealing the pale inner wood. It looked weirdly painful, despite trees not having nerve endings. "Sorry about that, trees. It was us or you, though, and you weather a bullet wound better than we do. Probably." She looked back down at Kieran's oblique profile. "Does getting shot hurt a tree?"

He went still, staring at the splintered wounds for a frozen second before Charlie found herself being grabbed and rolled beneath him.

"*Umf,*" she grunted, squashed between his considerable body weight and the rock-hard ground. She was pretty sure there was a pine cone jabbing into her right shoulder blade too. "What are you doing?"

He ignored her question, his gaze scanning the surrounding area, his face set in grim lines.

Before Charlie could politely request that he stop squishing her into the unyielding rocky ground, her leg buzzed. With some wriggling, she managed to retrieve her cell phone from her pocket.

"At least I didn't break another phone." She lost and broke and drove over enough electronic devices on the regular that she wasn't sure if her sisters would provide her with another one, and she didn't want to have to pay for a new phone just because she needed to save a rather ungrateful Kieran's life.

When she finally managed to get the screen within viewing range, she saw another text from Rory.

All clear

Relief swept over her, and she gave Kieran a poke in the ribs. "Let me up, Keeks. Rory says we're all clear."

"Keeks?" His massive form didn't budge, and the press of his very heavy and attractive body was starting to give her hormones some inappropriate ideas.

"You didn't like Kiki, so…" She shrugged as well as she could while being pinned to the ground.

"What's wrong with Kieran?"

"Too long. Now move. We need to see if Rory has footage of the person shooting at us."

"It's two syllables. Two." Despite his grumble, he shifted off of her, rolling to his feet with an easy fluidity. "Exactly the same number as *Kiki*."

Shaking off the distraction of watching the way his muscles flexed beneath his clothes as he moved, Charlie shoved herself up with far less grace. "You okay?" she asked, belatedly realizing that they hadn't checked for any injuries. She scanned over his body and then what she could see of hers. Adrenaline could hide pain pretty well—at least until it wore off and a person realized their arm was missing.

"I'm good. You?" His gaze raked over her, and she could almost feel a physical stroke following the track of his eyes.

Not seeing any blood, she hopped in place a few times, checking for any pain and also to expend a little of her pent-up energy. "Fine. Finer than usual, even. Let's go find out what Rory saw."

They made their way through the woods toward the gun shop. Charlie prided herself on going with the flow, but getting shot at wasn't something she experienced on a daily basis—which was probably a positive—so she found herself to be a tad jumpy. Every crack of a twig or chirp of a bird made her flinch, and her head swiveled back and forth as she tried to take in the entirety of her surroundings in one glance.

A huge hand enveloped hers, closing around her fingers with a gentleness she'd not expected. Surprised, she swiftly turned her head toward Kieran, who was looking as cranky as usual, possibly even more than usual, which was understandable, with the shooting and all.

"We're okay," he grumbled, the tone not matching the words at all. It was so unexpected for him to attempt to reassure her that she was struck silent for a solid thirteen seconds, until a shrill whistle came from a tree across the parking lot.

Charlie, to her infinite embarrassment, jumped at the sound, her head snapping around to locate the source. Kieran overreacted even more, yanking her behind him as he fell into a crouch that seemed to scream that he was ready to wrestle any foes into submission.

"Yo! Charlie!" a voice shouted, and she felt even more ridiculous for the way she was acting.

"Not now, Bones," she called back, turning toward the gun shop door. "There was gunplay this time."

"We heard it!" Bones yelled back from the tree she and Rhys had chosen for a reconnaissance spot. "We didn't see who shot at you, but we just wanted to tell you that it wasn't us! Any of us! Dave can't hit the broad side of a barn with a firearm, and the rest of us like you too much to shoot your head off."

"Good to know, Bones." Charlie gave a wave over her shoulder without looking toward the treasure hunter's tree. "I appreciate you not wanting to kill me! Except for Dave, but I guess that's fair, considering the whole Grand Junction incident."

An offended yelp came from behind a different tree, drawing her attention to the poorly camouflaged man attempting to hide behind it. "You promised you'd never bring that up!"

Kieran's strangled cough-laugh had a bit of a snarly edge to it this time, which Charlie could appreciate. The treasure hunters were a lot to take sometimes—most of the time—even when they weren't all acting like fairly benign but also incompetent stalkers.

Charlie paused before turning back to the tree holding Rhys and Bones. "Who's the sixth?" she called.

"The sixth?"

"There were five treasure hunters—you two, Dave, Tassie, and Lachlan. Now there are six of you. Who's the late arrival?"

There was quiet, only broken by faint muttering as, Charlie assumed, Bones and Rhys discussed the sixth treasure hunter. "There isn't a sixth," Bones finally shouted.

Charlie rolled her eyes. "We can count, you know. The secret's out. You might as well tell us who it is, since we'll figure it out soon enough."

"No one else was supposed to come." Bones sounded a bit cranky. "Just us five. We drew names and everything. Rhys is going right now to see who it is. Don't worry. We'll get them to leave."

Charlie was happy to let the treasure hunters take over

solving that particular mystery. She had enough on her plate. "Sounds good. They were heading toward the main drive when the bullets started flying. Before you chase them off though, make sure to ask them if they know who was shooting at us. They might be working together, so be careful, Rhys!"

There wasn't a response—not that she'd expected one—so Charlie headed into the gun store with Kieran on her heels. Rory was still in the same spot behind the counter, her expression set in grim lines as she leaned toward the laptop screen.

"Thanks for the heads-up," Charlie said, sliding across the counter again. With a pointed look, Kieran used the half door between counters to join her behind Rory's stool. Charlie shrugged. "My way's more fun."

How he managed to roll his eyes while holding his scowl was quite a feat, but Rory's growl drew her attention.

"Where'd they go?" Rory tapped the touch pad with enough force for it to be considered a slam. "They're here." She moved to a point on the video footage and pointed at the screen.

Even with Rory's helpfully jabbing finger, Charlie had to lean in and squint to make out the figure crouched in the trees. "Dave needs to take lessons on camouflage from this person."

Rory ignored her comment, paging through the footage screen by screen as small flares lit up in front of the figure. "Now they're shooting." The following screenshots held nothing but trees, no matter how close Charlie got to the screen or how hard she squinted. "Now they're gone. Vanished. I haven't been able to pick up any trace of them on the other views, and I have A. Lot. Of. Cameras." Each word was punctuated by a hard finger tap to the touch pad, until the whole laptop quivered beneath the attack.

"Easy there, tiger," Charlie said soothingly, giving her a pat on the shoulder. "You warned us in time, and that's the important thing. We'll find whoever it is—hopefully before they get another crack at us."

With a final wordless growl at the screen, Rory twisted around on her stool to face them. "I'll go over all the footage again, make sure I didn't miss anything. The gun was a pistol. Possibly a nine millimeter or forty caliber, but that's all I can tell by the sound."

"Did you see where the sixth treasure hunter went?"

Rory quickly found the right spot in the footage that showed the figure running through the front gate before disappearing out of range of the camera.

Charlie realized she was craning her neck, trying to follow the running form, as if she could magically see past the limits of the screen. "Do you have any cameras farther down the drive?"

"Yes." Before Charlie could get excited, she noticed that Rory was looking annoyed again as she switched her laptop over to a black screen. "Nonfunctional. Either someone took it out, or it picked the wrong time to stop working."

"Hmm." Charlie exchanged a speaking look with Kieran. "Seems pretty coincidental."

"Yes." Rory had moved past annoyed and now sounded flat-out pissed.

Charlie's phone vibrated with a call. "Hopefully this isn't

someone else telling us we're about to get shot at." As she pulled the phone from her pocket, she instinctively ducked, feeling less abashed about it when both Kieran and Rory did the same. Glancing at Fifi's name on the screen, Charlie wondered if she'd somehow sent a distress call through their sister bond earlier. If so, Fifi had taken her time responding.

"You guys hungry?" Fifi asked once Charlie accepted the call.

"Well, I guess that's a no to the functioning psychic sister bond."

"Sooo…you're *not* hungry?"

"No, we *are* hungry." Belatedly, she raised her eyebrows in question at Kieran, who gave her a definite nod. "Just not what I thought you were calling about. Barbecue?"

"Since it's pretty much our only choice unless we want frozen burritos from the gas station, then yes. Meet you at Levi's in ten?"

"More like thirty. We need to finish up here, and the gun store is in the boonies."

"Simpson *is* the boonies."

"So, we're in the boonies of the boonies then. Boonies squared." Charlie gave Rory an apologetic look, but Rory just stared back at her blankly, apparently unconcerned by the description and not understanding why Charlie was grimacing at her.

"Find anything out?" Fifi asked.

"I guess." It felt like a week had passed since they'd interviewed Kevin. "Lots more questions than answers though. You?"

"Eh. As much as chewed-on bones can tell a person."

"Speaking of chewed-on bones, we'll see you at Levi's in a half hour then."

Fifi gave a somewhat guilty–sounding snort of laughter. "Is your angry firefighter coming?"

"Of course." Charlie didn't bother asking. "I gave him a nickname. He's my sidekick now." She side-eyed Kieran to see his reaction, but his only response was an audible sigh. His cranky expression didn't change. "See you then."

"Bye."

Charlie ended the call. "Want to go to Levi's with us?" she asked Rory.

"No."

Charlie laughed. "I like your directness."

Flushing a little, Rory sent her a sideways look, as if checking her sarcasm levels. "Sorry. I have to work. Store's open until seven tonight."

"I was serious—not offended in any way," Charlie assured her. "And thanks for saving our lives and for setting up the interview with Kevin."

Rory gave an uncomfortable nod in response, never looking away from the laptop. "Hang on a minute, and I'll print this out for you."

"What's that?" Charlie peered at the screen over Rory's shoulder.

"Kevin emailed that list of names."

"That was quick," Kieran said, leaning over Rory's other shoulder.

Charlie beamed at him. "Never underestimate the threat of me showing up uninvited."

He gave the smallest cough-snort, and Charlie grinned.

EIGHT

Charlie hadn't realized how hungry she'd gotten until they walked into Levi's and the smells of barbecued meat and fried things hit her. Between the sheriff's interrupted interrogation, the meeting at the fire station, and the whole getting-shot-at thing, she'd managed to miss not only lunch, but also second breakfast *and* her usual midafternoon snack. Her hungry gaze tracked the server who was carrying a large tray laden with plates of food toward a table in the corner.

Charlie took a step in her direction. "Think they'd mind if I just nabbed a plate, maybe two? There's a ton of food. I'm sure they wouldn't even notice if a little is missing."

Kieran just gave one of his snorts, not even bothering to disguise his amusement with a cough anymore. Charlie felt like she'd leveled up in her relationship with him. Now, instead of being somewhere around an adversarial acquaintance, she'd moved up to warily-tolerated-yet-temporary colleague.

His arm wrapped around her middle, sweeping her out of

her intended path toward the food-laden server. "Over there," he said, confusing her until she spotted Fifi and Bennett, already seated at a table.

With a final longing glance at the food, Charlie made her way toward her sister and brother-in-law. Kieran kept his hand on her lower back as they wound their way through the tables, either because he was feeling uncharacteristically affectionate toward her, or because he didn't trust her not to make an attempt to steal someone else's food. She was leaning toward the latter, but she couldn't even blame him. She was, after all, very hungry.

"Why are you both on that side of the table?" Charlie asked once they'd reached Fifi and Bennett. She plopped into the chair across from her sister. "Is that a married-people thing?"

Fifi gave Bennett a sappy smile and patted his arm. "We both hate having our backs to the crowd. It's one of the many things we have in common."

Now that she'd mentioned it, Charlie felt the tickle of unseen eyes on her shoulder blades, making her twitch. Fifi must've read her mind, because she lost her lovesick expression and sprawled her leg to the side.

"Nope. No room over here."

Giving in with a sigh, Charlie settled back in her less-than-optimally placed chair. Kieran was hovering, as if waiting for an invitation, so she kicked the last seat away from the table and waved at it. "Might as well sit. Fifi isn't moving, and Bennett probably won't let you sit on his lap." Just in case, Charlie raised a questioning eyebrow at her brother-in-law.

"No."

With a sigh, Charlie gave the seat next to her a pat. "We'll just have to trust these two to let us know if we're about to be ambushed."

Kieran slowly settled into the last seat. "Not used to trusting someone else to watch my back."

"That must be tough with the jackals at the station." Charlie hadn't been impressed by the way several of the other firefighters had treated Kieran. Except for the chief, Ian and Rory had been the only ones who seemed willing to give him the benefit of the doubt, and even they'd been wary.

His shrug was more of an uncomfortable twist of his shoulders. "Can't blame them. They all trusted Dad." He glanced at Fifi. "Sorry about that."

"Not your fault." Fifi waved a hand as if being kidnapped wasn't that big a deal. Charlie had to admit that it was becoming fairly common in their family, but that didn't mean it wasn't terrifying and horrible for all the sisters. "You're not responsible for your dad's actions. We had to learn that the hard way about our mom—and poor Norah about her dad too. If you end up being a militia mole and snatch Charlie, then we'll be having a different conversation." The sweetness of her voice just made the warning that much more threatening, and Charlie grinned at her sister.

"If he kidnaps me, he'll regret it even before you catch up with him." The thought of all the ways she could torture Kieran made her smile widen, especially when he side-eyed her warily.

"What can I get you folks?"

The server's voice made Charlie jump, and she glared at

Fifi and Bennett. "What happened to warning us about an ambush?"

"She's not ambushing you." Fifi rolled her eyes in a very non-penitent way. "Ambushers don't bring you food."

"You never know," Charlie said darkly, but then pasted on a smile as she turned to face the startled-looking server. "Ribs, please, and mac and cheese."

She waited impatiently as the others ordered. The server had barely made it out of eavesdropping distance before Charlie jumped back into their previous conversation. Kieran was actually talking about himself, and every tiny nugget of personal information he dropped was fascinating.

"So you had no idea that your dad was in the militia?" she asked.

"I knew he was interested in the Freedom Survivors," he said, surprising her once again by his willingness to share. Maybe low blood sugar lowered his defenses. "He likes firearms and isn't the biggest fan of the government, but I didn't know he was actually a member."

"Are you two close?"

His mouth curled down in a way that seemed more sad than angry, which made Charlie instantly feel guilty for probing. "Guess not as close as I thought."

"What's your mom think of all this?"

"She died when I was nine."

The flat way he shared that heartbreaking information made it hit harder, like a kick to the stomach. "Sorry." Feeling the urgent need to erase the sorrow she could see in his eyes, even if that meant he returned to his usual crabby self, she bumbled on. "Siblings?"

"No."

That made everything that'd happened to him seem extra tragic, since her sisters were her bedrock. "Well, I'm just stepping in it all over the place here. Should we talk about the murder? That might make you feel better."

He twitched one eyebrow higher than the other. "The murder I'm accused of committing?"

Charlie actually groaned out loud at that but went still when he laughed. It was like a hummingbird flying close to her, Charlie thought. When she heard his rare and beautiful laugh, she didn't want to move in case she scared it away.

"It's fine. We can talk about Cobra." He looked up at Fifi and Bennett, who were watching the two of them, looking fascinated and a touch horrified.

"Why are you looking at us like you're watching a train crash?" Charlie asked.

Bennett and Fifi shared one of their annoying silent-speaking looks. "Because listening to you dig your hole deeper and deeper is just like watching a traffic accident," Fifi said as B nodded in agreement.

Kieran gave an amused snort, which made Charlie jump and look at him. He seemed to be inordinately amused tonight. It must've been the low blood sugar. The tiniest smile faded as he asked, "What'd you find out from Belly?"

"First of all," Fifi started as Charlie settled back, glad that the focus was off of her inability to make polite conversation. "The coroner is hilarious, and I promised her we'd go join her after this is all over for ladies' night at the Springfield Bar. She couldn't give us too much information, though, just because the remains had been treated pretty roughly, between the murder and the elements and wild animals and such. Cause of death was likely a blow to the head, and she's thinking time of death was four to six months ago. He was last seen about five and a half months ago—"

"Right after you fought him at the grocery store," Charlie interjected, holding back her snicker when he glared at her out of the corner of his eye.

Fifi, well used to her sister's sidebars, continued smoothly, "So law enforcement is now assuming Cobra's death was some-time between four and five and a half months ago, but most likely soon after he disappeared."

"Well, that narrows it down a little, I suppose," Charlie said doubtfully, although she was trying to look at the bright side of things. "You only need to find an alibi that covers six weeks. Too bad you weren't in jail with Clint."

Kieran very slowly turned his head until he was staring at her. "Yeah. Too bad."

"Since we can't turn back time and get Kieran to commit a crime in order for him to have an airtight alibi," Fifi said in her peace-keeping tone, "let's focus on finding the real killer."

Charlie pulled the list Rory had printed out of her pocket and unfolded it, flattening the creases as best she could. "So we interrogated a very Kevin-like Kevin at Ro—"

"Here you go!" The cheerful voice of the server interrupted her, and Charlie quickly yanked the list into her lap.

"Seriously, Fifi? B?" She glared at the two across the table, who looked like they were holding back laughter. "You're the absolute worst back-watchers of all time."

"You really are."

Shocked that Kieran backed her up on this, but also triumphant, Charlie swung her arm toward him as if presenting evidence. Unfortunately, she used a little too much force and whacked him on the chest with the back of her hand. "See? Kiki agrees."

"Not if you call me Kiki."

The server's gaze jumped from person to person at their table, looking bewildered. "Um…okay. Who ordered the pork?"

———

Once she'd inhaled half of her food, Charlie's brain turned back to the mysteries at hand. Retrieving the list of names from her lap with her left hand, she waved the fork in her right one to get the attention of the others at the table. "Okay, Kieran, this is probably going to be more on you, since we're not townies. Tim Helling?"

"Which one?"

"There's more than one Tim Helling in the Freedom Survivors?" Charlie thought that was a bit odd, since Simpson wasn't a highly populated place.

"Yeah. They're father and son."

"Oh." She glanced down at the list again. "It doesn't say Tim Junior, so we'll go with father, but keep the son as a possibility." No one seemed to object to that, so she continued. "Does either strike you as especially murderous?"

"No." When he thought, the space between his eyebrows wrinkled in a slightly different way than when he was straight scowling. Charlie forced her gaze off of Kieran's adorable face wrinkles and back onto the list. She was starting to worry that she was getting a bit obsessive about Kiki...possibly even ranging over the border into creepy stalkerhood. She needed to focus on the case, especially since Kieran was still talking. "They're both a bit strange, but that's not unusual out here. My gut says they're harmless, but don't take them off the list."

"Okay. Terry Buck."

"A bit too dumb and lazy to commit murder and get away with it. Besides, I think he was pretty tight with Cobra before..." He waved a hand instead of finishing the sentence.

"Before Cobra got his head bashed in?"

"Yeah."

"Archie Innis."

"Too drunk."

"But we don't know when Cobra was killed," Fifi protested. "No one's drunk *constantly*."

"Archie is," Kieran said. "He's the Liverton Riders' lawyer—or he used to be."

"Daryl Alexander."

"Can't see it. Kid's a follower and scared of his own shadow."

"Maybe if Clint gave him orders from jail?"

"Maybe." Kieran's tone was skeptical though.

"Saul DuBois."

"Hmm."

Charlie perked up when he didn't completely shoot down the possibility like he had with the others on the list.

"I can see it. Saul has a mean streak, and he and Clint have always been tight."

"I'll put a star by his name." Glancing at her occupied right hand, Charlie quickly amended that. "I'll put a *mental* star by his name. This mac and cheese is amazing, and I'm not going to put this fork down until it's gone."

"Doubt he'll talk to any of us," Kieran warned. "DuBois is angry and suspicious, especially of women."

"Where's he live?" Bennett asked, pushing his empty plate aside.

"West of town—wait." Kieran got that thinking furrow between his eyebrows again, and Charlie very carefully did not look at it. Looking at the man just encouraged the obsession, and she was already fixated enough on him as it was. "He and his wife are separated, so last I heard he's staying at the compound."

"The militia compound?" An idea was forming in Charlie's brain. A very *fun* idea.

"Yeah." His glance was wary, so he must've caught the glee in her voice.

"Wouldn't it be nice if the compound walls had ears…and eyes?"

Kieran's gaze grew flinty in a way she hadn't seen since the first time she'd met him at the coffee shop—truly hard, not just a thin, candy shell of pretend hardness over a warm and gooey center, which is how he usually looked at her now. "My dad won't tell us anything. Besides, he's locked up."

Ohhh. The flinty eyes made sense now. "Not your dad, but thanks for offering him up." She gave his knee a pat, relieved when the hardness softened with bewilderment. Seeing him truly shut down made her realize how much she liked those glimpses into his soft, squishy middle. "No, I was talking about *our* eyes and ears."

Fifi smiled huge. "It's time, isn't it?"

Charlie loved her sister all the time, but right now she felt an extra zip of fondness as she grinned back at her. "Yep. It's time for me to do a little breaking and entering."

"You?" Fifi's smile disappeared. "If anyone gets to invade the compound, it's me. Bennett and I staked out the place for *days*."

"You found a body," Charlie scoffed. "Don't act like it was all stake-out boringness."

"Finding a body is *not* a good time."

"No, but it's an *interesting* time, which means I should get to sneak into the compound."

"*We* should," Kieran interjected.

Charlie looked over at him. "Like...all four of us? That might be a little noticeable, don't you think?"

She could almost see him fight an eye roll. "Not all four of us. Two would be best." His gaze moved to Bennett. "You up for it, Green?"

"Course." Bennett gave Kieran a chin lift of a nod, and the two exchanged a look so smugly male that Charlie could only stare for a solid four seconds.

Oh no. They did not *just try to pull that.* Charlie's gaze met Fifi's in a moment of perfect sisterly mind melding. "Felicity

Florence, did your stalker and my angry firefighter just try to exclude us from a break-in that we initiated?"

"Why yes, Charlotte Calamity, I believe you are correct."

As if they'd rehearsed the move, both slowly turned to dead-eye stare at the men next to them. Bennett and Kieran shared a hunted look.

"Whatever should Charlie and I do while we wait for the two of you to return?" Fifi asked, as sugar-sweet as cotton candy. "Get manicures while we talk about how *brave* and *strong* our men are?"

Charlie batted her eyes with slow, menacing blinks. From Kieran's grimace, she was coming off more threatening than vapid. "OMG, Fifi, we are *sooo* lucky to have such big, powerful men to push us out of the exciting parts of our investigation so we're stuck with the boring, tedious, *safe* busywork that won't cause us to break a nail." She forcefully fluttered her eyelashes again, and Kieran actually flinched away from her this time. Turning to Fifi, she said in a normal voice, "Seriously, though, my nails are a mess. Mani and pedi after we solve the murder and bring Mom in?"

"Oh God, yes." Fifi spread her hands out in front of her and screwed up her face. "My cuticles look like they've been in a war zone."

"So back to taking a look inside the compound..." She focused on her sister, happy to ignore the guys since they were currently being ridiculous. "Two teams of two, do you think? Distraction and invasion?"

"Molly and John can be here in a few hours, and I'm sure

they'd love a little break in the mountains." Fifi pushed back her plate and pulled out her phone. "Should we let them know to plan a distraction? Molly will have an excellent plan or five, I'm sure." Her thumbs hovered over the screen, ready to text their sister. Bennett let out a small sound, as if his wife had elbowed him directly in the heart.

Carefully keeping her gaze off of her brother-in-law, who was sure to have his penitent-puppy expression on, Charlie had to bite the inside of her cheek to hold back a laugh. Fifi was hilarious when annoyed. Ignoring Kieran's laser-beam stare that she could almost feel burning into her cheek, Charlie gave a thoughtful nod. "That should work. They can use my grenade."

"*I* gave you that grenade." Bennett sounded so hurt that Charlie almost caved, but her sister's sharp kick to her shin under the table renewed her resolve.

"You gave her a *grenade*?" Kieran's growly voice was even harder to hold out against than Bennett's sad one, but she fought the urge to reassure him by explaining that it was just a flash-bang.

"On the other hand," Charlie determinedly said to Felicity, "I should keep it in case we run into trouble and need our own distraction."

"Good point."

Bennett heaved a huge sigh, and Charlie recognized the sound. The groveling was about to commence. "I'm sorry, Fifi, for trying to exclude you from the action, and I feel terrible if that dismissal made you feel like I was trying to diminish you or your abilities in any way. My only intent was to protect you from danger, which was misguided on my part, since I am well aware that you are very capable of protecting yourself—as well as those around you—in almost all situations."

Charlie bit down again on her now-sore cheek as another laugh tried to escape. His apologies always sounded like they'd been drafted by an attorney. In fact, knowing Bennett and his difficulty with social interactions, he very well might have hired a lawyer to write up a boilerplate apology. Charlie tried to see his palms, to check if he'd written notes on them in Sharpie for when he got himself in trouble, but his hands were under the table.

"And?" Fifi demanded, although she was making eye contact with her husband again, which was a good sign.

Bennett's contrite expression turned slightly panicky, and he darted a look across the table at Charlie, who discretely pointed at herself. "Oh! And I apologize to Charlie, who can also take care of herself, unless it involves caring for electronics of some sort. Then she's probably screwed."

Charlie's plan to graciously forgive her brother-in-law dissolved as she scowled at him. Apparently, Fifi found that dumb apology addendum acceptable, because she yanked Bennett by the front of his shirt into a kiss.

Holding up a hand to block the lip action across the table from her view, Charlie turned to Kieran, who was scowling—which was normal—but also looking slightly panicky—which was unusual. "What?" she asked him.

"Do I have to do…that?" He waved a hand at the couple Charlie assumed was still attached at the mouths. She wasn't about to drop her hand to find out.

"Do what? The apology or the kissing?" As soon as the words were out, she felt her face get warm and hoped that the low restaurant lighting hid her blush.

The intent way he stared at her didn't help cool her down, but she managed to hold his gaze. After an indeterminate amount of time of staring into Kieran's gorgeous blue eyes, she knew she had to say something or self-combust into a fiery inferno of embarrassment and lust—mostly lust—but she also knew that she wouldn't be able to form words if she was looking at him.

Going against her better judgment, she dropped her hand and looked over at Fifi and Bennett, knowing that there was no better lust-killer than watching her sister make out with her husband. Unfortunately—or fortunately? Charlie wasn't sure—the two were no longer kissing but were instead talking quietly with their faces close together.

"No," she said to Kieran without looking at him. "You don't have to do that. It's not like we're a couple, much less married." She kept her long-term plans regarding him to herself. Feeling a bit more composed, she turned back toward him. "If you're smart, though, you'll learn from this. No taking over my investigation."

"But it's *my* investigation?" Since he sounded more bewildered than belligerent, Charlie smiled at him fondly, reaching up to pat his prickly cheek.

"Sweet, innocent Kiki. You'll learn."

"Who wants dessert?"

At the server's cheerful question, Charlie jumped, turning

to glare at the couple across from her. "That's it. Next time, *my* back's to the wall, even if I do have to sit on B's lap."

A quiet growl from Kieran brought her head around in surprise. Feeling a warmth spreading through her insides at the realization that he was *jealous*, she leaned back in her chair and smiled.

It was *nice* being wanted.

NINE

CHARLIE SIGHED HAPPILY AS SHE watched the explosions light up the night sky. "Fifi and B do the *best* distractions."

Kieran grumbled something too quietly to hear, even though he was crouched right next to her. She figured he was still salty about not getting to wear his ski mask. To give him credit, he'd abandoned it quickly when she'd explained that it would make them look more suspicious if any of the militia members spotted them during the break-in. Since the incident at dinner, when Kieran and Bennett had attempted to make their manly, protect-the-womenfolk plan, the two men had been very well-behaved, suppressing their takeover tendencies quite admirably.

Thanks to Fifi's plotting and Bennett's personal arsenal, the militia guards—and everyone in the compound, actually—had been thoroughly distracted as Charlie and Kieran slipped in through the front gate. Charlie had already called lock-picking before they'd even left Kieran's truck, so they hadn't had to tussle over who got to do the actual breaking in. She doubted he'd ever needed lock-picking skills, however. As a firefighter, he would've just used an ax or the Jaws of Life or something if he needed to get into a locked building.

They'd made it all the way to the main building, and the light show was still ongoing.

"That's a lot of exploding, even considering Bennett's stash," Charlie whispered with a slight frown, mentally revising exactly how prepared her brother-in-law was at all times.

"Think they targeted the militia's weapon stockpiles." Kieran was smiling a little at the thought.

"Oh, how absolutely lovely." She adored the idea that the militia supplied their own distraction materials. "Ready?"

When she received a clipped nod in response, she headed for the side door, excitement fizzing through her. To her disappointment, the only lock on that entrance was a simple button on the knob, so her skills were wasted.

"Not even a dead bolt she huffed under her breath, glancing over her shoulder at Kieran when she thought she heard his quiet laugh. His expression was back to his usual scowl by the time she'd turned her head, but the cranky look was so familiar and endearing that she offered him a huge grin. "Breaking's done. Let's do some entering."

Slipping inside just far enough that Kieran could follow her, she stayed close to the wall and let her eyes adjust to the dimmer interior. Even though she was expecting it, the feel of his wide, warm hand on her shoulder startled her. Again, that reassurance of having this large, capable man at her back was unexpectedly comforting, even though it would've never occurred to her that this—that *he*—was something she'd ever need.

Surely not need, she corrected herself, brought up short by the unfamiliar thought. *Want, okay. Enjoy, sure. But need? Really?*

Focusing on the felony she was in the process of committing, she pushed all the squirmy emotions Kieran awoke in her to the very back of her mind to deal with later. Her eyes had adjusted to the dimness, so she crept forward into the empty industrial-style kitchen. The appliances hunkered against the shadowed walls, and the quiet seemed unnaturally deep after the improvised fireworks show outside, settling heavily over Charlie. She could still faintly hear the *crack*s and *boom*s, but everything was muffled by the thick walls.

Shaking off her unusually introspective thoughts, she moved more quickly toward the swinging doors that led, she assumed, to the dining area. A cautious peek confirmed that the big room held several rows of tables and benches. It was brighter than the kitchen, thanks to the windows set high along one wall.

Seeing no signs that the space was occupied, Charlie slipped into the dining room, holding the swinging door open for Kieran. In the dim light, he looked larger and more hulking than usual, but somehow friendlier. Charlie realized that this was because she couldn't make out his expression so well.

Amused by her thoughts, she felt a rush of affection for her breaking-and-entering partner and gave him a fond pat on the arm. Noticing the question in the way his dark shape cocked his head, she just gave a forget-about-it wave and started to weave through the long tables to the closest exit.

Cautiously, she cracked open the door and peered at a large space modeled after a hunting lodge. Dead animal heads mounted on the wood-paneled wall cast extra-creepy shadows, and the huge, empty fireplace looked like a monstrous, gaping mouth.

What is wrong *with you tonight?* Charlie gave her arm a pinch. *Monstrous, gaping mouth? Are you a Victorian-horror writer now?*

She distracted herself from her oddly imaginative mood by checking the scattered armchairs and couches for any stray militia members who'd resisted curiosity and stayed inside. Charlie was grateful for their paranoia, since even this room only had narrow windows placed high in the wall. They worked well to keep members from being spied on, but it also made it impossible to see what was going on outside without actually leaving the building.

Creeping through the room, she hesitated at a cluster of chairs gathered around a coffee table constructed of peeled pine branches. The coffee table seemed like the obvious spot, but that was the problem. It was *too* obvious. Kieran gave her a nudge and pointed up at the ceiling.

At first, she thought he was indicating the exposed timber beams a good twelve feet above their heads, but then her gaze landed on the hideous chandelier made of elk antlers suspended at a much more manageable height.

Manageable, that was, with a little help from the giant next to her.

Leaning so close, she could smell his woodsmoke and, oddly enough, new-car scent. Mentally filing that away to tease him about later, she breathed directly into his ear, "Give me a boost?"

As soon as the words were out, he was crouching down. Expecting him to go down to all fours to make himself into a step stool, she startled when his head nudged its way between her thighs. Swallowing a surprised yelp, she felt her eyes widen as he stood, easily hoisting her onto his shoulders as if she weighed nothing at all. Once he was at his full height, and Charlie was at her much-more-than-full height, she enjoyed the feeling of towering over the room…as well as the sturdy strength of Kieran's shoulders under her thighs.

Pulling out one of the tiny listening devices, she stuck it firmly in an antler crevice, mentally thanking Norah for making the bugs self-adhere. As enjoyable as it was to sit on Kieran, Fifi and Bennett's distraction wouldn't keep the militia members distracted forever. With a regretful, silent sigh, she patted the top of his head, surprised by the softness of his short hair. He crouched again, and she dismounted, giving him another pat in thanks… and also because she couldn't resist touching him once more.

On her feet again, feeling especially short, Charlie took another look around the dim room. A smile spread across her face as she carefully made her way around a leather couch to a snarling taxidermied bear standing against the wall. Going up on her tiptoes, she carefully reached into his toothy mouth and stuck the tiny camera on the back of his strange-looking tongue. After making sure the lens was pointing out toward the room, she withdrew her hand and gave the hideous beast a light pet on the top of his snout.

"Good boy," she mouthed soundlessly.

A double pat on her shoulder had her turning to look at Kieran, who waved toward the corner, where a set of stairs led downward. After one last sweeping gaze over the shadowed room, she gave a nod and moved toward the top of the steps. Best to save the rest of the electronic devices for other areas.

Kieran maneuvered in front of her, so it was his turn to have his arm pinched. He jumped, turning to stare at her. Although she still couldn't make out the details of his expression, she could almost smell his offended surprise.

In answer to his silent question, she grabbed him and pulled him back next to her. He gave an almost soundless huff. Although it was whisper quiet, the sound was still packed full of exasperation. Contrary as she was, Charlie grinned while keeping a close eye on him to make sure Kieran didn't try to shoulder his way in front again.

As they descended, the darkness lightened, which concerned Charlie. More light meant people—plus more chance of them being spotted and outed as intruders. The silence was reassuring though. It was probable that people left lights on as they went to investigate the explosions outside.

At the bottom of the stairs, she turned left as Kieran turned right, but it was only a moment before he rejoined her. Although it would've been more efficient if they'd split up to each explore half of the lower level, she felt that same reassurance that he had her back, just in case. Besides, she'd watched enough horror movies and Scooby-Doo reruns to know that splitting up was always, *always* a mistake.

Doors lined the hallway, a few cracked open to allow strips of light to run along the carpeted floor. She paused before the first door—this one ajar but dark inside—but she couldn't hear any sounds of other humans. Flattening herself against the wall, she checked to make sure that Kieran wasn't in the line of possible fire. He'd mirrored her on the other side of the doorway, and she gave him an approving nod. Although she couldn't imagine firefighter training included surreptitious compound searches, since their work was more along the lines of loudly hacking their way into a burning building with the owner's express permission, Kieran was doing a bang-up job of sneaking around.

She gave the door a light push, and it swung open easily, revealing a large, dorm-style bathroom with rows of urinals, a few toilet stalls, and an open bank of showers. It smelled about as clean as Charlie would've expected a militia bathroom to be, and she wrinkled her nose in distaste as she moved to the next door—this one closed—in the hall.

This revealed a large closet, stacked with piles of bedding and towels on one side, and cleaning equipment and supplies on the other. She wondered why they had the latter, since the bathroom hadn't shown any sign of their use—and that was with the lights off. What horrors would the unforgiving LED lights reveal?

With a small shudder, she eased the door closed and slipped across the hall to the closest door. This one had lights on inside, so her adrenaline ramped up in response to the possibility that this room might not be empty. She and Kieran fell into position on either side of the slightly open door as automatically as if they'd already searched fifty rooms.

This time, she slipped inside as she pushed open the door, muscles tensed, ready to dive to the side if she heard the distinct sound of a shotgun shell being racked. Instead, all she found was an empty bedroom, the covers on the bed rumpled and tossed aside, as if someone had risen in a hurry. As her gaze raked over the basic furniture—bed, dresser, nightstand, lamp—a worrying thought hit her. How were they supposed to tell which was Saul's room? Would they need to search through every member's underwear drawer looking for their embroidered initials?

Even as she thought it, she pushed the concern aside. Surely friends of the leader of this gun-loving cult would have the fanciest rooms—or even a suite. There had to be some pretty good perks if his friends were willing to kill for Clint.

Kieran was still in the doorway, angled so he could see if anyone was coming down the hallway. Charlie slipped by him and crossed the hall diagonally to the next door. Except for being a bit tidier, that room was a mirror of the first, so she moved on to yet another door.

By the sixth small and empty bedroom, Charlie was starting to get antsy, and judging by the muscle jumping along Kieran's jaw, he was feeling the same way. Skipping over the next four doors, she headed straight for the last room at the end of the hall.

This one was closed, and no light was escaping from the crack beneath the door. She fell into position, shooting Kieran a quick smile when he did the same. Slowly turning the knob, she pushed the door open…well, she *tried* to push it open. Something was holding it closed.

Charlie looked at the door and mentally kicked herself for missing the dead bolt Her heart began to thrum in her chest as she realized what this meant. Either someone was inside, or the occupant of the room locked it behind them, which meant there was something inside that was valuable or private. This felonious outing might prove to be more than just a bugging expedition. They might actually get some information about the militia and its members' crimes.

She slowed down her racing brain, knowing she was getting ahead of herself. The room's occupant could just be private or even had locked their door out of habit. Pulling out her lock-pick kit, she held it up toward Kieran, who gave her a tight nod before returning his attention to the hall behind her.

Knowing he had her back—and much more competently than Fifi and Bennett had at dinner earlier—steadied her hands and let her focus on the Yale Premier Single Cylinder YH82 dead bolt in front of her. Counting the time off in her head, she picked the lock in a fairly decent time of thirty-seven seconds. Not her best, but not bad under the current conditions.

Giving Kieran a light nudge on the side of his thigh to let him know she'd finished, she returned to her position by the door. Once he was in place as well, she turned the knob once more. This time, the door swung open silently.

When everything stayed quiet, Charlie slipped inside, mentally cursing the darkness as her eyes, accustomed to the semi-lit hall, struggled to make out the room's interior. If someone was waiting to attack, they'd have a nice, stationary target since she wouldn't be able to see them coming toward her. Her adrenaline told her to keep moving, to make herself a more difficult target, but her common sense reminded her that she didn't know the furniture layout, and braining herself on an inconveniently placed dresser was not a solid plan.

Although it felt like it'd taken a year, her eyes finally adjusted to the low light, and dark shapes gradually revealed more detail, illuminated through the wide-open door. Charlie's gaze immediately landed on the queen-size bed, where a single person—judging by the shape of the lump—took up a portion of mattress. She went still, waiting for whoever it was to leap up either screaming or shooting—or both.

When neither of those things happened, Charlie crept around to the side to get a better view. Once she saw the light hair spread over the pillow and the full lips parted on heavy, sleeping breaths, she knew who was sleeping in what Charlie had assumed was Clint's bed.

Gabrielle Jones, Cobra's widow.

The presence of the woman filled Charlie with new doubts. Was this actually Cobra's old room that his wife inherited? If so, there was no point of leaving any monitoring devices in here. In fact, it would feel creepy and intrusive to be recording Gabrielle when she wasn't one of Clint's henchmen—or henchpeople.

Unless she is?

Charlie's brain worked a million miles an hour as she hurried over to a bookshelf holding more bits and pieces than books. She stuck a bug on the bottom inside edge of the front cover of a dusty hardback and then crossed the room to add one to the back of the dresser mirror. She spent an extra few seconds deciding the best position for the camera. Although inside the return air grille was tempting, she didn't want to take the time all that unscrewing and replacing the grille would require.

Her gaze landed on a teddy bear sitting on the top shelf of the bookshelf, and she grinned as she headed for it. The bear had an open mouth, lined with black felt, and she adhered the camera inside his fuzzy maw before stepping back to admire the stuffed-bear symmetry of her spy cameras.

"Charlie, company."

Although Kieran had breathed the warning, her name barely loud enough for her to hear, she still startled as if he'd shouted, knowing he wouldn't have said *anything* unless it was urgent. Turning toward him, she saw him ease the door closed and then charge across the room in her direction.

Someone was coming.

She went still, the newly darkened room turned to pitch around her. Kieran's form loomed right in front of her, black against black, and he took hold of her arm. Keeping the layout of the room in mind, she made a mental list of various possible hiding spots. The options weren't great. There were two doors in addition to the one they'd entered—private bathroom and closet, she assumed. Bathrooms were terrible for hiding in— there were never any concealed spots except the obvious and immediately discoverable ones, and any windows tended to be tiny. She might be able to wriggle through a small opening, but Kieran needed a bigger exit.

Closets typically had even fewer windows than bathrooms, but they tended to have lots of clothes and things to hide behind, plus it was less likely an unsuspecting militia person would accidentally stumble over them. As clichéd and not great as it was, the closet looked to be their best option.

By the time her internal debate was done, Charlie's eyes had again adjusted enough to be able to at least make out shapes and forms. Kieran gave her a nudge, having reached the same conclusion, judging by the way he moved toward the first of the two doors just as the faint sound of voices reached her ears.

Forcing herself to keep her pace slow—since tripping over a random duck decoy or pair of discarded cargo pants at this point would be not only stupid but dangerous—she picked her way through the near-darkness. The voices grew loud enough for Charlie to make out two distinct tones, although they were still too muffled for her to understand any of their words.

Kieran silently opened the first door. The glow from a night-light reflected off a toilet and pedestal sink, and he just as quietly closed the door again. The voices grew louder, and Charlie could pick out a word here or there. Taking a deep breath, she soundlessly exhaled, trying to keep her heart from pounding and blocking out everything else. She had a feeling she'd need all her senses to get them both safely out of the compound.

"…check…doubt she…like the dead."

One of the voices steadily increased in volume and clarity, as if the person was getting closer to them, and she looked at Kieran, even though his face was just a featureless black blob. Charlie hurried to grab the doorknob on the second door, pulling it open as a heavy knock landed on the bedroom door.

"Gabby? You asleep?"

The latch clicked as someone turned the doorknob, and a slice of light from the hallway cut into the darkness of the room. Charlie realized there was another danger besides being caught by the guy from the hall. The loud knocking for sure woke up Gabrielle. All she had to do was turn her head to see Charlie and Kieran lurking in her room, pretending to be invisible.

Grabbing blindly for Kieran's hand, Charlie dove into the even deeper darkness of the closet—or what she *hoped* was a closet. Thankfully, the press of fabric on her face was a good sign. She wiggled around to face the door—or rather to face Kieran's looming form, which was wedged between her and the exit—cringing at the rustle of clothes her movement caused.

Kieran pressed back against her even more tightly as he closed the door, and she tried to move back to give them both some room, but the mass of clothes behind her was like a semisquishy but immovable wall. What felt like the corner of a hanger dug into the back of her neck, and she shifted to the side to avoid it.

"Shh!" Even though Kieran barely breathed the command, it was still loaded with bossy.

She went still except for her index finger, which gave a reprimanding poke to his ribs—or where she guessed his ribs were. He jolted but didn't make a sound. Charlie had a feeling she'd be hearing about it once they were free of the closet—and the whole compound.

"Gabby?" The voice was muffled through the closet door, but still too close for comfort. It also made Charlie realize that if the militia members were returning to their rooms, that meant the distraction was no longer doing its job, and the guards were also likely returning to their posts. Getting out of the compound was going to be...tricky. "Gabby!"

The sudden increase in volume made Charlie jump, although she couldn't move very much. She even had to turn her head to the side so she didn't squash her nose on his rock-hard back. That meant that every one of her inhales took in a mouthful of his warmth and faint smoke and distinctive new-car scent, and she made yet another mental note to ask him what exactly made him smell like anticipation and celebration and fresh-from-the-factory plastic.

A hand on her hip made her start, but Kieran's gentle squeeze was reassuring, and she was oddly glad when he kept his fingers where they were instead of releasing her. His hold, along with the press of his back against her front, grounded her in the thick darkness of the closet.

"Wha?" A sleep-thickened feminine voice penetrated the closet door, and Charlie closed her eyes in frustration—not that there was any visual difference between closing her eyes and keeping them open. Now that the bedroom's occupant was awake, they were going to have to figure out how to escape the closet before they could even worry about the reposted guards. "What's going on?"

"Sorry to disturb you," the man's voice said, quieter now that Gabrielle was awake. Charlie couldn't tell if it was a voice she'd heard before or not. "But there was some trouble in the armory. I didn't see you out there with everyone, so I wanted to make sure you were okay."

"Yeah, I'm fine." From the continued thickness of Gabrielle's voice, Charlie was pretty sure the woman had used a sleep aid of some sort. "Thanks, Terry."

Terry! He's on the list! Charlie poked Kieran's ribs again, and his fingers tightened warningly on her hip. She squirmed just a little, careful not to disturb the clothes again, but unable to stay still. His grip and silent reprimand should've bothered her, but it didn't. No, that wasn't right. She *was* bothered, but in an excited, fizzy-bubbles-in-her-middle type of way.

Giving herself a mental slap, she forced herself to be still and did her best not to smell him—or at least not obsess about smelling him.

"No problem. Everything's under control out there, so go back to sleep."

"Okay." From the way Gabrielle mumbled the word, she was halfway back to dreamland already. Charlie was impressed. Whatever the woman had used to help her sleep must be some pretty strong stuff. If Charlie had been woken up in the middle of the night because there'd been a problem in the militia's armory, she would've been bouncing off the walls for the rest of the night.

There was a pause, and Charlie strained her ears, trying to pick up the click of the latch that meant Terry was gone—or out of Gabrielle's bedroom, at least. She was listening so hard that she jumped a tiny bit when instead of leaving, the man spoke again. "Thought I told you to keep this door locked, Gabby."

Gabrielle must've had her head in a pillow, because Charlie couldn't make out her response.

"No, you didn't. It was unlocked." Terry made an annoyed sound. "Never mind. Just lock it after me."

Charlie was pretty sure there was no way the woman was leaving her bed. Terry must've realized that, because he heaved a sigh that she could hear in the closet.

"Fine. I'll lock it with my key. Try to remember to secure it in the future though. None of the members will bother the president's lady, but I don't trust some of the new recruits." He paused again, but Charlie didn't hear any response from Gabrielle. That was good for her and Kieran, since the quicker she was sleeping, the quicker they could get out of her bedroom—and into the hall, another potential crocodile pit now that the members were back. "Night, Gabby."

This time, when silence fell over the bedroom, Charlie was pretty sure Terry was gone. Even though he hadn't said anything incriminating, his presence made their break-in seem worth the hassle.

Although she probably should hold off on deciding if their breaking and entering was worth it once they were out of the compound and not still wedged in a tiny closet.

They waited long enough that Charlie started obsessing over how good Kieran smelled again, but finally, his back muscles flexed against her cheek and the door soundlessly cracked open. Charlie tensed with anticipation, more than ready to escape the small space. She wasn't normally claustrophobic, but being this close to Kieran wasn't good for her peace of mind. This was definitely not the time to get silly over some guy's smell, no matter how luscious it was.

She leaned forward, not even caring that all that did with Kieran in the way was to mash her more firmly against his back, eyes fixed on that thin crack of slightly brighter darkness outside the closet. Kieran shifted, but before he could open the door wider and step out, there was a grumbly groan from the direction of the bed.

Charlie tensed, and Kieran closed the door a little too abruptly. The bump of wood against wood and the click of the latch sounded like a bomb blast in the small space. She froze and felt Kieran do the same, the body in front of her as solid as a stone gargoyle. Faint rustling sounds drifted through the closet door and then the shuffle-flap of bare feet against a hard floor.

Charlie's nerves tightened like a violin string, twisting tauter with each step Gabrielle made toward their very pathetic hiding place. At the sound of a doorknob rattling, Charlie grabbed two handfuls of Kieran's shirt. He wasn't immune to the tension, since his fingers had tightened on her hip until it felt like he'd leave five impressions in her skin when he finally released her.

The snap of a door closing broke Charlie out of her paralysis. "Bathroom," she breathed against his still-tense back.

His exhale was audible—barely, but it still made it obvious how wound up Kieran had been by the close call, as well. She went to jab him in the ribs to urge him to move, but he was already swinging open the door and stepping through it, leaving her poking finger to meet only air. It wasn't nearly as satisfying as picking on Kieran had been.

Knowing that they likely only had seconds before Gabrielle would be leaving the bathroom, she scooted out of the closet right behind Kieran, careful to close the door soundlessly behind her. The bedroom seemed much lighter after the black box of the closet, so Charlie was able to pick her way quickly to where Kieran was leaning against the door to the hall, his ear flat to one of the panels.

He must not have heard anything, because he twisted the dead bolt and opened the door a tiny crack. The silence from the hall seemed heavy, and Charlie's imagination conjured up an image of the entire militia crouched right outside Gabrielle's room, ready to leap at them the second they stepped into the hall.

The mental picture was vivid enough that she held her breath as Kieran opened the door wider and slipped out, only starting to breathe again when she followed him into the blessedly empty hallway. Although it felt like they'd been in Gabrielle's room for days, the hall looked just the same as it had a few minutes ago.

She pulled the door silently closed behind her, grimacing a little as she hoped that Terry wouldn't check on Gabrielle again that night. Without a key, there was no way to lock it from the outside. Pushing the worry from her mind—since they had several other more pressing concerns at the moment—she caught up with Kieran. She hated following behind him. It felt as if she were cowering behind him, letting him take the fire so she'd have an opportunity to duck and run if things got dangerous. She'd much rather go first, throwing herself headlong into trouble and protecting the people she cared about by giving them a chance to run.

The thought stuck uncomfortably in her brain. Of course she wasn't putting Kieran on the same level as her beloved sisters. She'd just met the guy. All her teasing about keeping him and marrying him were just a joke, although his incredible, cranky attractiveness was very real. He was her partner for the break-in, and that's the only—and quite understandable—reason she felt protective.

As they reached the base of the stairs, stretching up into darkness, Charlie spared a wistful look to her left. They hadn't gotten a chance to explore the other half of the basement living quarters, much less leave a few bugs. Although she knew they were out of time, she still wished they'd been able to cover more ground.

There was a soft *thunk* of a lock disengaging, and then Charlie was flying through the air, only the hard band around her upper arm keeping her aloft. As she landed, she stumbled on the stairs and struggled to regain her balance before it didn't matter anymore, since Kieran had her pinned against the stairway wall, the railing digging painfully into her back.

Footsteps—heavier and more distinct than Gabrielle's had been—echoed through the otherwise silent hall, gradually getting louder. Charlie fingered the bumpy surface of the grenade in her pocket, wondering if it was time to use it. Causing a commotion in the basement of all places seemed a good way to get them trapped, however.

Kieran tensed, making her realize she was once again pressed against him, although they were front to front this time. They were so close that she felt his hand dive into his jacket pocket, making her wonder if Kieran had a flash-bang of his own he was considering using.

The footsteps were coming impossibly close, and she knew someone would be stepping into view at any second. Her muscles tensed in readiness as her brain whirred, coming up with plan after plan only to discard them. She'd do what she always did—wing it. She always survived—at least she had in the past.

She decided to jump on whoever it was, using surprise to her advantage. Even if he was armed, she could probably take him down if he wasn't expecting her to leap out of the stairwell. Kieran's hand squeezed warningly, but she had no clue what exactly he was warning her about. This would've been an excellent time for telepathic communication, but Charlie had never shared any traits with superheroes—except maybe an appreciation for spandex.

The footsteps paused, and Charlie stopped breathing. Had she been exhaling too heavily? Had her boot sole squeaked against the concrete step? Was her heart loud enough to be heard outside her body? It had to be her who'd given them away. Kieran was silent as a rock next to her, so she knew he hadn't made a sound. She tensed even more, knowing this would be a hundred times more difficult if her opponent was ready for her attack.

TEN

INSTEAD OF AN AMBUSH, SHE heard the click of a latch. The footsteps continued, but after the thud of a door closing, they grew faint.

All her breath left her in a silent gust. Just another person who had to use the bathroom. Kieran leaned heavily against her for a fraction of a second, as if relief had drained his strength right out of him, before he collected himself and climbed the stairs on silent feet. She followed, knowing there'd be a time to collapse in relief and that was when they were fully clear of the compound. For now, she concentrated on being as silent as a ghost—one of the good, incorporeal ghosts, not a nasty poltergeist.

At the top of the stairs, Kieran paused for a second to scan the area before making his way through the big, shadowy room. Charlie followed, allowing him to lead for now, mainly because he'd just saved her bacon in the basement by yanking her out of sight of the bathroom visitor just in time. She'd give him a few minutes, then take over the lead.

They moved a lot faster than they had when they'd come through the first time, since they knew the way now and getting out was their priority. The dining room and kitchen were thankfully still empty, and Charlie wondered where everyone was. They'd only heard Terry and possibly one other person return to the basement when they were in Gabrielle's bedroom, so the majority of the militia members had to be wandering around the compound somewhere.

She strained to listen, but she couldn't hear if anything was happening outside the house. Either their distraction-makers had left, seriously toned down the noise levels, or been captured. Charlie's stomach lurched at the last option, so she pushed it back into a dark corner of her brain. *No sense in worrying about something that probably didn't even happen*, she told herself.

They crept toward the exit on the far side of the kitchen. Kieran cracked open the door and paused as Charlie's phone vibrated against her leg, startling her. She grabbed it out of her pocket and checked the screen, which seemed dangerously bright.

"Are you checking your phone?" Kieran hissed, making her glance up from the text she was reading. He'd stepped outside and was holding the door for her.

Responding with a quick OK, she dropped her phone back in her pocket and slipped through the doorway. "Fifi," she said with just the tiniest bit of condescension. He deserved it for the scorn in his whispered words though. Did he think she was scrolling social media during their break-in? "They're out."

As she said the hushed words, a thrill of danger coursed

through her. She and Kieran were on their own inside enemy territory. There'd be no help from her sister and brother-in-law. The idea was both unnerving and exciting, and her view of the compound grounds suddenly sharpened from a rush of adrenaline hitting her system.

Kieran gave a tight nod before turning the simple knob lock and closing the door silently. Charlie listened, hearing not-so-distant voices and a faint roar and crackle she was pretty sure was fire. As if to back up her guess, the acrid burn of smoke hit her nose. She couldn't see anyone, so she joined Kieran as he made his way along the building, staying in the deeper shadows along the exterior wall.

As they reached the end of the building, Charlie saw a flicker of movement to her left. Kieran took a step away from the cover of the wall, as if to cross the open area between the main building and the closest outbuilding—a ratty-looking pole barn that, by its smell, housed some kind of livestock. Grabbing two handfuls of the back of his jacket, Charlie yanked him back.

A man emerged from another, smaller building to their left, letting the door slam closed behind him. Jogging down the porch steps, he looked around before heading toward the now-faint voices. Charlie's heart pounded as she froze, her hands still keeping their hold on Kieran, feeling horribly visible, like she glowed with light, even when she knew they were hidden in the darkest shadows.

Hopefully they were hidden.

Charlie didn't even breathe until the man disappeared around the corner of the building he'd come out of. Then she had to fight to not let every bit of air out of her lungs in an audible rush, but it was hard. Relief made her limp. If she hadn't yanked Kieran back, the man would've seen him for sure. Something told her that these militia guys had a bit of a nervous trigger finger, especially right after Fifi and Bennett's distraction.

Right on the tail of the wave of relief, annoyance followed. If Kieran wasn't going to protect himself, she was going to have to do it. With her still-tight grip on his jacket, she hauled him back and stepped in front of him. He must've been feeling a little sheepish from his error in judgment since he let her bodily rearrange their order.

After taking a look around that was likely unnecessarily thorough, she led them quickly across the open area to the close shadows of the livestock shelter, then to a hay barn that was listing to the side, then to an old well house that was so small it barely provided any cover. The front gate was within sight, lit by a sodium security light, and, to her frustration, manned by two guards.

When they'd waltzed in through the front gate earlier, Charlie had arranged the chain and padlock to appear as if it were securely locked. Once they reached the gate, they'd need to remove the unfastened padlock and pull off the chain before they could get through. That was going to take time—not much, but enough for the gate guards to tackle them...or shoot them a bunch of times.

Kieran nudged her shoulder and pointed in a different direction, away from the front gate. She knew immediately what he was wordlessly suggesting, that they make their way to the unmanned section of fence and climb over it. She made a face. If she had to, she'd climb the fence, but it was ten feet tall and topped with razor wire. Even with gloves and wire cutters, it'd be a beast to go over.

Besides, she had a better idea. Well, a *different* idea. She couldn't guarantee that her plan was *better*. Definitely more fun though.

With a short shake of her head, she pulled her secret weapon from one of her pockets. Pulling the pin, she launched the grenade toward the two guys standing next to the gate.

"Wait!" Kieran hissed, but it was too late for that kind of back-seat strategizing. The plan was in motion, and it was going to work perfectly. She hoped.

Squeezing her eyes closed, she turned and reached up to clamp her hands over Kieran's ears, feeling a little guilty for not giving him any warning or earlier instructions on what to do if she spontaneously introduced a flash-bang into their getaway.

"No, cover your own—*Charlie*." He bit off his words as he flattened his hands over her ears, which was a really nice thing to do, something that she definitely would get sappy over later. Beneath her closed eyelids, the world lit up a painfully bright white. Even with his huge hands covering her ears—and basically her entire head—the *boom* filled her head, making her whole body ache with the force of it.

Not giving herself time to recover—since that would defeat the whole purpose of a stun grenade—she dropped her hands and turned to run for the gate. Even though her eyes had been closed when it went off, the flash had still completely ruined her night vision, so she hoped there weren't any holes or rocks in her path to trip her up.

In the illumination by the gate, she saw that the men had managed to stay on their feet, although they were both bent over, one pressing the heels of his palms against his eyes, and the other with his hands flattened against the sides of his head, as if he could retroactively protect his ears.

Charlie hit the gate, grabbing the chain link with one hand to keep from bouncing back while reaching for the padlock even before her feet had stopped moving. A twist and one side of the chain was released, falling against the gate with a clatter that sounded muffled since her ears were still reeling from the explosion.

She yanked the chain but it caught, the end tangled in the links, and she had to use a precious three seconds to free it. Even with her compromised hearing, shouts were audible, and she hoped they were from the two still affected by the flash-bang, rather than backup militia guys who hadn't been knocked silly by the blast.

The chain slithered free, and she shoved the gate open and began running down the dirt driveway. She glanced behind her to check on Kieran, skidding to a halt when she saw he wasn't behind her. He was still at the entrance, messing with the gate.

"What are you doing?" she yelled, running back toward him. No sense in being quiet anymore. After all, that flash-bang probably woke even Gabrielle up. The two gate guards were still incapacitated, but there were reinforcements coming—a whole crowd of them by the sound of it.

"Locking them in," he snapped, finishing fiddling with the chain and padlock and sprinting toward her. When he caught up with Charlie, he reached out to grab her hand, pulling her along as if *she* were the cause of the delay.

"They have the key, doofus," she said, her legs working faster than when Fifi promised judgment-free ice cream to whichever sister finished their run the fastest during training.

"It'll take them a minute to get it open. We can use that time to, you know, *get away*."

She spared him a quick, envious scowl before she focused on the dark road. Now was not the time to trip and go sprawling face down on the rural mountain road. She'd watched enough horror movies to know that. "You're not breathing hard at all."

That huff was definitely a laugh. "Firefighter training is brutal. I'm just glad I'm not hauling a hundred pounds of gear right now."

"Don't...tell Fifi." Unlike Kieran, Charlie was definitely sucking air. Her body urged her to slow, but the shouts and rattling of the gate—did that mean they'd unlocked it already, or was that just one of the guys shaking the fence in frustration?—kept her moving as fast as she could go.

"Tell her what?" He turned his head to look at her without slowing his pace.

"Watch where you're running!" she yelled at him, then had to pause to suck in some hard breaths to replace the oxygen she'd just wasted. "Don't...you watch...horror movies? Focus!"

"Fine." Although it was too dark to see his expression, she

knew he was smirking. She could just *feel* it. "So what am I supposed to keep from your sister?"

"Fire…fighting…training." She just had to make it around the next curve and then up the tiniest hill to get to where they'd left his truck. "No details. Fifi…doesn't…need to know."

"Okay." Despite his response, his tone told her he didn't understand why she wanted him to hit the mute button about that. He hadn't been tortured by her training sessions on a daily basis for years, so of course he didn't get it. As long as he kept his mouth shut about practicing running while carrying a hundred pounds of gear, they wouldn't have a problem.

As they rounded the turn, there was the truck, the scarce moonlight reflecting off its shiny bits. Charlie had never been so glad to see an inanimate object in her life.

"Your truck…is…*beautiful*," she gasped out with the very last of the air in her lungs.

"I know."

She sprinted up the slope—which somehow didn't feel like the "tiniest hill" she remembered from when they'd arrived—and headed for the passenger side of the truck, not even arguing about who was going to drive. Oxygen was too precious. She yanked open the door and dove inside, grabbing the far side of the seat to haul herself up.

The engine rumbled, warning her she'd better get secured before they took off or she'd end up on the floor. Twisting around so she was actually sitting in the seat, rather than sprawled across it, she braced herself on the dash just as Kieran stomped on the accelerator.

"Seat belt!" she ordered, clicking her own into place.

Keeping one hand on the wheel as they charged down the road, he reached for his seat belt with his other. A sharp curve was coming up fast, and Charlie decided she'd rather the driver have the use of both hands. She leaned over, grabbed the seat belt from him, and snapped it into place.

"You could...probably turn...your lights on," she said pragmatically, still puffing a little. "They already know...we're heading to Moose Peak Road...since we don't have any other choice. Plus, lights might help us...not die." Settling back in her seat, Charlie affected a look of relaxed unconcern, hiding the fact that her right quad and calf muscles were clenching as she pushed on a phantom accelerator.

Without saying a word, he followed her suggestion, and the road lit up in front of them. It made the drive both less and—oddly—*more* terrifying, since everything they could possibly smash themselves into—rocks, trees, even small cliff faces—was brightly illuminated. From Kieran's expression—his standard scowl, which Charlie decided was his relaxed face—and his easy grip on the steering wheel, he wasn't too stressed about hurtling down a mountain on a dirt road that was barely more than two strips on the rocky ground.

Since he wasn't outwardly concerned, Charlie relaxed back in her seat and enjoyed the ride. After all, sitting in Kieran's cushy truck was a thousand times better than running, even if she wasn't driving. Her leg twitched again in co-driving solidarity as he barely slowed before twisting the wheel, sending the truck rocketing around the hairpin turn.

"Very nice."

"Thank you."

Pulling out her phone, Charlie texted Fifi an update.

Only seconds later, her sister's response popped up on Charlie's screen. Glad you're out. Any tail?

Briefly thinking about all the jokes she could make and discarding them all, Charlie just sent a shrug emoji and then added, Not one we can see yet.

Let me know if that changes. We'll head to the HS—meet us there.

Charlie frowned at her phone. High school?

Honeymoon suite!

Charlie could almost hear her sister's exasperated sigh through the text. *Ohhh, right,* she thought, before texting, Ohhh, right.

"We're meeting Fifi and her husband-stalker at our hotel in Rosehill."

"Okay," he grunted, not saying anything else, even though she waited for him to ask the usual question.

"Don't you want to know why that's Bennett's nickname?"

"I'm a firefighter." Kieran guided the truck around another curve so tight and fast that the truck juddered and hopped before smoothing out on the straightaway.

Charlie blinked at him. She wasn't accustomed to being

thrown off her game. Usually, *she* was the one who discombobulated people, not the other way around. When it was clear he wasn't about to elaborate on the relevance, she asked, "What does that have to do with anything? Or do you just like announcing the firefighter thing to gain hotness points?" *Not that he needs any more of those.*

Despite the tricky driving conditions, he slid her a sideways look. "Hotness points?"

"Sure, you know." When it became clear that he, in fact, did *not* know, she made up a little example. "Say you go to a bar, looking for a hookup."

That got her another side-eye, but she ignored the incredulity in it and pressed on.

"You see a beautiful woman at the bar, so you sit down next to her." Charlie had to consciously stop grinding her teeth, weirdly jealous of this imaginary person. *Why did I have to make her so gorgeous?* "She glances at you, rates you about a four or five on the hookup-able scale, and turns back to her chocolate martini."

He makes a sound in the back of his throat—a choke or possibly a gag. "Chocolate martini?"

A gag then. "Not important—also, don't yuck other people's yum. Let her enjoy her chocolate martini without feeling like you have to make a negative comment. Anyway, moving on. In order to up your score, you introduce yourself." She lowered her voice to as much of a growl as she could manage. "Hey, beautiful. I'm Kieran Crabbypants Byrne. I'm a firefighter."

"Sullivan."

"What?"

"My middle name."

"Gotcha." She dropped to that low register again. "Hey, beautiful. I'm Kieran Sullivan Crabbypants Byrne. I'm a firefighter." She smacked her hands together. "Bam! Suddenly, you're a solid five and a half on the hookup-able scale. It's like magic."

The two-track road they were on ended in a T intersection, and Kieran slowed the truck just a hair before turning left onto the new gravel road. The tires slid, rocks pinging against the undercarriage, but then they managed to grab the road and propel the truck forward. Turning around in her seat, Charlie squinted into the darkness behind them.

"I can't see anyone following, but that could just be because it's dark. There aren't a whole lot of streetlights out here in the middle of nowhere." Turning back around to face front again, she felt her body being pressed back against the seat as Kieran stomped on the accelerator, blasting them forward. "Not that I don't love going fast, but Fifi did warn me that a few of the more dickish deputies like to speed trap this road, and being pulled over will not help our main goal of, you know, getting away."

Although he made a grumbly noise, he slowed down. "I don't sound like that."

Apparently, the grumpy sound he'd made had been due to her impression of him, not her request to reduce his speed. "Of course it's just a reenactment, since I wasn't there at the bar, but I have a feeling I was pretty spot on."

"I don't...I—it would never happen." He sounded flustered

enough to make Charlie grin. Now it was her turn to throw him off his game. The universe had righted itself. He huffed. "Besides, that's not what I meant. I wasn't looking for…hotness points."

"Mm-hmm…" She purposefully made the sound as skeptical as she possibly could, loving that she had him fumbling for words. Talking with Kieran was always stimulating, but this was an extra side of fun.

"I wasn't," he grumped, sending her such a glare that it buzzed through her, waking her nerve endings. The adrenaline hadn't subsided yet, so her whole body vibrated with the thrill of Kieran and the break-in they'd just done. She wouldn't have been surprised if she was lit up like a sparkler. "I just meant I already know the whole story about your sister and Green."

She cocked her head at him, honestly not making the connection.

"Firefighters gossip, remember?" he said. "Not much happens around here—"

She interrupted him with a barked laugh. "Except for lots of murder-y crime-ing."

He waved a hand as if dismissing the incredibly felonious recent history of the town as irrelevant. "Not much has happened *lately*, so the story of a bounty hunter and PI chasing a skip and getting kidnapped was the main topic of conversation—still is the main topic. So I don't use the firefighter thing as a hookup tool." He curled his lip, as if the last two words tasted gross.

Feeling fizzy with all sorts of energy, she wanted to poke the grumpy bear. "What do you use then?"

"What?"

"What's your hookup tool?"

"I don't *use* a hookup tool."

It was completely believable to her that he didn't need any help getting all the action he'd ever want, but adding to his adorably flustered state was just too tempting. "So, you just frown at the ladies, and they come running? That's a bit hard to imagine, isn't it?" *It's so easy to imagine.* In fact, it was easy enough that her jealousy of these hordes of women she'd just made up flared up again.

"No—I mean, that's not how... I don't..." He gave up with a frustrated huff.

Charlie couldn't hold back her laughter anymore. "Sorry. I have a lot of sisters. We're the *masters* of teasing. I couldn't help myself."

His grumpy sound was her kryptonite, and she couldn't stop herself from reaching across the seat to squeeze his knee. She meant it as a friendly gesture, a sort of way of telling him that no harm was meant, but her fingers wanted to linger on the rock-hard muscle. His leg jumped just the tiniest bit under her touch—as if he'd quickly controlled the motion—before the truck lurched forward, rocking her back and making her realize she was being weird.

"Sorry," she apologized, moving her hand back to her own leg as she glanced at the speedometer and cleared her throat. "Sheriff deputies with a grudge against my family."

The reminder—and possibly the removal of her hand—made him lighten up on the accelerator, and the truck slowed until it was going the speed limit. It felt impossibly slow, especially out in the dark emptiness, where it seemed like she and Kieran were the only people in the universe.

That wasn't true though. She turned around, peering into the darkness behind the truck. The running lights didn't do much for visibility behind them, but she squinted, undoing her seat belt so she could turn completely.

"What are you doing?" Kieran snapped. "Put that back on."

"I will." She leaned closer to the rear window. "Just confirming something first. Yep. Someone's following us."

"Sure they're militia?" Kieran asked as she returned to facing front and rebuckled her seat belt. "Could just be a random car."

"With their lights off?" she asked skeptically, and he grimaced, speeding up again. "Know where you're going?" She grabbed her phone and opened a navigation app. "I can give you directions."

He shot her a flat look. "I'm a firefi—" He snapped his mouth closed before finishing that sentence, but Charlie still laughed.

"We're back to that?"

"No, I'm just saying that my job requires me to know how to get around this area," he grumbled as Charlie grinned at him. She had no idea why she liked him so much—especially his growling, especially, *especially* when she was winding him up—but she really did. Keeping his gaze straight ahead so she was smiling at his scowling profile, he continued. "Besides, map software is notoriously unreliable in this area, especially since cell reception is spotty."

As if he'd just cursed her, the last bar disappeared from her phone, and the dreaded *No Service* message appeared instead. "Humph."

He laughed outright at her disgruntled sound. "Don't worry." A small, smug smile stayed in place, and she completely forgot about her phone. "I know how to get us there—*and* I'll lose our tail in the process."

"You're adorable."

"What?" His tiny grin slipped away as he stared at her, horrified.

"Oops." She knew she didn't look repentant, but she couldn't stop grinning at him. Besides, she hadn't lied. "Sorry. I meant to say that you're very competent."

This mollified him enough that he returned to his usual scowl.

Curious if she could get him back to his happy smile, she tried again. "Very geographically aware."

He didn't smile, looking more baffled than anything, but she couldn't stop. She was discovering all sorts of fun games to play with Kieran.

"Your driving is good. Not as good as mine, but it's still good."

That just received a grunt.

"And your posture is excellent."

"Okay."

"That's rare in the time of smartphones."

"Hang on." He cut the truck's lights, and the dark outside seemed impenetrable.

"Why?" Despite her question, she grabbed for the handle above the door with one hand and braced her other on the dash.

"You didn't mention I'm also great at evasion techniques." Cranking the wheel, he drove them right off the road.

ELEVEN

The truck bounced and lurched across invisible obstacles, and Charlie's arms strained to hold her in place, even as her seat belt locked tightly across her chest. "I appreciate the heads-up about the need to hold on," she said sincerely. "Apparently, it's leg *and* arm day today."

His expression was hard to see, but he gave a chuckle that sounded a bit...well, diabolical. Contrarily, it made Charlie smile. Then another bounce of the truck almost made her bite her tongue off, so she set her teeth and braced for the next hit.

It came with a bump, plus a crunch and the twang of wires breaking.

"Did you just run over a piano?" she asked once the rear tires had settled back on the ground and she dared to relax her jaw to speak.

"Yes." His tone was completely deadpan, and she loved it so much. "Next is the cello. We're taking out the entire Simpson Symphony Orchestra."

She opened her mouth to respond, but another lurch made her teeth clack together painfully. "Oof," she said. "Freaking tuba."

He laughed again, and she beamed at him, rough ride through the unyielding darkness forgotten for the moment. As someone who could appreciate a good adrenaline rush, she recognized a like mind. The man was becoming a little too perfect, and if he kept laughing, she was going to get an inferiority complex. The idea made her immediately snort with amusement, since her self-esteem was quite solid.

Her arms ached as they hit another bump that launched the truck into the air for a moment before the front wheels, then the back, landed with a bounce. They rolled through another natural speed bump, then another. The jouncing was beginning to make her head ache.

"Before my insides get churned into butter, what's the ETA?" She tried to make her voice casual, but even she could hear the tension in her words.

"ETA to where?"

"Oh, just…" She paused as the truck launched off an especially large bump, automatically counting the seconds before the wheels touched ground again—well, it was more of a slam than a touch. She hurried to get the rest of her words out before the terrain jarred her any more than she already was. "Let's start with any paved road."

"Depends."

Her teeth ground together for more reasons than one this time. "Depends on what?"

"How long they look for us." Twisting the wheel, he pulled up next to an enormous boulder and stopped, turning off the truck and killing the dash lights.

It was suddenly very dark inside the cab. They both fell silent, and the only sound was the occasional *tick* from the engine as it cooled. As her eyes adjusted, the sky outside the windshield lit up with billions of stars. Staring, Charlie felt both awed and slightly panicky. The universe felt a bit *too* big at the moment, so she focused on Kieran. At the sight of his bulky, shadowed form, she immediately relaxed. For a grumpy bastard, he sure made her feel safe.

Safe, but also…not, she thought nonsensically as the hummingbirds in her stomach buzzed and swooped in a way that didn't feel bad, just strange and novel. The awkwardness that kept her mouth shut was new too, and she didn't think she liked caring what another person thought of her.

Scrambling to think of something—anything—to say to banish those weird emotions, she grabbed her cell phone out of her pocket. "Fifi! Needs to know! That we're here!" Her voice sounded too loud and definitely too peppy in the enclosed space.

She could feel Kieran's confused gaze on the side of her face as she focused on her phone screen, relieved to see she had cell service again—just a measly single bar but hopefully enough to text.

Hiding from our tail by a large boulder the size of a small boulder. Debrief without us, and we'll see you in the morning.

Instantly, an ellipsis appeared, showing that Fifi was typing. Charlie kept her eyes locked on the screen, hanging on desperately to the normality of texting her sister so she didn't have to deal with the man next to her or all the churning feelings he caused.

No debrief jokes? What kind of animal would you be?

Charlie winced. Kieran had really thrown her off her game if Fifi was using the emergency *is this really you or did someone kill you and steal your phone* question.

Otter, she quickly answered, but then paused. Wait. Did I end up picking octopus?

Despite her answer—or maybe because of it—Fifi seemed reassured. Stay safe and text when you're in your room—don't care how late it is.

I'm always happy to wake you and B up.

Fifi shot back an eye-roll emoji.

With the conversation over, Charlie was back to her original situation—alone in a dark truck with a guy who seemed to be giving her *feelings*, of all things. Letting out a sigh she carefully kept soundless—the only thing worse than having emotions, after all, was Kieran knowing about them—she decided to make some small talk. How hard could it be?

"Why do you stay in Simpson when everyone treats you like you're going to bite their faces off?" she asked. *Okay, so maybe small talk isn't my forte.*

Even in the dimness of the truck, she saw him flinch, as if she'd punched him. The reaction and his silence reminded her that not everyone was an open book like she was. She'd happily talk about just about anything, and her sisters often reminded her that other people had actual boundaries, unlike her. She didn't mean to ignore people's boundaries. She just forgot that they existed.

Feeling bad for conversationally punching him, she dug around in her brain for a whole different conversation, one that hopefully was less intrusive than her last attempt. "Did you know this big rock was here when you drove off the road? Or should I be grateful that you saw it before we ran into it?"

He didn't respond for a few seconds, and Charlie had resigned herself to passing the time until the militia gave up searching for them in silent boredom when he finally spoke. "I knew it was here. I hike this area."

"Yeah?" Relieved she wouldn't have to entertain herself, since she was *not* good with extended stillness, Charlie turned to face him, bending her left leg and pulling it up onto the seat in front of her. "National forest borders our backyard in Langston, so Fifi has us do most of our training in there. I can't say that if I didn't have my sister screaming at me like a rabid drill sergeant, I'd hike for fun, but running in the woods is much better than on a treadmill."

"You live with your sisters?"

"Yep. All four of them—plus their assorted stalkers." When he made an odd choking sound, she clarified. "Their husbands and boyfriends, I mean. We keep the actual stalkers outside. They can come into the garage when it's cold though."

His laugh still sounded strangled, but it was more clearly a sound of amusement, rather than a choke. It was as if his laughter muscles had atrophied from lack of use, and he was relearning how to use them correctly.

"I don't know why I stay," he said, and it took Charlie a startled moment to realize he was answering her first question. "Habit, I guess? I grew up here. It's my home."

Charlie understood having a home she'd never want to leave, but their house in Langston was a safe place, filled with people who loved her—well, at least it was now that their mom wasn't there anymore. From her admittedly limited point of view, it felt like Simpson—although a fun, murder-y little town for most people—was a hostile place for Kieran, so she was struggling to get why he wouldn't drive off into the sunset without a backward glance.

"Okay, but is it a home you actually like?" she asked, trying her hardest to be tactful but not sure if she was succeeding. "I mean, *I* like it here, but I have the skin of an armadillo."

"Are you calling me sensitive?"

Charlie peered through the gloom, trying to tell if he was serious. It seemed unlikely that he was teasing her, but his voice was so deadpan that she honestly couldn't tell. She decided to just be honest. "Well, yeah."

This laugh came even more easily, encouraging her to keep talking.

"I know you're an ultra-tough firefighter, since you've told me that about a thousand times—"

He interrupted her with a huff. "*Two* times, and I've never said I was 'ultra-tough,' *and* I didn't tell you I was a firefighter to brag about it."

She continued as if he hadn't said anything. "But I also know you have a squishy, soft middle."

Air left his lungs in an audible *whoosh*. "Squishy middle? Squishy *middle*? I had the second-highest score on our last fitness ability test." Grabbing her hand, he pressed her fingers against his abs. "Does this *feel* soft and squishy to you?"

"I didn't mean that you were *literally* soft and squishy," she explained, even as the motion of his ab muscles flexing beneath her fingers distracted her from what she was saying. "Just that your emotions are…mmm. Sorry, what was I saying?"

"How not squishy I am?" There was a smug note in his voice that should've come off as obnoxious but instead turned her on—although that could've been the heat of his skin radiating through his shirt or just the entire package that made up Kieran Sullivan Byrne.

"Hmm…" It was almost impossible to make her hum sound skeptical, but she somehow managed it. "I don't think I can conclusively determine that without further study."

He went still under her hand, which she couldn't seem to keep from stroking his abs—not that she really tried too hard. This time, his hiss of breath wasn't caused by irritation, judging by the way he leaned closer to her. There was a click in the sudden silence and then a second one before she felt her seat belt loosening and retracting. She didn't have time to ask what he was doing before he was sliding across the seat, lifting and turning her with a startling quickness and ease.

Suddenly, he was now where she'd been sitting, and she found herself on his lap, straddling him, their faces so close together that she could feel the warmth of his breath on her mouth. Her head spun from how quickly he'd moved her—or possibly from their close proximity.

"Wait," she said, almost not recognizing her own voice. Surely that husky-voiced siren wasn't her? "What about the guys searching for us?"

Without looking away from her, he lowered the passenger-side window, letting the brisk mountain air rush in. Instead of clearing her head in a chilly wake-up call, the sweep of cold air just made everything more exciting and real. Forcing herself to listen to the world outside the cab of the truck was a huge effort, but she managed—at least for a few seconds. There was silence, only broken by an occasional soft breeze. Otherwise, the night was still.

"Did they give up looking for us already?" she asked as Kieran closed the window. They'd broken into the compound and—if Charlie was interpreting the explosions properly—Fifi and Bennett had even blown up a goodly chunk of the armory. Couldn't the militia guys have spent more than five minutes trying to find the culprits? "What kind of poor excuse for anti-government extremists are these people?"

"Doubt they even saw us leave the road," Kieran said, still not breaking their locked gaze. All this eye contact was making her skin buzz with adrenaline and something else—something less familiar but that she still could identify as desire. "Probably still think they're chasing us down Moose Peak Road. Once they reach the highway, they won't know which way we went. We'll just need to wait until they return to the compound."

"Hmm…" It was hard focusing on their conversation when the eye contact was all kinds of intense. "It's still early. Should we meet Kiki and B for debriefing after all?"

"No."

Her lips curved up at that flat negative, but before she could respond, his lips were on hers, and her entire body lit up like he'd set it on fire. Her fingers, somehow still resting on his abs, curled into fists, grabbing handfuls of his shirt in a futile effort to ground herself. He shifted under her, leaning closer, his fingers burrowing into her hair so he could cup her skull as if he was holding something precious and breakable. Despite his gentleness, he kissed her with a barely banked ferocity that should've scared her.

Luckily, Charlie wasn't easily scared.

She eagerly met each kiss with her own, almost giddy with the thrill of finally kissing this man on his scowling face, nipping at the lips that snarled grumpy things. Who knew that his kisses would be so sweet?

Jerking her head back, she sucked in a breath, just now realizing that she'd stopped breathing while they'd kissed. "Told you that you have a squishy center."

His growl made her shiver and lean closer, eager to start the kissing again, but it was his turn to pull away. "Nothing squishy about me."

Charlie wanted to argue, but she knew that would just prolong their kissing hiatus, so she held back the words for probably the first time in her entire life. Instead, she just smiled at him and made a noncommittal sound as she pressed their lips together—or at least, she *tried* to press their lips together, but he held her back.

"What did that sound mean?" he grumbled, the warm air from his words hitting her damp skin, making it feel as if his voice could actually caress her.

She shivered again, wondering if there was a limit to how turned on she could be. Squirming in his lap, she tried to close that tiny distance between them, but still he held her back. He wore a stern expression which shouldn't have pushed her lust buttons even harder, but somehow it did.

"Charlotte Calamity Pax."

Even her hated full first name didn't sound so bad in his growly voice. "Yes?"

"Why aren't you arguing with me?"

Her laugh came out sounding husky, almost sultry. She wasn't sure who she was becoming after having been exposed to lip-to-lip contact with him, but she kind of liked the sexy seductress—especially if her transformation meant more making out with Kieran. "You *want* me to argue with you?"

"Yes—no—*argh*." It was so fun to see him all flustered like that. "You're holding back just so I'll keep kissing you."

"Well…yeah." Darting in, she nipped his lower lip and then retreated again, eating up his reaction, his indrawn breath and full body jolt. She loved the way she could affect him. "If I argued, this"—she bit lightly at that full lip again—"would be delayed."

"Good point."

Then his lips were on hers again, and he was kissing her as if she were the only source of life, and he'd fall over dead if he stopped. That feeling of being irresistible and the reason he was going out of his mind with desire was intoxicating and addictive. Who would've thought that she, Charlie Pax, would cause a man to lose his entire sanity with just the power of her lips?

At that point, she had to stop thinking, because his enormous, hot hands were sliding under her shirt and against her skin. Her nerve endings lit up until she was surprised the truck cab wasn't glowing like an enormous firefly.

As his fingertips brushed the bare skin directly under her bra, she couldn't hold in the tiny sound that escaped—a sound that was embarrassingly close to a moan. Although it was muffled against Kieran's mouth, she knew he had heard it, since his lips turned up under hers. Even though she couldn't actually see his small smile, she just knew it was obnoxiously smug.

Pulling back, she nipped his lower lip in retaliation, but by the way he chuckled, dark and deep, he didn't find that to be any kind of punishment.

"You're like a little Chihuahua," he murmured, his mouth brushing against her throat. That felt very nice, so she raised her chin, giving him more access to her vulnerable neck. "All yappy and bite-y." He set his teeth against her skin, pressing so lightly that all she felt was a pleasurable zip of sensation running up her spine.

The Chihuahua comment couldn't stand, however, so she made a valiant effort to *not* melt into a puddle of goo at the sensation. "Well, you're a bulldog. All muscle-y and grumpy-looking, but a total sucker for scritches." Proving her point—and satisfying her deep need to touch him everywhere—she ran her hands over his head, letting her short fingernails lightly scratch at his scalp. From his groan and the way his eyes went heavy-lidded, he liked her touch just as much as she loved touching him. "See? I'm surprised your leg isn't thumping the floor."

"What?" His eyes popped open, although she noticed he didn't move his head.

"You know…" She kept getting distracted by how soft his hair was, despite the short cut. "The twitchy leg thing a dog does when you find just the right itchy spot." She gave him a scratch behind one ear and couldn't hold back her laugh when he growled and wrapped his arms around her, squeezing her tightly against him.

"*That* isn't my itchy spot," he teased—actually *teased*—and she melted as she laughed even harder.

Wrapping her arms around his neck, she hugged him back. Although her body was still buzzing with unsatisfied need, she was surprisingly content. "Kieran Sullivan Byrne, I like you a lot."

"Didn't plan on it, Charlotte Calamity Pax, but I like you too."

The gruff way he admitted it made her feel even more special, and her arms tightened around his neck until he gave a groan of protest and patted her shoulder. "Did you just tap out?" she asked, giggling again as she loosened her hold. This clingy-monkey behavior was not like her, but for some reason, she couldn't seem to keep her hands off of Kieran.

"I did." There was no shame in his admission. In fact, smug satisfaction was thick in his voice. "You've wrestled me into submission."

"Hmm…" She studied his face in the dim moonlight. "What should I do with a submissive Kieran?"

So close to him, she saw his eyes spark with heat before lowering to half-mast. "I have a few suggestions."

Ignoring the answering hungry flare in her lower belly, she pretended to think. Despite all the times she wondered what it'd be like to kiss—and do more—with Kieran, she hadn't expected the reality to be so explosive. The intensity was new and bewildering, and as much as she wanted to continue their make-out session, another part of her needed to hole up in her room and just process.

It wasn't a familiar sensation, since she normally was a huge fan of jumping in without a plan and letting any future consequences sort themselves out later. The urge to retreat to think about her emotions felt almost as alien as her urge to stay on his lap until the morning sun peeked over the mountaintops. Shoving the whole tangled mass of confusing thoughts into a corner of her brain to stew over later, she gave Kieran an impish smile and lunged for the driver's seat.

"Nope," he said, catching and returning her to his lap with an ease that made her even more attracted to him—a feat she thought was impossible. At what point would her desire for him max out? She was beginning to wonder if it ever would. It would continue to build and build until her head—or other parts of her—exploded. "Not driving my truck."

"But I haven't done any off-roading in forever. Isn't it my turn to take out the last half of the symphony?" She gave him her best puppy-dog eyes, a look she borrowed from her twin, since she didn't have one of her own. All it did was make him laugh and hug her.

"No." Sliding out from underneath her, he started to shift over to the driver's seat but paused to kiss her—hard and quick. "Your *on*-road driving scares the crap out of me." Reluctantly, he moved to the other side of the seat.

"C'mon," she said, even as she pulled on her seat belt, knowing the argument was lost. It'd been a long shot anyway. "I'm a great driver."

"I know." He rolled down the window to listen once more, and they both were silent for several minutes. The only sound was the slight whine of the wind, and he closed the window before speaking again. "You're good, and very fast, and like to push your car's limits."

Those all seemed like positives to Charlie, so she asked, "And?"

"You'd probably get us back to town safely, but it wouldn't matter, since you'd give me a heart attack in the process. I'd be dead anyway."

She rolled her eyes as he started the truck. "You're a firefighter. Aren't all you guys adrenaline junkies?"

"It's different."

When she realized that was all he was going to say about the matter, she huffed. "That's not an answer. Why's it different to be in a truck with me as I'm driving—*very competently*—down a mountain than it is for you to run into a burning building?"

He shot her a sideways look. It didn't matter that the darkness made it hard to see his expression. She could positively *feel* the irritation in that glance. She didn't care though—if he wasn't going to let her drive his truck, he was going to have to explain exactly why.

"Hmm?" she prompted when he stayed silent.

"Because you're in the truck with me." He bit off the words like he was mad at them.

She stared at him, all sorts of emotions fizzing around in her belly. "So you don't care about endangering yourself, but you're worried about…me?"

He grunted an affirmative—or at least what sounded like an affirmative to Charlie. The butterflies in her stomach turned into huge pterodactyls, and she had no idea what to say in response to that. "Oh. Okay."

Kieran snorted—one of his amused, choked ones. "That's all you have to say about that?"

"Uh…" Her brain needed some time to chew on the fact that Kieran actually cared about her enough to worry when she was in danger. It was one thing for him to say he liked her in the middle of making out, but a whole other thing to be protective. Her sisters were the only ones who'd ever cared enough about her to worry about her, so his admission was a bit of a shock. Her brain wasn't quite back online, but he was still waiting for more of a verbal reaction, so she had to say something. "Um… thanks?"

Although he choke-laughed again, he didn't press her for more, just started up the truck. As he backed out of their hiding spot next to the large boulder, Charlie sank back in her seat as a pleasant feeling spread from the pterodactyl party in her middle until even her fingers and toes were warm with the knowledge that someone outside her family cared about her. Despite the foreignness of the sensation, it was a wonderful feeling, and she sank into it like it was a warm bath.

I wonder if this is what it's like to be...content.

TWELVE

They spent the drive to Rosehill in comfortable silence—at least, Charlie thought the silence was comfortable, until Kieran parked the truck outside of her hotel. Under the yellow glow of a streetlight, she saw a muscle in his jaw was twitching.

"How did I manage to annoy you?" she asked, feeling an answering twinge of irritation. "I haven't even been talking!"

He turned to stare at her. "What? I'm not annoyed with you."

"Oh." Her righteous indignation seeped away. "What's with the twitching then?"

"Twitching?"

She gestured toward her own jaw. "The angry muscle right about here. It was twitching."

To her utter shock, his face flushed. "No, that's because… Uh, it wasn't because I'm annoyed at you."

Now she *had* to know what'd made Kieran Byrne actually *blush*. "So what's making you twitchy?"

"I'm not—" He cut himself off with a grunt, glaring at her with narrowed eyes. "Okay, *now* you're aggravating me."

She laughed. "I knew you'd get there eventually. I am talking again, after all. So, let me guess what's stressing you out. Is it because you realized you drive like a grandpa?"

To her surprise, the tight lines of his face softened with amusement. "The important thing is that we survived the drive."

"Yeah, we did." His smile was impossible to resist, and she grinned back at him. "We also survived breaking into the militia compound, planting some bugs, *and* a high-speed chase, so yay us."

"It wasn't really a chase—" He stopped his pedantic correction as his gaze snapped to the rearview mirror. "Sheriff."

Charlie twisted around in time to see a sheriff's department SUV pulling up behind Kieran's truck. "Seriously?" She didn't even care that the word came out as a full-on whine. "I was hoping to get a couple hours of sleep tonight."

"Were you?"

The odd tone in Kieran's voice caught her attention, despite the fact that the sheriff was in the process of getting out of the SUV behind them. "I was," she said slowly, trying to puzzle out why wanting to sleep for a few hours before facing the next day was making him act so strange and out of character. "Why are you acting like that's not a normal thing to want to do?"

"I'm not." The words came too quickly to be believable, though, and his blush was back. "I just wanted…uh, I wasn't sure—" A sharp rap of the sheriff's knuckles on Kieran's window cut him off, and Charlie tried to hold on to her patience as he lowered his window.

"Hi, Sheriff," she said as sweetly as she could. "Would you mind giving us a couple of minutes? We're in the middle of a very important conversation."

Summers looked startled for just a fraction of a second before her impassive mask fell back into place. "No. Your conversation can wait."

"Can it though?" Charlie had a feeling that she wasn't ever going to learn the cause of Kieran's blush, and her Spidey senses were telling her that the reason was *fascinating*.

"Yes." The sheriff sounded a touch harried before she regained her composure. "Where have you two been tonight?"

"None of your business," Kieran grumped.

"Making out," Charlie said at the same time. When his answer penetrated a second too late, she offered him an apologetic grimace and turned back to the sheriff. "What he said."

"It *is* my business if you were burglarizing the Freedom Survivors' compound."

"Of course we weren't," Charlie lied easily. "And since when do militia guys call the *cops*? I guess government agencies are only evil until one of the militia guys gets their feelings hurt."

"Criminal trespass, damage to property, arson," Summers continued as if Charlie hadn't spoken. "You're in a lot of trouble. Multiple felonies means a long stretch of prison time."

"Well, you're going to have to do some sheriff-ing and figure out who the culprit was then," Charlie said, doing her best to sound bored.

"If it wasn't you, it had to be your sister and her husband."

Kieran gave an irritated grunt, and Charlie squeezed his leg.

She was getting annoyed too, but she fought to keep any trace of it out of her expression as she forced a light laugh. "Those two had a just-married date night, so you're going to have to find a different suspect. Except for going out to dinner, I imagine they haven't left their honeymoon suite."

"Not much of an alibi." Summers smirked, although it didn't look natural—more like the sheriff was trying to get a reaction from them. That settled some of Charlie's fears that there was actual evidence that any of them had been in the compound.

"It is when we're followed by an entire team of fortune hunters," Charlie said, matching the sheriff's smirk with one of her own. "Plus half the town watches us wherever we go. We won't have any problem finding witnesses that put us far away from the compound." *I hope.* The fortune hunters weren't *friends* exactly, but they still owed her for disappearing before the coffee shop fire. Despite Charlie's doubts, her words must've struck home, judging by the way the sheriff's face fell for just a moment before she blanked her expression again. "They'll also tell you that Kieran kisses like a *beast*, and that can be a bit disconcerting to know about a work colleague."

"Are we done here, Sheriff?" Kieran asked in a way that was more of a statement than a polite question.

Her nod was stiff. "For now. Don't leave the county."

Charlie couldn't resist. "Oh, we won't. After all, we have a murder to solve first." It was Kieran's turn to squeeze her leg just above her knee. Although she knew he meant it as a warning to watch her mouth around the sheriff, her lady bits took it as a sign of interest. Summers's frown brought her back to earth, and she quickly gave her most innocent smile. "Kidding, of course. There'll be no mystery solving. We're just going to enjoy the changing leaves and mountain views as we lounge around, ignoring any clues we might stumble across, and definitely not committing any felonies in pursuit of the truth."

When she stopped talking, the sheriff was scowling and Kieran sighed heavily. With a final warning glare, Summers turned away and headed back to her SUV. Charlie watched her as Kieran closed the window. It wasn't until the sheriff drove around them, turned at the next intersection, and disappeared from their view that Charlie spoke.

"I'm ninety-nine percent sure she doesn't have any concrete evidence that we were involved."

Turning his head, Kieran studied her. For once, his usual scowl wasn't in place, which made her a bit anxious that she couldn't read his expression.

Maybe she wasn't quite that sure. "Ninety-five percent?"

The sound he made was a laugh and a sigh mixed together, which didn't reassure her. Kieran was acting strange. Where was her consistently grumpy and quarrelsome firefighter?

"What's wrong?"

"Nothing's wrong." Even though he said the words with conviction, he still didn't look right. This person gazing at her with amusement and fondness was not the cranky guy she'd first met. "You just like to walk the cliff's edge, don't you?"

She studied him, looking for clues in his expression, not sure why she cared if he meant that as a compliment or a complaint. "Yes?" Hating how she was turning her statements into questions, she shored up her wavering confidence and flashed him a smile. "The view's best from there."

His eyes softened even more, his expression so far from the scowling Kieran she was used to that she couldn't pull her gaze away from his. He appeared almost tender, and that was blowing her mind a little—even as she found herself leaning toward him. "Yeah, it is," he said in a tone she'd never heard from him before. She wasn't able to analyze his strangely gentle mien, however, since he cupped the back of her neck and drew her even closer, closing the last few inches to bring their lips together.

Unlike the explosive, ferocious kisses they'd shared earlier, this was…soft. He touched his mouth to hers carefully, as if she was something fragile and precious. Oddly enough, despite his gentleness and the lack of tongue action, her mind went as blank as it had when they were trying to burrow into each other's bodies. Her hands found his face, cupping either side of his jaw, her fingertips stroking his stubbly scruff.

She had no idea how much time had passed when he withdrew just enough that their lips separated, but she could still feel the warm air of his breath brushing her skin. Her gaze locked on his. As much as she adored his grumpy scowls and angry, narrowed eyes, this soft Kieran was even more mesmerizing. This was the squishy middle part of him that no one else got to see, but he'd stripped away his sharp spines just for her.

Charlie felt honored and also a little worried. She wasn't tactful or perceptive or careful—how was she supposed to avoid damaging Kieran? When his defenses were in place, his hard shell of grumpiness firmly encasing him, he was protected from her. Now, though, with his soft underbelly exposed to her, she could hurt him so easily—and she'd rather punch herself in the face than hurt Kieran Byrne.

"Get some sleep," he said huskily, his growly, bossy tone overlying the tenderness. She felt his face move as he spoke, and she realized she still cradled his jaw. With a sigh, she allowed her hands to drop, giving him one last caress as she pulled away. Her fingers only made it as far as his chest, however, balling his shirt in handfuls as if she was locking in, ready to resist being pulled away from him.

"Fine," she huffed, making him laugh in a grumbly way that rumbled along her spine and made her tighten her grip on him. "You're not helping things. That laugh of yours is dangerous."

His smile was wide and open, sending another zing of concern through her that she was going to damage this gentle side of Kieran. Her fingers loosened their grip, but then she tightened them again, yanking him toward her for one more press of her lips against his—just for a blissful second. She knew if she didn't pull away now, she'd be latched on to him for the rest of the night, so she forced herself to release him.

"You're ridiculously addictive," she said, opening her door, hoping the chilly mountain air would return some common sense to her brain. Instead, it just made her want to cuddle up to his warm body again. "It's annoying."

His soft laugh sent a fizz of attraction through her.

"Not helping." With a huff, she jumped out of the pickup.

He was grinning at her, not at all bothered by her accusation. "Good night, Charlie."

"Night, Kiki."

Even the nickname couldn't make him lose his smile completely, although he drew his eyebrows together in a mock scowl. The combination of soft and grumpy made him even more irresistible, and she groaned as she slammed the truck door.

She was in so much trouble.

———

"These people are so dull." Lou heaved a dramatic sigh and leaned back in her chair.

Charlie couldn't argue with that. "Welcome to Stakeouts and Surveillance 101. Ninety-nine-point-nine percent of the time it's eye-crossingly boring."

Fifi made a sound of agreement from her spot on the bed, where she and Bennett were cuddled together. They'd offered up their honeymoon suite for a communications center, since the coffee shop wasn't an option, and half of the murder club was busy. Only Lou, Rory, and—for some random reason—Ian had joined Fifi, Charlie, and Bennett to spy electronically on the militia compound. "Welcome to the exciting world of bounty hunting."

"I'd say I'll stick to barista-ing, but that's gotten a little *too* exciting lately. Plus, you know, I'm out of a job." Lou kicked her socked feet up and placed them on Rory's lap. Rory looked down at the feet and then at Lou's face, her expression baffled.

"You're supposed to massage them," Lou said helpfully. Rory gave one of the feet now living in her lap a tentative poke with one finger, making Charlie laugh.

Ian, Rory's objectively gorgeous husband, tossed a balled-up scrap of paper at Lou's head. "Quit harassing my wife. If she massages anyone's feet, they should be mine."

"Ow," Lou said when the tiny ball bounced off her head.

Ian rolled his eyes and took a sip of his coffee. "There's no way that hurt."

"Why are you here, anyway?" Lou asked, glancing at her cell phone. "Didn't you say you have to get to work? You'd better go put out some fires." She snorted. "*Literal* fires."

"I'm going." Ian leaned over to press a kiss to Rory's temple, making her smile even as she kept her eyes focused on the laptop screen showing the militia compound's two video feeds. "Just wanted to make sure Rory was comfortable before I left."

It was Rory's turn to snort. "He wanted coffee."

Ian grinned around his cup, not denying it in the least.

"That reminds me," Charlie said as she jumped off her perch on the table. Pouring coffee into a paper cup, she added creamer and sugar.

"Who's that for?" Ian asked, because of course he did. He was a firefighter, after all, and they were all incredibly nosy.

"Why can't it be for me?" she asked rather than answer him. She was not a blusher, but for some reason, the back of her neck felt hot.

As if he could smell gossip, Ian's eyes lit up. "Because it's definitely not. Who're you hoarding coffee for, Ms. Tough Bounty Hunter? Someone you have a crush on, maybe?"

"Mind your business." Now the strange, prickling heat was spreading to her face. Despite that, she couldn't hold back a smile.

"Aha!" Ian crowed. "There is someone. Who is it? You can tell me. I'll keep your dirty, dirty secret."

Charlie slanted a look at Rory, who gave a tiny shake of her head.

Ian must've caught it, because he clutched at his chest with his free, non-coffee-holding hand. "How could you betray me like that? My own wife!"

"You'd keep an important secret," Rory said, not looking at all disturbed by Ian's dramatics. "But something like this? The entire fire department will know by noon who Charlie's dating."

Still grumbling—although Charlie noticed that he didn't deny it—Ian leaned down again, this time to teasingly bite at Rory's neck, making her laugh. Although Rory's uncharacteristic giggles were almost unbearably adorable, Charlie was distracted by a knock on the door of the suite. She hurried over, completely losing any control she'd had over her sappy grin.

"I have a feeling I'm going to find out anyway," Ian said quietly to Rory, but Charlie ignored him. The firefighters could talk all they wanted. She had no problem with the entire world knowing that she and Kieran were a thing. Kind of a thing? A potential thing? Shaking off her mental attempt to define what they were starting, she checked the peephole and then yanked open the door.

"Hi." That was all she managed to say, since most of her brain was occupied by just staring at him, taking in the huge, cranky hotness that made up Kieran Sullivan Byrne.

He lifted his chin in response to her greeting as his gaze ran over her like a warm, rough hand, making her skin feel all buzzy.

She wondered if he was having the same issue, if just the sight of her had affected his ability to find and say words. The thought was rather delicious.

"Oh, it's Byrne." Ian's voice had gone a bit flat, the teasing note disappearing.

Kieran flicked a look over her shoulder, giving Ian the slightest of nods before refocusing on Charlie.

The interruption brought her out of her Kieran-induced fog, and she held out the coffee she'd just poured. "Here. Saved you one. I know this is like liquid gold around here now."

He glanced down at the coffee and one of those rare, authentic smiles touched his mouth. It was impossible not to grin back at him as he took the cup from her, allowing his fingers to brush along hers in the process. "Thanks." His voice had turned husky, and the rough sound made her shiver in delight.

"Come in." Stepping back, she swept her arm out to the side. "We're watching the fascinating video feed from the compound."

His gaze shot to the laptop as he stepped into the room. "Yeah? Anything useful?"

"No." She closed the door behind him. "I was being sarcastic. It is not at all fascinating. As Lou said, the Freedom Survivors are boring." She gave Ian an irritated look. "Knock it off."

Everyone else in the room looked at Charlie in surprise, except for Ian, who maintained his poker face as he returned her glare with an icy one of his own. "I have my reasons."

"Stupid ones." Resisting the urge to stand in front of Kieran to protect him from Ian's misplaced distrust, Charlie boosted herself up on the table where she'd been sitting earlier. "He's not responsible for something his dad did."

"She's right," Rory said before Ian could respond, and he jerked his head around to stare at her. "We can't stop our parents if they go off the rails. You of all people should understand that."

His mouth tightened as the silence in the room stretched with tension, but then Ian let out an audible breath. "You're right." Turning back to Kieran, he pulled his shoulders back as if bracing for an uncomfortable task. "Sorry, Byrne."

Kieran gave a grunt, his scowl almost hiding how uncomfortable he felt. Charlie could see it in the tiny muscle jumping in his jaw and the way he shot a quick, almost entreating look at her. She couldn't resist the appeal, so she launched into speech, grabbing at the first topic of conversation that came to mind.

"While we watch the very boring militia dudes go about their very boring day, we should probably talk about Mom."

Although Fifi groaned, she said, "Yeah, you're right. Clock's ticking. I'm surprised she hasn't shown up yet, honestly. Maybe she doesn't need the key after all."

A familiar figure running through Rory's woods flashed in her recent memory, and Charlie frowned. "Maybe she is here. We still don't know who the sixth treasure hunter is."

Fifi's groan was even louder this time as she tipped her head back. "Of course that's Mom."

It did make an annoying amount of sense. "So she needs the key, after all."

"Be ready for her to break into our hotel rooms."

"Pretty sure she already did that last night." Even though

she'd been exhausted as well as distracted by the Kieran-shaped cloud she'd been floating on, she'd had an uneasy feeling when she'd entered her room the night before—enough so that she did a complete search of the space before she could even think about going to bed.

Lou made appropriately horrified noises as Fifi sat up straight, eyes lit with outrage. "Did she find it?"

Charlie fished the key out of her zipped pocket and held it up so her sister could see it. "Duh, of course not. I'm keeping it on me. She'll have to resort to full-on robbery to get her crime-ing hands on this."

"She'll try it," Fifi warned.

"I know." An old and bitter pang of sadness struck Charlie, surprising her. She hadn't thought her mom had the ability to disappoint her anymore. One of the militia members on the screen crossed over to plop down on the couch, and Charlie watched his movements, using the time to rewrap her emotions in some muffling blankets. Once she was pleasantly numb again, she looked away from the screen. "I have about fifty decoy keys on me, but we still need to find the lock before she gets ahold of this key. She's ditched us too many times for us to trust that we'll be able to tail her."

"As fascinating as this is," Ian said, his usual easy manner returning, "I've got to get to work." Pressing another temple kiss to his wife, he topped off his coffee, gave the rest of them a chin lift of farewell, and left the room, closing the door behind him with a click.

"Okay." Fifi picked up the conversation as if they hadn't

been interrupted. "Are we assuming the lock is somewhere around Langston?"

"Probably Denver," Charlie said. "Mom would've had to stash the necklace before getting arrested."

"Unless she handed it off to Zach or another partner in crime," Bennett suggested.

It was a good theory, but Charlie knew her mother too well to see that happening. "Jane wouldn't trust anyone with the necklace, especially Zach."

Fifi nodded. "Rightly so. The guy would've been gone like a shot, taking the prize and leaving Mom to face the consequences."

"So we're going to assume she locked up the necklace some-where in Denver," Lou said before her mouth pulled down in an exaggerated frown. "That's a lot of possibilities."

"Not necessarily," Kieran chimed in. As pathetic as it was, Charlie was glad for the excuse to look at him. Her crush had officially entered ridiculousness territory. "Where was she picked up by police?"

"Just a mile northwest from the victim's hotel." Bennett had been investigating Jane when he'd met Fifi, so it made sense he knew a random detail like that.

Charlie grabbed her phone and opened a map app. "Do you know the exact address where the cops arrested her?" she asked without looking away from her screen.

"Sixth Avenue and Colorado."

Of course he does. She grinned. "You're proving once again how handy you are to have around."

An almost inaudible protest from Kieran had her glancing his way. For some reason, his scowl was firmly back in place.

"What's wrong?" she asked.

"Nothing," he grumbled. When she didn't say anything or look away, the tips of his ears turned a bit pink. "Just...it was *my* idea."

Charlie was forced to suck in her cheeks in order to hold back her laugh. It didn't help that Lou had obviously heard his mumbled complaint and was snickering, but Charlie somehow managed to keep a straight face. "You're very handy too."

Although he huffed as if he hadn't been fishing for praise, his scowl lightened. Charlie waited until her head was tipped down at her phone again before she allowed the tiniest smile to escape. Maybe it was strange of her, but she liked that he wanted her approval. It made her feel important to him. Focusing on the map app with an effort, she zoomed in on the area between where her mom had been arrested and the hotel where she'd stolen the necklace and frowned.

"It's so residential," she said.

Lou stood and moved closer to Charlie so she could see. "Maybe she didn't go far. Would the hotel have locked storage units people could use?"

"We'll check." Charlie made a mental note to call the hotel later. "If not, they might know the closest place that does."

Kieran leaned over her shoulder to look at the screen, his body so close to her back that she could feel the heat radiating from him. "There's a shipping place. Maybe the key is for a mailbox."

Fifi came over to stand behind Charlie's other side, resting her chin on Charlie's shoulder. "Hmm…that's in the other direction. Would Mom have been able to make it all the way over here in time? She's not a fan of physical activity." She pointed at the intersection where Jane had been picked up, getting her finger too close to the screen, making the map zoom in.

"Fifi, no touching," Charlie complained mildly. The map now showed a sliver of the opposite side of Colorado Boulevard, where—according to the map icons—two restaurants, a laundromat, and a gym were located. She moved to return the map to its original position when Rory sat up straight.

"The militia widow is awake."

Everyone's attention turned from the map to the laptop, and they all crowded around the table. Charlie dropped her phone into her pocket, shouldering her way between Fifi and Lou so she could see the video feed. Gabrielle was indeed getting out of bed, shoving her mussed long hair over her shoulder before she stretched. She dropped her arms as she looked toward the door, her lips moving.

"Turn it up," Charlie said, reaching for the laptop even as she said the words. Cranking it up to maximum volume, she leaned closer to the screen as Gabrielle's bedroom door opened and a skinny, white man stepped inside. He yanked off his baseball hat, leaving his hair mussed around his protruding ears.

"Sorry to bother you, Ms. Jones, but we were wondering if you'd talked to Clint about the break-in last night?"

Charlie turned her head so she could meet Kieran's gaze. From his expression, he was wondering the same thing she was.

"Why would Jones's widow be chatting with the new cult leader?" Fifi asked as if she could read Charlie's mind.

"Shh!" Lou waved a hand at Fifi, her gaze locked on the screen. "We'll miss what they're saying."

"It's recording," Fifi muttered under her breath, but Lou just shushed her again. Charlie gave an amused snort and received her own chorus of *shh*s from Lou, Bennett, and—annoyingly—Fifi.

"I have," Gabrielle said. *"He's sure the visiting PIs are involved."*

"Bounty hunters," Charlie and Fifi said at the same time.

"Shh!" the others hissed at them.

"That's what Saul thought too," the skinny man on the screen said. *"What's Clint thinking we should do?"*

"Besides, I *am* a PI, so she's not totally wrong," Bennett said, and then dodged Fifi's swatting hand.

"I'll meet everyone upstairs in an hour and tell you what he said." Gabrielle made a shooing motion toward the door. *"No sense in having to repeat everything."*

"Oh, okay." The skinny guy retreated quickly. *"I'll let the others know."*

"Thanks, Daryl."

"Daryl," Charlie repeated. "Isn't he one of Clint's friends from the informant's list?"

"Yes," Rory answered.

"Gabrielle's lying," Kieran said. "Unless we missed her having a phone conversation?"

"Nope," Fifi said. "She's definitely lying. Someone's been monitoring the feed since early this morning, and I even ran through all last night's footage of her bedroom. She's been asleep until just a minute ago, and her phone is way over there." She pointed at the dresser on the screen where a phone sat, plugged into a charger. "There's no way she could reach it without getting out of bed."

"So…" Charlie said slowly as the wheels in her mind spun. "Maybe it's not Clint giving orders from jail."

THIRTEEN

FIFI WAS ALREADY NODDING. APPARENTLY, their psychic-sister link was up and working. "Even though Clint couldn't have killed Cobra, it still might've been someone wanting to take over the militia."

"After hearing about how Cobra treated his wife, I can't really blame her," Charlie said. There were mutters of agreement all around.

Charlie could barely contain her impatience as Gabrielle got ready. She appreciated that the woman got dressed in the bathroom after showering, so that she didn't feel like more of a creeper than she already did for setting up a camera in a stranger's bedroom.

Finally, Gabrielle took her phone off the charger and tucked it in her pocket. She stood by the closed door for several seconds, her shoulders curling in and her head bowing, making her look like a completely different person than the confident woman striding around her bedroom a few minutes earlier.

"What's she doing?" Rory asked, leaning closer as she frowned at the screen.

"Getting into character." Kieran's voice was flat and filled with antipathy. Charlie couldn't blame him. The woman was trying to frame him for murder, after all—or at least allowing it.

"That's wild," Lou breathed, sounding a bit impressed. "She's like an actor before a play."

Gabrielle swung open the door and scurried out, looking for all the world like a timid, beaten-down mouse who'd never commit murder or manipulate an entire militia.

Once she was out of range of the bedroom camera, Rory maximized the feed from the camera lurking in the taxidermied bear's mouth on the main level. Charlie mentally complimented herself on her camera placement, because almost the entire room was within view. A half dozen men were milling around, including skinny Daryl. Except for one surly-looking man, they all rushed over to Gabrielle when she arrived, solicitously helping her get settled on the couch. Once they'd all taken their seats, Gabrielle spoke, her voice soft and hesitant. Rory maxed out the volume on the bug stuck to the antler chandelier.

"Clint is very...angry about last night," she started. *"He's sure it's the PIs visiting from Denver."*

"Bounty hunters from Langston," Charlie muttered, only to be shushed. "Well, if I'm being accused of something, they should at least get their details right."

"Accused?" Kieran gave one of his harshly amused grunts. "We *did* break in."

"And blow up most of their arsenal," Fifi said absently.

"Local law enforcement should thank us for that. No one on that compound should have a grenade launcher in their sticky little fingers."

"If you guys don't zip it, I'm going to start gagging people," Lou warned, and they all settled in to watch the video feed.

"*...this time,*" Gabrielle was saying. "*It's obvious—Clint said it's obvious—that the coffee shop wasn't enough. We need to end them this time.*" As if she'd realized how strong her voice had gotten, Gabrielle ducked her head. "*He'd like to hear your... ideas? On how to accomplish that?*"

"*I don't like this,*" one of the men said, but Charlie barely heard him over the pounding in her ears.

"The coffee shop?" she repeated, rage surging through her. Unable to stay still, she turned abruptly and began pacing the floor. "*She* was the one who almost killed us?"

"Be mad about it in a minute," Fifi said, her eyes still fixed on the screen. "We need to hear what their next attempt will be."

"*The sheriff already has her eyes on us because of Cobra, and now Clint wants us to murder a bunch of PIs?*" The sour-looking guy—the only one who hadn't rushed to fawn over Gabrielle—was talking when Charlie managed to dial back her anger enough to pay attention to the video feed. "*Guess he won't be happy until we're all in prison with him.*"

Gabrielle glared at the man for just a split second before looking down at her knees. "*You know Clint wouldn't set you up, Saul. He just trusts that you can pull this off without getting caught.*"

"Ooh." Lou gave a dramatic wince. "Did you see those deadly eye lasers?"

"She's definitely the boss." If Gabrielle hadn't been in the process of convincing a bunch of militia guys to *murder* them, Charlie might've been a little impressed. Gabrielle had likely knocked off her abusive husband—or at least taken advantage of his death—and was now ruling the militia in his place, all without any of the misogynistic members knowing they were taking orders from a woman. Since she was, in fact, planning to *murder* them, however, a fresh flame of anger burned any admiration Charlie felt for Gabrielle right up.

"How does Clint want us to do this then?" an older guy with some unfortunate facial hair asked. *"Blow 'em up?"*

"We don't have much as far as explosives go after last night," Daryl said doubtfully. *"I suppose we could just…shoot them?"*

"How're we supposed to do that without getting caught?" Saul huffed.

"Tank, you're our best sniper." Gabrielle's breathy voice held an extra heaping of admiration. A stocky guy who'd been quiet so far lit up at her compliment. *"We'll just need to find out where they're going to be and then get you into position beforehand. There'll be enough commotion after for you to slip away."*

Saul gave her a suspicious look. *"Shouldn't you run this by Clint before you start making plans?"*

Her head dipped again as her voice softened enough that Charlie had to strain to hear her. *"This was one of Clint's ideas."*

Although Saul didn't look convinced, he kept his mouth shut—for the moment, at least.

"Won't I need an alibi?" Tank asked, not sounding that bothered by the idea of shooting several innocent—well, relatively innocent—people.

"I'll go talk to the sheriff about Cobra's case at the same time. Saul can wait in the car in a hat and sunglasses, and I'll make sure to mention to the sheriff that Tank drove me and give her a glimpse from a distance. If the sheriff vouches for you, that'll be an ironclad alibi."

"What about my alibi?" Saul whined.

"The fact that everyone knows you can't hit the side of the barn from ten feet away," one of the guys said. Everyone besides Saul and Gabrielle snickered.

"Just tell everyone you're planning to go hunting." Gabrielle was losing her breathy, innocent tone as irritation seeped into her voice. Charlie was a little surprised she'd managed to pull off the whole stealth-leadership thing, since she had a hard time staying in character. It was possible that the Paxes were testing Gabrielle's patience, however. They were good at that. *"After we get back from the sheriff's office, you can drive to Connor Springs and wander around town, making sure lots of people—and security cameras, if possible—get a glimpse of you."* She paused and when she spoke again, the trembling uncertainty was back. *"That's something that Clint would do, I think."*

Saul didn't look happy. *"The timing won't line up."*

"Fine." The word came out as a snap before Gabrielle caught herself. *"Daryl, you'll drive Saul's truck to Connor Springs before the op, get the license plate on some cameras but keep your face hidden. Saul, someone else can give you a ride there later, and then*

you and Daryl will swap places before you put your face on every camera you can find. Will you do that for us, D?" Her voice was sheer sweetness, and even on the camera feed, Charlie could see Daryl positively melt.

Guys are kind of dumb, generally speaking. She glanced at Kieran, who met her gaze with a curious frown—one that deepened when she gave him an apologetic grimace for mentally slandering his gender.

"How will I know where they'll be?" Tank asked.

The camera angle was just right to show Gabrielle's slow, smug smile. *"I'll find out from Lou Sparks. She's buddied up to them, and she never shuts up. All I'll need to do is bring them up, and she'll babble away, telling us everything we need to know."*

"Wow." Lou leaned back in her chair. "I mean, she's not exactly *wrong*, but it'll still be fun to foil her plan."

Charlie's brain spun at a hundred miles an hour as a plan began to take shape. "Rather than foil it, how about we *redirect* it? Lou, how're your acting skills?"

"Rusty but still solid." Lou grinned. "I love when you Pax sisters visit. It's always so much *fun*."

———

"Sooo…"

Charlie groaned softly but with great feeling. "Of course you're going to start this when I'm stuck in a ceiling with you."

Despite the dim light in the ceiling soffit, she clearly saw her sister's wicked grin. "This is the perfect time to get all the details. What else do we have to do while waiting for our wannabe assassin to show?"

"We could talk about the case?" Charlie suggested, even though she knew it was no use. Fifi had a firm grip on this topic, and she wasn't about to let it go. Charlie was surprised her sister hadn't pressed her for details earlier actually.

"Orrrrrrr…we could talk about you and your grumpy firefighter."

"Orrrrrrr," Charlie mimicked her sister, "we could talk about you and your stalker husband."

"Sure." As soon as Fifi cheerfully agreed, Charlie winced at her mistake. "Sometimes, Bennett likes to do this thing with his ton—"

"Okay!" Charlie yelped louder than she should have. She was just that desperate. "What do you want to know?" Before her sister could speak, she quickly qualified that question. "I know nothing about his tongue abilities." She paused. "Fine, I know *some* things about his tongue abilities, but nothing I'm going to share with you."

"So you two have…?"

Charlie couldn't see very well in the dim light, but she could almost *feel* the way Fifi was suggestively bouncing her eyebrows and had to laugh. "No. Just made out a little."

"Yeah? How was it?"

"Nice."

"Nice?" Fifi sounded disappointed. "With all his smoldering attitude, I figured it'd be better than *nice*. *Good*, at the very least."

"Fine." The word burst from Charlie as she realized she'd been dying to talk to someone about the previous night. "It was *amazing*. The militia guys could've run right up to his truck, and I wouldn't have noticed." She paused. "Okay, I would've noticed, because I'm not an idiot, but I wouldn't have cared, which also makes me sound like an idiot, so I guess I'm an idiot now. Kieran's lips sucked out my brain apparently."

"Um...ew?" Fifi commented after a moment.

"You asked for it, wanting to know all about my *feelings*."

"I'm fine with hearing about your feelings, but the Kieran-lip-sucking thing is gross."

"Obviously, you've never made out with Kieran if you feel that way." Charlie blinked at the conflicting emotions raging through her from the thought of her sister kissing the fireman, gave up on trying to make sense of her new, Kieran-muddled self, and laughed. "But I don't really want to talk about my feelings either. Can we *please* discuss the case?"

"Fine," Fifi said, but then ruined it. "I just need to say one last thing first."

Charlie groaned.

"I'm happy for you." Fifi reached over and gave Charlie's arm a pat. "I feel so grateful for finding Bennett, who makes me really happy and...brain-sucked, so I'm hoping you'll find that too."

"Is brain-sucked really going to be a thing?" Even as she asked, Charlie knew it was too late to stop it.

"Yes."

Charlie sighed before giving her sister a return pat. "Thank you. I'm glad you found someone who makes you happy, and I appreciate that you want me to be equally brain-sucked. *Now* can we talk about the case?"

"Want to go check out lockboxes around where Mom was picked up once this is all over?" She gestured awkwardly at the soffit space around them, stirring up the dust.

Charlie squeezed her nose to stop a sneeze as she nodded but then shook her head. "Someone'll have to stay here to deal with the aftermath."

"The guys can."

With a snort, Charlie squinted through the near dark at her sister. "Yeah, and those two will happily stay here and answer the sheriff's questions as we jaunt off to Denver without them? The only reason they're not crammed in here with us is that they're the size of small bears."

Although Fifi made a grumbly sound, she didn't argue—she couldn't, because Charlie was very right.

There were a couple of distant thuds from outside, and they both went still, listening. Charlie peered through the crack she'd made from popping up a ceiling tile a bare inch, but the space beneath them stayed empty and still.

"Should we send Molly, Norah, and Cara to Denver?" Charlie asked in a whisper. As much as she hated to delegate anything to do with Jane's case, they were running out of time. Their mom's first court appearance was tomorrow, and in order to keep their house, they needed to make sure she actually *appeared*. In the meantime, a murderous militia was literally gunning for them, so there were a lot of balls in the air.

"Let me text them." Fifi wiggled around, retrieving her phone from wherever she'd had it stashed and tapping at the screen. "Nope. They're all up to their eyebrows in the latest case from Barney." The glow from Fifi's phone highlighted her frown. "They will if we really need them to, but they're really close to bringing the skip in, and you know Barney's just looking for any excuse to cause some last-minute shenanigans. Plus, we need to keep him happy, just in case we aren't able to bring Mom in on time."

"Ugh," Charlie groaned. "I'll be so glad when all of this is over and we can tell him to shove his entire being up his own—" Her phone vibrated against her leg, cutting her off. She shifted carefully so she could pull it out and look at the screen, not wanting to put any pressure on the fragile ceiling tiles surrounding her. The metal framework she rested on supported her weight, but she wouldn't trust the tiles to even hold up her phone. Reading the text, she felt a thrill of anticipation as she nudged her sister and held the phone in front of Fifi's face. Here we go.

Slowly and carefully slipping her phone back into her pocket, she pulled the gun from her hip holster and aimed it through the tiny crack she'd made by popping up a ceiling tile. Next to her, Fifi mirrored her. Steadying her breathing, Charlie waited.

The floor below creaked, heavy footfalls and even heavier breathing echoing through the attic storage space. *For a militia guy, he's not very stealthy,* Charlie thought, adrenaline powering through her, making it hard to stay still. She controlled her body, however, not even allowing herself to twitch a toe.

Tank came into view—or at least the top of the dirty ball cap he was wearing did. Crouching by one of the dirty windows looking out onto Simpson's main street, Tank set down his duffel bag and unzipped it.

It was nearly impossible to wait, but Charlie didn't want any ambiguity afterward. It needed to be obvious why he'd come, why he'd bribed the sports-store manager to give him access to their second-story storage area with the window that looked directly down on the blackened coffee shop.

She held herself still, waiting until Tank had opened the window, taken out his rifle, and aimed at the street below. Apparently, the saying about good things coming to those who waited was true, because Tank bent over, sticking out his ample rump.

Charlie grinned. He couldn't have presented a better bull's-eye if he'd drawn some concentric circles on it. She almost felt guilty for shooting such an easy target, but then she reminded herself that Tank was only there to kill them. Lou had happily babbled to Gabrielle about Charlie and Fifi's plan to visit the site of the coffee shop fire in order to look for clues. He wasn't innocently looking out the window. The guy was an assassin, lying in wait.

Ever so carefully, Charlie took aim and pulled the trigger.

He jumped and yelped, one hand reaching back. Before he could do more than that, Fifi sent her own shot into his other butt cheek.

Tank yipped again, and his rifle clattered to the floor as he whirled around, his hunted gaze scouring the storage space.

Charlie could almost see realization dawn on his face as his eyes turned to the ceiling. Groping for the rifle on the floor behind him, he stared right at their hiding spot.

"Ready?" Fifi whispered, but Charlie was already in motion. Of course she was ready. She was *always* ready. Dropping the gun, she grabbed the water pipe in front of her and pulled her knees in, crashing through the ceiling tiles as she swung from the pipe like she was a kid on the monkey bars. She got a glimpse of Tank's wide eyes and pale moon face—as well as the gun he was swinging in her direction—before her boots connected with his chest.

He hit the floor like a felled tree, the crash loud enough to be heard from the street, and Charlie went down with him. She tried to catch her balance so she landed on her feet, straddling him, since that would look rather awesome, but her foot sank into his gut instead. As the air left him in a *whoosh*, she lost her balance and crashed down on top of him.

Shoving off of his bulky form, she scrambled to her feet. It was too late though. She could hear Fifi laughing behind her.

"I suppose your dismount was more graceful," Charlie grumped, crouching next to the motionless man.

"Infinitely." Fifi joined her on the other side of Tank's limp form. "Plus I stuck my landing."

"Good for you."

Fifi ignored Charlie's sour grapes and took Tank's pulse. "Did you knock him out, or did the sedative from the darts kick in?"

Charlie shrugged, although she stayed alert to any sneaky

move by Tank. "Or he's faking it. Your guess is as good as mine."
Poking his arm, she sighed. "It's going to be a pain in our asses
to roll him over to cuff him."

Fifi nodded. "It would've been so much more considerate if
he'd passed out on his stomach."

A thunder of boots on the stairs made them both stand and
turn toward the door, ready just in case the people about to join
them weren't friendly. When Kieran was the first one through
the doorway, Charlie relaxed and grinned at his scowling face.

"Excellent," she said when Bennett followed right behind
Kieran. "You're just in time to help us roll him over."

Kieran's gaze flicked over her as if doing inventory, making
sure all her parts were in the proper order. When he met her eyes
again, his severe frown softened into a smile. As always, a happy
Kieran made her heart skip a beat. Without saying a word—or
waiting for Bennett, who was doing a more hands-on check of
Fifi's well-being—Kieran strode over to Tank and turned him
over onto his belly.

"Whoa." Charlie was impressed...and turned on. "You just
flipped that huge man like a pancake."

"He's not even breathing hard," Fifi said with proper awe
before looking at Charlie. "And you said it was just fine."

"I admitted it was better than fine," she muttered. When
Kieran narrowed his eyes at her suspiciously, she offered him a
sunny smile. "Want to go to Denver?"

"Yes."

"Hey!" Fifi protested. "We should at least rock-paper-
scissors for it."

"Why bother?" Charlie made short work of cuffing Tank. "I'll win anyway. You always go with rock."

Although Fifi huffed, she didn't argue with that fact. "I get flustered."

"Tell the sheriff hi from us!" Charlie grabbed Kieran's hand and hustled him toward the door before Fifi could say anything else. "I'll text if we find anything!"

As she hurried down the stairs, Kieran crowded close behind her, so when he spoke, it was right against her ear. "You okay?"

Turning her head, she nearly fell down the rest of the steps when she saw how very reachable his lips were. Kieran steadied her easily, which didn't help her distraction. "Very."

As if he could read her mind, a tiny smug smile touched his lips. It would've been obnoxious if it hadn't been for the affectionate, almost tender look in his eyes. "Good. Let's go find a necklace then."

FOURTEEN

As she climbed into the passenger seat of his truck, hurrying at the sound of approaching emergency sirens, Charlie frowned at the VW Fox across the street. She was sure Rhys's Jeep was somewhere close by as well. "Maybe I should drive."

"Nope." Kieran started the engine.

"How are you at dodging treasure hunters?"

"Fair to good." He pulled out into the street and immediately turned left into an alley. Only seconds later, a sheriff's department squad car flew past the entrance to the alley.

Internally, Charlie snickered at the "good" comment, remembering her conversation with her sister about his makeout skills, but she forced herself to stay poker-faced. "You'd have thought Fifi and Bennett would've given us a minute to get clear before they called in the cops."

"They may've been a little salty about having to stay here on cleanup duty while we get to go search for the necklace."

"Then Fifi should get better at rock-paper-scissors," Charlie huffed although she wasn't really annoyed, especially since it seemed as if they'd escaped detection.

Kieran made a strangled sound in his throat, the one that sounded like he was simultaneously holding back a laugh while also growling in annoyance that he'd allowed himself to be amused. It was so especially specific to Kieran that it was quickly becoming one of Charlie's favorite sounds. He steered the truck carefully through the alley, maneuvering between two trash bins that made the space so tight Charlie found herself sucking in her stomach, as if she could make the truck narrower that way. Even though she knew it was a ridiculous thought, she held her breath until they'd made it safely through.

As he turned onto a street that wasn't much wider than the alley had been, Charlie caught a glimpse of white in her side mirror. "Bones is on your tail."

"The one who drives the VW?" His gaze didn't even flicker toward the rearview mirror, as if he trusted her judgment so completely that he didn't even have check for himself, which pleased Charlie an inordinate amount.

"That's Bones." She turned around to get a better view out the back of the truck cab, but the other car hadn't emerged from the alley yet. "She's also the one who's apparently dating Rhys now, which is a good thing."

He flicked her a questioning glance as he turned left again. "Why's that?"

"Because it makes them happy," she explained without taking her gaze off the road behind them. There still wasn't any sign of Bones's car, but she felt like she needed to be extra vigilant since Kieran was trusting her to watch his back. At his skeptical-sounding snort, she reached over blindly to tap his arm. "I'm serious! I'm glad they're happy. I'm not a *monster*."

Even without looking at him, she could *feel* Kieran's skepticism.

"Fine. Rhys is the only competent one of that bunch. Hopefully love will distract him."

His laugh came easier that time as he turned right onto the main road through town. A half mile behind them, Charlie saw the flashing emergency lights from a handful of sheriff squad cars.

"Oop, our buddy Tank's bad day is getting even worse." She grinned, happy about her part in that.

"Good." His voice was so coldly furious that she spared a glance at his profile. "He deserves all that and more."

"Awe," she cooed, disguising the very real flutter of butter-flies with a slathering of teasing sarcasm. "Your vengeful side is adorable."

He shot her an exasperated look. "He was trying to kill you, Charlie."

"I know, and that *is* super irritating." To her surprise, Bones wasn't behind them yet. It was possible Kieran had lost their tail by just basically going around the block, but Charlie doubted that. No, it was more likely that Rhys had a devious plan. Figuring the white VW and green Jeep would pop up again later, Charlie left her rear-window vigil and turned to face front.

"Irritating? More like enraging." His cold look of death was back, and Charlie smiled at him as she reached over to give him a consoling pat right above his knee. He glared at her hand as if it had personally offended him, so she left it there just to be contrary. "Why aren't you enraged?"

She considered the question, enjoying the feel of the tense muscles beneath her palm. "I used to get enraged, but it happens too often now. I have to save my fury for special occasions, like when Fifi was kidnapped, or when Norah was strapped into that bomb vest."

He made a choked sound as his quadriceps clenched even tighter under her hand. She watched the play of emotions on his face, fascinated, until he relaxed into something that looked like resolve. "You'll give me a list."

"Okay." She waited for more information, but he just gave a satisfied lift of his chin at her answer, so she had to ask for clarification. "A list of what exactly?"

"People we need to kill once this is over."

"Oh yes." She beamed at him, feeling like her heart was going to burst. The man was perfect. Not only was he requesting a mortal enemies list, but he knew how to prioritize. All the new and confusing emotions she'd felt since watching Kieran patiently wait for a squirrel to cross the street made sense now, her thoughts clarifying into one crystal-clear, unquestionable truth. "I love you."

He startled, and the car jerked slightly to the side before he straightened the steering wheel. His mouth opened, but nothing came out before it closed again.

Charlie grinned even wider, rather proud she'd managed to discombobulate Kieran. "You don't have to say anything."

She meant that. She was content to have told him. Things only bothered her when she kept them inside. Now that the words were out, everything would fall into place—maybe not exactly how she wanted it to, but she was hopeful. When he shot her a dubious look, she laughed. "I mean it. I didn't say it to make you uncomfortable. Just go to your happy place of scowling silence."

He huffed a sound that was halfway between amusement and bewilderment, then he did as she suggested.

Humming tunelessly, Charlie pulled out her phone and checked her messages. Seeing that Molly had checked in, Charlie sent a text that the plan had gone off without a hitch. Her sister responded immediately with a whole line of emojis, which likely meant she was on a stakeout and bored. Charlie snickered. *Better Moo than me.*

"What's funny?" Kieran asked, still sounding stiffly panicked.

Charlie gave him a fond smile. "Just enjoying the fact that I'm not bored out of my mind on a stakeout." She realized that she was never bored when she was with Kieran. Just more proof she'd been telling the truth about loving him.

"How do you know?" The words burst from him, sounding much too serious for the topic at hand.

Eyeing him curiously, she shrugged. "stakeouts are almost always boring."

"No. How do you know…?" His side-eye was projecting so much desperation that she felt bad for him, but she wasn't able to help him out when she honestly had no idea what he was asking. "You know, about the love thing?"

Despite his utter seriousness, she had to bite the inside of her cheek to keep from laughing. The *love thing*? "I just…know?" She was well aware that she wasn't the most introspective person, so she shrugged as she struggled to describe the process, since there really hadn't *been* a process. He looked so desperate, however, that she tried her best to explain. "The feelings are just… there. Similar to how I feel about my sisters, but I also want to have sex with you."

He made another choking sound and then was silent long enough for her to check that he was still breathing. He was, although he looked a little bit shock-y.

Squeezing his leg where she still rested her hand, she asked, "You okay?"

"No."

This might work out to her advantage. "That's too bad. Need me to drive?"

His laugh sounded strangled, as if it had been torn from him against his will—even more than usual. "No. I'm fine to drive. You just need to explain this better."

With a huff of frustration, Charlie lifted her free hand in the air and then let it drop. She knew it would've been more dramatic if she'd used both hands, but she wasn't willing to give up her hold on Kieran's leg. She really liked touching him. That was probably a love thing too. "Why do I have to explain it at all?"

"Because it doesn't make any sense!" His voice rose, and she blinked at him in surprise. As much as he'd growled and grumbled, she'd never heard him sound quite this hysterical before.

"Of course it doesn't make sense," she said, keeping her voice soothing despite her exasperation. She wasn't a philosopher. Why was he asking *her* of all people to explain romantic love? "It's not supposed to make sense. It just...is. People love and are loved. It's not convenient—I mean, this is probably the worst time for me to have gotten all squishy and distracted, since Mom's first court appearance is tomorrow, and we don't have her *or* the necklace." Panic crept in as she started talking faster. "She's going to skip out on her bail, and then Barney will take the house in the most sneering, offensive way, and then all of us are going to be out on the street, and then Dad's house will be razed so Barney can build something gross, like a hotel where you can shoot mountain lions from your balcony or something like that, and—"

"Hey, enough with that nonsense." Kieran's voice was gruff, but his hand was gentle as it curled around hers. He probably just wanted to get her to stop digging her fingers into his leg, but she still appreciated the gesture. "We still have what? Eighteen hours?"

Charlie did the mental math. "More like fourteen."

"Plenty of time."

She stared at him but then laughed, feeling the anxiety drain out of her as she did so. Apparently, the way to figuratively slap Kieran out of his hysterics was to indulge in some of her own. *Good to know.*

"You still haven't convinced me."

She squinted at him, thrown off guard by the ninety-degree turn in conversation. "Convince you about what?"

"That you...love me." He gave the word *love* an upward inflection, as if questioning its very existence.

"I don't have to convince you," she huffed. "It's not a debate. I love you, which means the love rays radiate from me onto you, and you just stand there and absorb them. It's like the sun—if you're around me, there's no hiding from me or my love beams."

"Nope." His chin was set at a very obstinate angle, and Charlie was annoyed that she found it adorable, rather than obnoxious. No wonder her condition was called lovesickness. "Because I don't believe you."

Okay, maybe not so adorable. "Your lack of belief doesn't change an actual fact. I'm not freaking Tinker Bell." She was starting to get annoyed. This wasn't how she imagined her proclamation of love going—not that she'd ever really thought about how a proclamation of love would go, but still. "My love for you exists. It's a real thing. Nothing you can do about it." She finished off just a bit smugly, enjoying the way his jaw muscle worked.

"No way. It's impossible." His fingers squeezed the steering wheel, his knuckles going pale with strain.

This time, she couldn't help throwing both hands into the air. He was *that* infuriating. "Why is it impossible?"

"Because no one has ever loved me!" he roared.

Charlie blinked at him, letting his words settle into her brain before she spoke. She started to ask about his mom—surely his mom loved him, even if his dad was a sentient trash fire—but then she stopped. She of all people knew how disappointing parents could be. "So?"

He stared at her until she waved toward the windshield at the curvy mountain road he was currently supposed to be navigating.

"You might want to pull over before you drive us off the cliff and we both die a fiery death, which would be a tragic waste of a nice truck." She patted the dash.

Muttering something that sounded like a long and creative series of swears, he jerked the wheel to the right. Instead of just pulling over onto the narrow shoulder, he turned off the road completely.

"Is this an actual surface you're supposed to be driving on?" Charlie asked doubtfully as the truck lurched over rough ground.

"Yeah, there was a road sign."

"Hmm." Charlie didn't doubt him, but she did question Field County's Road and Bridges Department's judgment. The "road" they were on was barely a two-track trail, scattered with rocks and scruffy vegetation. They followed the twisting path through the trees until even the faint tracks ended, and Kieran put the truck into park and turned off the engine. "So...apparently a dead-end road then?"

"The road doesn't matter," he grumped, turning to face her. "We need to finish discussing this love thing."

"Arguing," Charlie corrected, "and there's nothing to discuss. The bargaining stage is over, and you need to just accept that I love you and move on. There. Argument over. Are you going to be able to turn around, or will you have to back all the way to the highway?" She eyed the evergreens clustered around them.

"You *don't*," he insisted, making Charlie sigh loudly as she refocused on him. "I'm not someone that people love."

"You *are*," she said with forced patience. Things were easier when people just accepted she was right immediately. "You, Kieran Sullivan Byrne, are a lovable person."

"No, I'm not." Despite the stubborn reply, there was an almost frantic intensity to the way he stared at her, as if he was desperate for her to convince him that he was wrong. Luckily for him, she was happy to do just that.

"What are you even talking about?" She didn't realize that she could roll her eyes so hard without them getting stuck looking at her brain. "You're ridiculously lovable. You're loyal and smart and brave, not to mention *this*." She swept a hand down, gesturing from the top of his head to his feet.

"What?" He glanced down at himself and then back at her, confused as if he didn't own a mirror.

Apparently, she was going to have to spell it out. "You, Firefighter Byrne, are very nice to look at. That's not a condition of love or anything, but it's definitely a bonus."

He scoffed. "Please, it's not like I look like Ian or anything."

She waved a hand. "Ian's objectively attractive, sure." His glower deepened, so she hurried to finish her thought. "You're *subjectively* attractive." He looked as if he wasn't sure how to take that. "I like how you look. I *really* like how you look."

"But I'm rude." His stare didn't change but continued begging her to convince him that he was wrong. In fact, his gaze grew even more intense. "I'm not nice. I'm angry."

She felt her mouth curl up in a satisfied smile. "I know. I love all those things about you. They're bonuses, not flaws. Everything about you works for me."

He stared at her, apparently out of counterarguments, which

was just fine with her. There were better things he could be doing with his mouth, especially here in the privacy of the trees on the dead-end road that really didn't deserve being called a road.

"Convinced I love you yet?" she asked. His answer wouldn't change how she felt, although she hoped it would erase that frantic panic she'd glimpsed in his eyes. No one should feel unlovable, especially someone like Kieran.

"No." Despite his answer, she saw the conflict in his expression and grinned. She was already wearing down his resistance. "If you do love me, you have terrible judgment."

"I have excellent judgment." To prove that, she unbuckled both of their seat belts and climbed onto his lap, facing him. His hands settled on her hips, feeling so natural there that she couldn't stop grinning. Despite all of his arguments, his body knew they belonged together.

Even as his fingers gently squeezed her hips, his eyebrows drew together. When he opened his mouth as if to argue further, Charlie kissed him. She was sick of talking. Ever since she'd first seen the surly firefighter at The Coffee Spot, she'd wanted him. After falling in love with him, that want had grown to a desperate need. Now that she had him underneath her, she wasn't about to let this opportunity slip away.

Just like his hands, his lips knew there were better things to do than to argue. Humming with pleasure, Charlie deepened the kiss as she reached for the lever on the side of the seat. With one yank, she dropped the seat back so it was almost horizontal. His surprised grunt was muffled against her mouth, but then he was kissing her again, and nothing else mattered.

Kieran released her hips, but before she could feel aggrieved at the loss of his touch, he buried his fingers in her hair. With both hands, he clutched her head tightly, holding her as close as he could physically manage. That lurking, frantic need she'd seen in his gaze during their entire discussion—argument—about his lovableness was evident in the way his fingers clutched at her and his lips pressed almost desperately against hers.

As much as he'd protested that she couldn't love him, she could feel how much he wanted to believe she could.

Her heart both broke and warmed at his silent confession, and she clutched him back, telling him over and over again how much she loved him with her lips and hands. As they frantically kissed—any technique thrown out the window, replaced by desperate need—she stroked his face and neck.

He groaned against her lips, and the vibrations shot through her entire body, leaving heat and oversensitized skin in their wake.

A tiny niggling thought wouldn't let her be, and she some-how managed to wrench herself away just enough to speak. As she did, the fading evening light reminded her of something important. "We can't do this out in public."

"We're not, unless you're counting squirrels as the public." He pulled her back into the kiss, but enough of her brain was not-mushified to remember that wasn't why she'd pulled away.

"Wait—we need to get to Denver. We only have fourteen hours."

He scowled. "Right." His gaze flicked down to her mouth,

and he leaned in, as if drawn to her against his will. "Just five more minutes."

Just the warmth of his breath on her lips was enough for her to forget any objections. "Okay."

Then his mouth was on hers again, and everything—her mom, the necklace, the treasure hunters, Barney Thompson— disappeared. The only two people that existed in the universe were Charlie and Kieran, and they were doing their best to merge into one being.

Charlie yanked at his shirt, almost desperate to feel his skin but not willing to stop kissing for a moment to concentrate on removing it. With a grunt, Kieran helped her pull it up until his belly and most of his chest was exposed, and then did the same to her. She didn't even notice him unhooking her bra, but the cool air brushing the bare skin of her breasts told her he'd managed it.

With a nip to her bottom lip, he ended the kiss. Before she could do more than pull in a breath to groan out a complaint, he'd latched onto her nipple. A string from where his mouth touched buzzed all the way to her low belly, electrifying her skin. She tightened her fingers in his short hair, unable to grip the handfuls she needed to hold him in place and never, ever let him get away.

Then he scored her lightly with his teeth, and it felt like the top of her head blew off. She heard someone babbling, promising all sorts of things if he just continued what he was doing, and she wasn't even embarrassed when she realized the words were coming from her.

She worked open the button and zip on his pants, needing more—more skin, more contact, just *more* of Kieran however she could get it. Without removing his mouth from her breast, he lifted his hips to help her as she yanked his pants and boxer briefs down over his hips. With her prize in sight, she left his clothes crumpled around his thighs and wrapped her hand around his erection.

His head jerked back as he hissed, and she instantly missed the feel of his mouth. Tightening her fingers just enough to make him clench his jaw, she leaned forward to kiss him.

Kissing wasn't the right words for it, though, not for what they were doing. It was too intense for such a fluffy word. They were trying to consume each other, to merge together and become one person with too many limbs so that they'd never be without each other again.

Kieran yanked her pants and panties down to the tops of her thighs so they were a disheveled matched pair, but it allowed enough access for him to slide two fingers between her legs. They slid easily through her wetness, a light tease of a stroke that made her nip at his lip in retaliation.

His rough chuckle was muffled, but she still felt the glow of it. Charlie was pretty sure she'd never get tired of making Kieran happy. His fingers disappeared, and she groaned her disappointment. When they were replaced by something bigger, something hot and hard at her entrance, that sound turned into a moan of encouragement instead.

Apparently, his Charlie-moan translator software wasn't fully updated, since he paused. "This okay?" He held her gaze intently. "I don't have condoms on me, but I haven't had sex for years, and we're required to be tested for STIs regularly for work. If you're not on birth control, though, or want to wait until after you see my last test results or just don't want to do this now or—"

She kissed him—short and hard and sweet—to stop the flow of words. It was disconcerting—and incredibly endearing—to hear Kieran actually *babble*, but she was too desperate for him to *awe* over it now. In fact, she could barely get coherent words to form, but she knew from his intent look that he wasn't progressing anything until she answered him in actual words.

"Yes," she managed to get out. "I have an implant. I want this. With you. Now. Please." She broke off as he pushed inside her, her ability to speak lost to pleasure once again.

He held her on top of him, controlling her descent. The restriction of her pants around her thighs kept her legs together, slowing the process to an erotic crawl that made her want to scream with impatience and, at the same time, with pleasure. She felt every tiny slide and twitch of his erection as Kieran slowly entered her, and she was so sensitive that it felt like every inch of her skin was buzzing. Charlie gripped his biceps, clinging on tightly, using him as her anchor to keep her grounded as she felt things she'd never experienced before.

She kept kissing him because she had to—there was no other option. She'd been in awe of his desperation for her, but now it felt as if she was just as frantic as he was. The power of the moment was shared equally between them, and leaving herself open was the scariest thing she'd ever done.

Once he was all the way inside her, he paused, his fingers digging into her hips. Reluctantly, she lifted her lips from his so she could meet his eyes, needing to know that he was just as invested in this moment as she was. When their gazes connected, she sucked in a breath.

His surly mask was gone, stripped away, leaving him so raw and vulnerable and open that it almost hurt to meet his eyes—but there was no way Charlie was looking away. She knew he could see everything—her desperate need for him and how terrifying she found that—just as she could see his. They were locked together in both their bodies and their gazes, and it was so much bigger and more overwhelming than she'd ever expected.

She clung to his arms as her body clenched around him, and his eyes snapped shut, breaking their gaze as his head tilted back. His groan of pleasure vibrated through her and her own eyes slid shut reluctantly, even though she wanted to continue watching him. She couldn't imagine ever getting tired of looking at him, but he started to move, and pleasure stole away every other thought.

Digging his fingers into her hips, he shifted her up and down, the burn from the almost-unbearable stretch just adding to her pleasure. He controlled the movement, and she was shocked that she was okay with that—more than okay. She loved just letting him move her, so that all she had to concentrate on was feeling.

And that was enough.

Too soon—but not nearly soon enough—he sped up their

movements, lifting her and then yanking her back down, his hips rising so he could drive that extra inch into her. All the pleasure building inside her grew until she knew she needed to either come or explode.

She decided on coming.

As she tipped over into ecstasy, she felt her body clamp down on Kieran, and his movements grew frenzied. His grip on her hips would've hurt if she were feeling anything except pleasure at the moment, and he slammed into her one last time before holding them together, his back arched off the seat. "Charlie!" His voice was guttural, almost panicked, and she clutched him tighter, despite her sated languor.

"I'm here," she murmured, which she realized was rather a ridiculous thing to say, since *obviously* she was here, since he was literally inside her at this very moment. It seemed to be the right thing, however, since he opened his eyes and smiled at her, his heavy-lidded gaze full of contentment and affection and other things she was a little too raw to think about too hard, so she didn't. He wrapped his arms around her, holding her tight.

She let herself sink to his chest and just float, knowing he'd keep her safe.

———

Too soon, the rest of the world came rushing back. Without lifting her head, she groaned into his chest. His arms squeezed around her, which felt nice until they got a little too tight, and she couldn't breathe. At her squeak of protest, he released her with a grumble that vibrated against her cheek, making her smile.

Everything—her mom, the necklace, their ever-shrinking deadline—came rushing back, and she groaned as she sat up—or tried to, at least. Her pants around her thighs hobbled her, and she dropped back onto his chest with a laugh. "A little help?"

He scowled, but she was pretty confident his current crankiness was due to the fact that fulfilling her request would mean they wouldn't be plastered together anymore. It was kind of sweet, really, that he was grumpy about the interruption of their snuggling. Despite his frown, he reluctantly returned both of them to a fully cleaned up and clothed condition before raising the seat with her still straddling him.

Charlie discovered she was just as reluctant to leave his lap as he was to let her go, but the beep of her phone made her huff out a breath and shift off him. Before she could fully dismount, however, he caught her hips. She froze, the feeling of his fingers pressing into the tender spots he'd formed making her want him all over again.

"Kiss me first." His bossy voice made her shiver in a very nice, not-at-all cold way.

A smile curled her mouth as she obeyed.

FIFTEEN

"Oops." She eyed the text message—well, messages. When Charlie hadn't answered immediately, Fifi had sent more texts... a *lot* more.

"Emergency?" he asked, shooting her a frown.

Reaching over, she poked his leg. "Focus on your driving, mister."

"Got it." Despite his distraction, he did seem impressively proficient at backing up as he reversed toward the highway. "What's the text?"

"Definitely not a crisis." Charlie's thumbs flew over the screen as she responded, although she didn't say anything about what had kept her ignoring her phone earlier. Charlie wanted to keep that close to her chest for a while, to cuddle the memory and enjoy the newness of their secret. "Fifi's just annoyed I didn't respond. I told her you insisted on an off-road adventure." She smirked at how very accurate that was as she pocketed her phone.

"Don't blame me—it was *your* fault."

"How was that *my* fault?" It was hard to put her fists on her hips while sitting in a pickup cab, but she managed the best she could.

"You're the one who makes the world disappear. I can't be expected to care about anything else when you're kissing me—much less when I'm inside you." He shrugged as if he hadn't just said something so aggravating yet so romantic that it took her breath away.

"As if you don't do the exact same thing to me," she grumbled, trying to hide the fact that her cheeks were hot and her heart was racing. When he didn't respond, she snuck a glance at his profile. She instantly regretted it when she saw the enormous, pleased smile on his face.

Happy Kieran was dangerous, but Charlie had always had a thing for danger.

———

An hour into their journey, her phone rang. "Hey, Lou. What's up?"

"So," Lou rushed out, as if the words had to escape or she'd explode. Although she sounded like that more often than not, her voice had even more urgency than usual, so Charlie sat up straight. "There's a new deputy, Carl Crill, and he interviewed Rory about the whole shooting thing that happened at her shop—which you completely neglected to tell me about, by the way—and she asked a few questions, and apparently Deputy Carl Crill is more of a firefighter than a cop because he spilled e-ver-y-thing. All the tea."

At her pause, Charlie made a get-on-with-it motion that Lou couldn't see. "So spill what he spilled," she urged, putting her phone on speaker when Kieran gave her a curious look.

"Apparently, Tank was trying to confess to Cobra's killing, but the sheriff isn't a dummy, so she realized he's way too dumb to be the mastermind behind everything, plus his story had holes you could drive a car through. I mean, he couldn't even carry out a simple assassination plot without getting shot in the butt with tranquilizer darts."

"That's true," Charlie said, unsuccessfully trying to picture the beefy guy as an evil genius.

Lou continued without seeming to need to pause to breathe. "He mentioned Gabrielle once and then turned pale and tried to cover his slip, so Summers brought her in for questioning. After hearing that Tank was claiming credit, Gabrielle *flipped out*. She not only confessed to killing Cobra and organizing the coffee shop fire, but also to trying to shoot you outside of Rory's store."

"I'd totally forgotten about that," Charlie admitted, shrugging at Kieran's incredulous look. "What? It's been a busy few days."

"There were a bunch of other illegal things she's been doing—well, the militia's been doing under her leadership— all without anyone knowing that *she's* in charge, not Clint. So she's been arrested for all sorts of things, as well as most of the remaining militia members, so we'll probably drop our petition, since the Freedom Survivors are basically no more—unless they continue doing their little meetings from prison, in which case it doesn't matter what they call themselves, since it doesn't reflect on Simpson, and—most importantly—we don't have to say or think about the name ever again—well, ever again after all the gossip dies down. Wild, huh?"

Charlie blinked, absorbing all the information Lou had just dumped on her. "Definitely wild. Thanks for all this, Lou. Tell Rory thank you too. I'm impressed she managed to get all that out of the deputy. I wouldn't have guessed her to be such a good interrogator."

Lou laughed. "It sounds like Deputy Carl was dying to share, so Rory just stared at him as all the information about the case came pouring out of his mouth. I don't think he's going to last long at the sheriff's department."

With a snort, Charlie said, "Definitely not. I almost feel bad for him when Sheriff Summers finds out what he did."

"We've got to get the scoop from these baby deputies while we can, before they figure out how to keep their mouths shut. Good luck with your lock searching. Call me the instant you find the one the key fits into, or when you find the necklace, or when you find your mom. Just call me whenever you have exciting news, got it?"

Charlie made a sound that wasn't really agreement but was close enough to pass for it, since Lou signed off and ended the call. She met Kieran's gaze briefly before he turned back to his driving. "Congratulations," she said. "You're no longer a person of interest."

"Does this mean I can leave town?"

Her heart gave an excited stutter, but she affected calm. "I hope so, since we already did a couple hours ago."

"No." He gave her another of his brief but meaningful looks. "Leave. For good."

"Where are you thinking of going?" Her nonchalant tone was failing, and the words came out more high-pitched than she was going for.

He obviously heard the excitement she was trying to hide, since the corner of his mouth tucked in like he was concealing a smile. "I don't know. I heard Langston is nice this time of year."

At that, she couldn't hold back her excited squeal, and only the thought of sending the truck flying off the road and over the cliff kept her from hurling herself at him so she could hug the snot out of him. "Really? I get to keep you?"

His growl-laugh made her heart sing. "Yeah. You get to keep me."

———

By the time they reached Denver, it'd been dark for a while.

"This'll be good," Charlie said, trying very hard to ignore how the minutes remaining until Jane's first court appearance tomorrow were slipping away at a terrifying rate. "We can wander around without too many people noticing us."

Kieran made a skeptical sound as he turned onto the street where the Cherry Creek mailing store was on, and she couldn't even be mad about it. The place was packed with cars and pedestrians enjoying the cool fall evening.

"Or not." She frowned thoughtfully as she studied the crowds, trying to come up with a plan. "Should we wait a few hours before going in? It's going to look suspicious if we try the key in every lock."

"Mmm," he grunted his agreement.

"Ugh. I hate wasting time, especially when we have so little of it left." When she realized that they were just grunting back and forth, she had to laugh, despite their current dilemma. She'd already called the hotel where the necklace had been stolen from. Although they did have safes in the rooms, guests had to clear them before checking out. There was no way Jane could be holding on to a room—she couldn't afford to pay for that many nights. The hotel clerk had suggested the mailbox place as the closest rentable storage. "Let's go to the intersection where Jane was picked up by police and check it out."

With a grunt of assent—which made her laugh again—he turned left and carefully eased down the crowded street. He parked in the small lot of a closed chiropractor's office just a few blocks from where Jane's dash from the law had ended. As they walked along the sidewalk, Kieran rested a hand at the small of her back, and she marveled at how that simple touch made her feel taller and braver and just about indestructible.

The streetlights were frequent and bright, plus they were supplemented by security lights mounted on people's homes. Charlie looked around, trying to put herself in her panicked mom's shoes. She had to have been freaking out carrying that necklace around with no safe place to hide it. If the cops had found it on her, there wouldn't have been any chance of her escaping justice. For a secret second, Charlie wondered if that might've been a good thing—no possibility of innocence meant no bail, and that would've meant she and her sisters could've avoided potentially losing their childhood home *and* not had to chase Jane all over the country. Sure, Jane would've definitely gotten prison time, but Charlie couldn't really see any downside to it. She gave an amused—but also sad and frustrated—snort, and Kieran's hand pressed a touch more heavily against her spine.

"What?" he asked.

"Just thinking about Mom and the necklace and what-ifs, and also how rich people never have to live in the dark."

He hummed in a way that made her stomach warm, because it meant he was truly listening to her and wasn't just impatiently waiting for her to stop talking like a lot of people tended to do. Between the flutter in her belly and the warm press of his hand against her lower back, she was hit by a rush of love so strong that she almost staggered. Catching herself, she turned her faltering step into a turn, pretending that she was getting a three-hundred-and-sixty-degree view of the area.

She eyed the houses and the few businesses, forcing her brain off Kieran and back on to what a panicking Jane might've been thinking that night she stole the necklace. "This should be easy," she complained. "Most of the buildings around here are private homes."

"Does she know anyone who lives around here?" Kieran asked, following the path of her gaze with his own.

"Doubt it." She swallowed a snicker at the thought. "She's more of a Dutch's clientele kind of person. Let's go check out that laundromat. Maybe they have some lockers available to rent."

His grunt of agreement sent Charlie into a spate of giggles, and Kieran gave her a questioning look.

"Not important." She waved off her grunt-caused laughter as she concentrated on crossing the busy avenue. "Plus I already know it wouldn't be funny if I tried to explain it."

With an unhappy rumble that almost set her off again, he strode across the road as if he were taking a stroll through the park. Traffic seemed to slow and stop for him, as if it knew how very cranky the man would be if he were to be hit. Charlie hurried after him, wanting to take advantage of his strange superpower.

He held the laundromat door open, and she thanked him as she stepped inside. Apparently, she had Manners Kieran with her this evening. A thorough look around the small space showed washers and dryers, but not much else. There definitely weren't any lockers—or anything that could hold a necklace and be unlocked with a key.

They quickly eliminated the two restaurants as potential hiding places for Jane's stolen goods, which left the gym.

"Except for the mailboxes place, this is probably the most likely," she said under her breath as they entered. Kieran grunted in agreement.

Two people stood behind the reception desk, a man and a woman, and Charlie made a beeline for the man. "Hello," she said cheerfully. "We're new to the area and would like a tour please."

The guy glanced at his coworker and opened his mouth. Before he could suggest that the woman give them the tour, Charlie shut him down.

"Chad!" she read the script embroidered on his polo shirt. "Wonderful! I was hoping you'd be here. Mark Jones said to have you show us around since you know the gym better than anyone." She shot a quick glance at the woman, who was looking bemused. "No offense. I'm sure you're great too. It's just that Mark's a good friend, and he wouldn't shut up about how great Chad here is."

"Uh…" Chad blinked. "Mark Jones?"

Charlie turned up the wattage on her smile. "That's the guy! He wasn't sure you'd remember his name, since you help out so many people here, but he was really impressed with the tip you gave him. Really improved his overhead lifts. So…tour?"

Chad seemed to gather himself. "My shift ends in ten minutes—"

"Just a quickie," Charlie interrupted. "We're pretty sure we're going to sign up, but we'd love if you showed us around—just the highlights. Norman and I are fast walkers." She shot a look at Kieran to see how he liked his new name, but his scowl was locked into place as usual. He did give her the tiniest side-eye glance, which she happily took as irritation. "I'm Claire."

Chad still hesitated, so Charlie broke out her best pleading puppy-dog eyes and made sure her dimples were showing.

"Sure," he gave in with a forced return smile. "Come with me."

As Chad rattled off information about the gym, he speed-walked to the weight room, then zoomed through the treadmills and elliptical machines to reach the spin and yoga classrooms on the other side.

"Any questions?" he asked in a tone that seriously discouraged asking anything, his gaze fixed on the exit door.

"Can we peek at the locker rooms real quick?" Charlie asked, breaking out the dimples and puppy-dog eyes again.

With an impatient sigh, Chad led them to the locker room doors. "I can't show you around in there," he said to Charlie, gesturing at the door marked "Women."

"That's fine." She shoved open the door. "I'll just check it out myself."

Inside, she hurried toward the bank of lockers, pulling the key out of an inside pocket as she did so. A woman sat on the bench in front of them, pulling on socks, and Charlie gave her an innocent smile—at least, she hoped it looked innocent.

"I forgot which locker I used," she said with a self-effacing laugh.

The woman gave a polite smile in response, but her eyebrows drew together. "Isn't the number attached to the key?"

"It must've fallen off." Charlie started on the top left as she spoke, since she knew her time was limited. She guessed she had a minute—tops—before Chad started fussing. The key slid into the first lock smoothly, and her stomach jumped with excitement—but it refused to turn. A key was in the next locker, so she skipped that one and tried the third. Same thing—the key slid in but refused to turn.

By the time she'd tried all of the top row of lockers, her heart rate had sped up and she felt sweat prickling along her hairline.

"You about done in there?" Chad yelled from outside the door.

"Almost!" she called back, her voice higher pitched than usual. The key grew slick in her grip, and she almost dropped it between the second and third lockers in the middle row. The woman on the bench gave her an odd look. Charlie forced another smile, but she was pretty sure it was closer to a grimace. "My boyfriend's impatient."

"Wasn't that Chad?" the woman asked, looking more suspicious rather than less. "I thought he was gay?"

"My boyfriend's with Chad." The key sank into yet another lock but refused to turn. "I mean, not *with him* with him. Just standing with him in the hallway." Three more lockers to go on the middle row. "Waiting for me." Two lockers. "Impatiently."

Chad thumped on the door, as if proving her words to be true, just as the key turned in last locker in the middle row, and the metal door popped open. Charlie went still for an instant before grabbing the plastic grocery bag inside. She shoved the bag and its contents into one of her cargo pants pockets, gave the inside of the locker a quick glance to make sure nothing remained, and then hurried toward the door.

"Sorry," she said breathlessly as she burst from the locker room. "I started talking to one of the members about the gym. Really nice woman. She loves this place. It was hard to get her to stop praising you guys. I think we've seen everything we need to in order to make our decision. Right, honey?" she widened her eyes at Kieran, trying to let him know she'd found something without being too obvious about it.

She must've succeeded, since he actually spoke instead of

grunted. "Yeah. Thanks for the tour." Grabbing her hand, he pulled her toward the front exit.

"Thank you, Chad," Charlie called over her shoulder, walking as fast as she could while still looking casual. "We'll be back in soon to sign up. I'll let Mark know that you were a great tour guide."

Chad looked baffled and still irritated, but he just shrugged and headed in the opposite direction.

"Found it?" Kieran asked under his breath, shoving open one of the front doors and waiting for her to walk through.

"Found *something*," she muttered, continuously scanning the area as they crossed the road and hurried back to the chiropractor's office where the truck was parked. She was feeling utterly conspicuous, as if the contents of the grocery bag were lighting up with flashing red lights. "Didn't have a chance to check what's inside, but the size and weight are right for the you-know-what."

"One down, one to go." When she shot him a confused look, he clarified, "Let's go find your mom." Instead of looking grim, he seemed almost eager for the chase.

She grinned at him. "It's like you're a boyfriend-bot, made in a factory to my very particular specifications."

"Thanks?"

"You're welcome." The words were distracted when she caught a glimpse of Dave trying to hide in the shadows behind a too-small hedge. The area was much too well-lit to hide Dave or his lack of skills. Swallowing a satisfied smile, she hurried toward the passenger door of Kieran's truck. "Let's go back to Simpson."

Kieran frowned but waited until they were both inside the cab before asking, "Why are we going back to Simpson? Shouldn't we turn the necklace in to the police first?"

"Nope. This'll only work if we have the necklace *and* Jane."

"There are five treasure hunters watching us right now." He started the engine. "Won't we be sitting ducks once we're in the middle of nowhere?"

"There are six, actually, and they're just where we want them to be."

The slant of his eyebrows conveyed his skepticism, but he didn't argue. Instead, he turned west out of the parking lot. "Simpson it is then."

"Thank you, perfect boyfriend-bot." She ignored the scowl he sent her way, her brain too busy with the details of her plan. She pulled the bag from her pocket and peeked inside before holding it open so Kieran could see. "All this hassle over some sparkly rocks."

His grunt sounded like agreement. "Not a fan of diamonds?"

"Nope. Waste of money." She tucked the bag holding the necklace back in her pocket. "There's too much fun stuff to buy instead."

"Like what?"

"Oh, better spy tech for Fifi, fun nerdy computer stuff for Norah, tuition for Cara, a new car for Moo—or at least a new paint job so people quit bugging her to sell them weed wherever she goes—"

"What?"

"You'll understand when you see it. Oh, there's a Target. Let's stop for travel snacks."

This time, his look was knowing. "Why do I have the feeling we're stopping for more than food?"

Leaning over, she kissed him on the cheek, her heart nearly bursting at his utter perfection. "Because you're a smart man."

With a smile he apparently wasn't able to completely fight off, Kieran turned into the Target lot.

SIXTEEN

"Quit fussing," Charlie scolded. "It looks good on you."

"I'm not really a hoodie guy," he complained for the hundredth time since she'd grabbed it off the rack at Target and held it up to his chest. "I run hot." He tugged at the neckline, also for the hundredth time, as if that would magically create more room for his admittedly thick neck.

"Yeah, you do. Are you more of a bare-chest-beneath-bunker-gear type of guy then?" she asked with put-on innocence.

He shot her a glare but quit yanking at the sweatshirt.

"We're almost to the hotel," she said, feeling bad for him. She of all people knew what it was like to be stuffed into something that didn't fit. "You can take it off then. In fact, you're welcome to take *everything* off."

"If you're trying to distract me, then it's working." His voice dropped to a deep grumble that did fun and interesting things to her insides.

"Once all this is over, want to go on vacation somewhere?"

"Yes."

He didn't even hesitate, his definite answer smooshing all the doubts that she hadn't even realized had snuck into her mind. "Excellent. Where should we go?"

"Anywhere with a bed and a lock on the door." His stare was so hot she was surprised it didn't burn her skin. "The bed's optional."

She shivered in anticipation. "Let's just stay at the hotel then. That way, we won't waste time traveling."

"Yeah." He sent her another one of those smoldering glances that sent her stomach butterflies into a tizzy. "Let's do that."

Kieran parked on the street a block from the hotel, and Charlie's pulse, which had already been pounding thanks to Kieran's impossible hotness, ramped up to a faster rhythm. She felt the familiar rush of adrenaline racing through her, and she sent him a wild grin.

"Ready?" he asked, his hand on the door handle.

"Always."

Opening her door, she jumped out of the truck. Once she and Kieran had closed their respective doors, a deep silence fell. The night was too quiet, as if it were holding its breath. Kieran joined her on the sidewalk, and they walked toward the hotel door, close enough that their arms were brushing.

Charlie loved having him next to her. She'd always prided herself on her independence, on the fact that she didn't need anyone to help her bring in skips or get her out of tight spots. The time she'd spent with Kieran showed her that, although she didn't *need* anyone with her, she wanted him there. In fact, his presence made her adventures even better.

Catching his hand, she gave it a squeeze. "I like you."

He gave one of his usual snarly choke-laughs. "I thought you loved me. Have I been downgraded?"

"Nah." She gave a laugh not because anything was funny, but because she was happy. "It's easy to love someone. It's harder to actually like them."

"That makes no sen—" He broke off with a grunt as a dark shape hit his solar plexus, taking him down in a rough tackle.

Charlie took a step toward him, rage surging through her at the sight of three people piling on top of Kieran's fallen form. Before she could start kicking some asses, someone hit her from behind, and she went down. Hands patted her down, ignoring her struggles, as at least two others held her face down on the sidewalk.

"Turn her," someone commanded, making Charlie grit her teeth. That voice was familiar—she'd known it her entire life—and even though she knew well that Jane chose money over her own daughters, it felt like a kick in the stomach to have it confirmed yet again.

The hands holding her down flipped her over onto her back, and Charlie kicked out at Jane, who barely managed to dodge in time. Tassie and Bones were the ones holding her down, and Charlie felt a strange sense of betrayal, as if the fortune hunters had broken the rules by teaming up with Jane.

"Lachlan, Dave," Jane yelled. "Get over here and help hold her down."

"We're a little busy…with this guy," Lachlan answered, his voice breathless with exertion. Charlie felt a grim satisfaction that Kieran wasn't making it easy on them, and that thought made her redouble her struggles.

"Hold still, Charlotte," her mom ordered, sounding annoyed as she dug into Charlie's cargo pockets.

Charlie's laugh came out as a gasp as she tried to knee her mom in the face, making Jane jerk back out of range. "Why should I make robbing me easier?"

Jane tsked. "Robbing you? I'm just taking back *my* property. You had no right to take it in the first place. Ah!" She made a sound of triumph as she yanked the grocery bag out of Charlie's pocket. She took a quick look inside before climbing to her feet. "Got it. Knock them out."

Bones grabbed double fistfuls of Charlie's shirt, lifting her upper body off the sidewalk.

"Can't believe I was rooting for you and Rhys," Charlie sighed in her best *not surprised, just disappointed* tone.

Bones hesitated, turning her face away slightly as she said sheepishly, "It's just that we'd really like to buy a house, and Denver real estate prices right now are outrageous."

"Do it," Jane snapped, and Bones shoved Charlie down, cracking her head against the sidewalk.

Her head spinning from the blow, Charlie resisted the urge to struggle—and her even greater urge to tell Bones her rationale for joining the evil team was *ridiculous*—and forced her muscles to go limp. Bones gave her upper body a shake. When Charlie remained boneless, she dropped her and stood.

"She's out," Bones announced as Charlie tried very hard not to move.

"The big guy is too."

Charlie's fingers twitched as worry swamped her. Was Kieran really unconscious—or, even worse, dead? Everything inside her wanted to quit pretending to be knocked out and go to him, to take his pulse and check his injuries. It was wrong for the giant to have fallen—Kieran seemed invincible, as if his constant scowl armored him, protecting him from anything that might hurt a mere mortal.

The thought made her want to laugh, relaxing her slightly. The guy wasn't a superhero. She'd become the very smitten kitten she would've mocked before meeting Kieran.

Car doors slammed, but her field of vision was limited to what she could see through barely cracked open eyes and a limply lolling head. All she could see were a few pairs of booted feet walking away. She listened instead, waiting until more car doors closed and engine rumbles had faded away into nothingness.

After what felt like an hour of silence—but was probably closer to four minutes—she opened her eyes a little more and took a surreptitious look around. When all she saw was Kieran's crumpled form, she couldn't stay down a second longer.

Rolling to her feet, she hurried over to his side. "You better be acting," she threatened, hating the slight shake in her voice. "Otherwise, I'm going to kick your ass. Well, I'll probably call for an ambulance, wait for you to be discharged from the hospital, check to make sure that you're feeling up to an ass-kicking, and *then* kick your ass, but you'll be sorry for scaring me eventually."

His huge form began to shake, which sent a dart of panic through her. *Is he having a seizure?*

His eyes opened and he sat up, grinning.

No on the seizure, she realized as relief swamped her. *He's just laughing.*

"How's your head?" she asked, not even able to be annoyed with him for laughing at her rambling threat. She was just too happy he was conscious and, by all appearances, uninjured.

That brought a return of his scowl as he massaged the back of his skull. "Sore, but it takes a harder hit than that to knock me out. How's yours?" His hand dropped to his side as he stood, his gaze raking over her with an intensity that made her stomach turn to mush for all sorts of lovely reasons.

"Samesies." She cautiously did a full-body stretch, checking in with all her body parts now that she'd been reassured that Kieran was fine. "A few bruises and scrapes, but they're kind of a big bunch of wimps."

The whine of a small car engine grew louder, and they both whirled to face the sound. Fifi pulled her car up to the curb next to them, Bennett in the front passenger seat, and rolled down her window.

"Get in, losers," Fifi said, her face lit up with the excitement of a chase. "We're going Mom hunting."

Charlie gave a *whoop* and ran around to the other side of the car so she could climb into the seat behind Bennett. Kieran got into the back seat beside her. "GPS's working then?"

"Like a dream," Fifi said as Bennett held up his phone as if to provide evidence. On the map on his screen, an orange dot moved steadily down a road heading out of Rosehill, one that eventually led to the highway that could take their quarry either east toward Denver or west toward Grand Junction. First, though, it would take Jane right through downtown Simpson.

Charlie didn't even have her door closed all the way before Fifi hit the accelerator and the car shot forward. Turning her head, Charlie met Kieran's gaze and grinned at him, adrenaline spiking. This was it. They had one last chance to capture Jane and save their home.

When Kieran smiled back at her, she suddenly felt invincible, as if *she* were the superhero. Of course they were going to bring in Jane.

How could they fail?

Kieran grabbed her hand. "I love you. Marry me."

She gave a snorted laugh that would've been embarrassing if joy hadn't filled her so completely, leaving no room for any other emotion. "Is that a command, Kiki?"

"Yes." The corner of his mouth twitched up. "One you have to obey."

"Mm-hmm." It was extremely hard to hold on to her skeptical expression when everything inside her wanted to squeal and scream all the yeses and throw her arms around him and never let him go. "What is this word? Obey?"

A laugh escaped before he locked down his scowl again. "Fine. Marry me?"

Smothering her inner squealer, she raised her eyebrows.

He gave an exaggerated sigh. "Please."

"Do you two have to do this here?" Bennett asked stiffly. "I'm feeling very uncomfortable right now."

"Ignore him," Fifi said, her eyes finding the rearview

mirror every few seconds, probably more than was safe as she flew around the curvy mountain road. "I feel like we're in our very own soap opera. Well, c'mon! Answer the man, Charlotte Calamity Pax!"

She couldn't hold back anymore. "Yes!" She did actually squeal with happiness, as well as throw her arms around his neck and hug him hard. He laughed again, although this time it wasn't stifled, but an open sound of happiness and love that seemed to wrap itself around her and cuddle her close. She'd never thought she'd ever crave safety, but then again, she never realized it could feel so good.

Pulling back, Kieran framed her face with his hands and just looked at her for a long moment. "It's a little terrifying how much I love you."

"Really?" She clutched his wrists as if to hold him in place. "I love you so much, but I'm not scared at all."

Kieran grinned at her. "Of course you're not." He gave her a short, hard kiss. "Because you're fearless." He kissed her again, longer this time.

Charlie couldn't stop smiling, even as she kissed him back.

Bennett groaned. "Please make it stop."

Fifi laughed and whooped.

Charlie pulled back just enough to speak. "It's weird having a cheering section while we kiss."

"You're the one who wanted to share our honeymoon suite," Fifi reminded her, not sounding at all abashed.

Charlie couldn't even think of a teasing comeback. She was too occupied by staring into her husband-to-be's eyes.

"Sorry to interrupt." Bennett did not sound sorry at all. "But could you check with Lou to make sure everything is in place on their end? Charlie? Charlie!"

"Okay, okay." She reluctantly pulled away, although she couldn't stop staring at Kieran and his ridiculously happy expression as she pulled out her phone. When she finally managed to peel her gaze away, she saw a text pop up on her screen.

Minor problem, Lou had written, bringing Charlie back down to earth with a metaphorical thump. Okay, fine. Slightly major problem.

"Lou says there's a problem. She's rating it as 'slightly major,'" Charlie told the others, sending Lou a few question marks as a request for more information. Several new texts popped up on her screen. "Daisy's deputy husband was called away. Apparently, there was a bomb threat at the elementary school."

"Uh." Fifi's fingers tightened on the wheel as she sent Charlie a concerned glance. "How does this plan work without our deputy roadblock?"

"It doesn't." Charlie's brain was already grinding away at possible new plans as she texted. "Lou wants to know how many minutes until Jane's in Simpson."

"Sixteen," Bennett said, his voice even tenser than normal. "Twenty-two max, *if* she goes the speed limit, which isn't likely."

"Even if she's not stopped in Simpson, she still has the GPS tracker," Kieran said, giving Charlie's jiggling knee a squeeze. Despite the situation, Charlie felt herself calm slightly at his touch. The man was magic, but she'd already figured that out. "We'll just keep following her and grab her when she eventually stops."

"No time." Charlie watched the ellipsis on her screen with renewed tension as she waited for Lou's return text. "Jane has to be at court in Denver by nine. She could drive for hours if she has a full gas tank, and the woman has a bladder of steel."

"She really does," Fifi confirmed.

New plan underway, Lou texted, and Charlie let out a breath of relief. May take time to put into place, so any extra minutes would be appreciated.

"Not sure how Lou expects us to slow Jane down, but I'll tell her we'll try," Charlie grumbled as her thumbs flew over the screen. "She said they're working on setting something else up."

"Can you catch up to her?" Kieran asked. "Get in front of her to slow her down?"

"If she knows we're behind her," Fifi said, "she'll go rogue—and she might find the GPS device. We've been chasing Mom unsuccessfully for weeks. If she loses us this time—now that she has the necklace—she'll be gone forever."

They fell into tense silence as Fifi maneuvered around the hairpin turns leading up to the pass.

"Twelves minutes out," Bennett reported, his gaze locked on his phone screen.

Charlie texted Lou the updated arrival time.

Need more time!!! Lou responded.

"Lou's used three exclamation points," Charlie warned. "They're not going to be ready in twelve minutes."

"Eleven now."

"B, love you like a brother, but that's not helping." Charlie leaned forward so she could look over his shoulder at the dot moving too fast across his phone screen. At least, it *had* been moving too fast. "Hang on… Did the dot just slow down?"

"Yeah."

Kieran nudged Charlie's side and showed her the traffic map on his phone. "A large vehicle is causing traffic to slow over this stretch." He pointed to a section of road that was highlighted red.

"Thank the gods for feather-footed, RV-driving tourists!" Charlie crowed, peering closer at Kieran's phone as Fifi gave an answering whoop. "What is that—about four miles? Five?"

"Just under five."

"Do the math, B," she urged, bouncing a little in her seat. "What's Mom's new ETA?"

"If the traffic stays at this pace, then twenty-seven minutes."

"Yes!" Charlie quickly texted Lou the update and got an immediate response. "She said they can work with that. Probably."

Brake lights lit the night as the vehicles in front of them slowed to a crawl, and Fifi brought their car in line with the others in the long, creeping caterpillar inching over the pass and down the other side toward Simpson.

"Oh," Charlie said.

"What is it?" Kieran looked around, obviously picking up on the startled disappointment in her tone.

"I just realized that it'll take us twenty-seven minutes to reach Simpson too."

He gave one of his snort-choke-laughs before gripping the back of her neck in an affectionate squeeze. "You'll survive."

Her own snort was skeptical. "We'll see about that."

———

Somehow, she did manage to survive the endless half hour before traffic loosened up just a few miles before the Simpson town limits. As they sped past the RV sitting on the short section of shoulder marked as a slow-vehicle pull-off, Charlie gave the driver a cheery thank you wave. It was likely they'd saved their bacon.

"Jane's less than a minute outside Simpson," Bennett reported.

Charlie fumbled a little as she texted Lou, adrenaline making her thumbs feel large and clumsy. Despite that, she managed to pass on the message, receiving just a thumbs-up icon in response. "Can't wait to see what alternative plan they came up with."

"Knowing Lou Sparks," Kieran said wryly, "it'll be a doozy."

"Doozy?" Charlie teased. "Okay, Grandpa."

Before he could respond, they went around the last curve before passing the WELCOME TO SIMPSON sign.

Charlie felt a delighted smile stretch across her face as utter chaos, lit by the pink and gold dawn light, came into view. "I take it all back, Kiki. This is, indeed, a doozy."

"What are those?" Fifi peered through the windshield at the milling animals. "Sheep?"

"Goats," Bennett corrected.

"That's Millie Iverson's truck and trailer." Kieran nudged Charlie over to get a better view between the front seats, but she refused to budge. This was just gorgeous, so perfectly chaotic.

"And her goats." He paused before speaking again, sounding rather awed. "All of them."

An ancient pickup and even older stock trailer were parked diagonally across the street, blocking the road. A large herd of goats milled around, completely surrounding Bones's white car. Charlie peered through the VW's back window.

"I don't think anyone's in there," she said, her heart giving a thud of dread. A memory of searching for Jane in the forest behind their house popped into her head. After all this, would they end up just losing Jane on foot?

Fifi slowed the car, and Charlie hopped out even before it had come to a complete halt. She scanned the scattered groups of early-rising townspeople watching the commotion, but she didn't see Jane or any of the treasure hunters.

Nor, come to think of it, did she see any of the murder club ladies.

"Lou?" Charlie called, weaving her way through the goats. It was trickier than she would've thought, their warm, furry bodies pressing against her legs and then skittering off to the side, her clear path suddenly *not* clear anymore, and she tripped over a goat that definitely hadn't been there a half second earlier. The pavement flew toward her face as she fell, but then she stopped before hitting the ground, her face just inches from the pavement.

Craning her head around, she saw that Kieran had caught her by the back of her shirt.

"Thanks, Ki." She grinned at him from her awkward position. "That would've hurt *and* been especially embarrassing. You know that Fifi would've gotten a picture."

He just grunted, and she knew she had it bad, because the surly sound sent a rush of love through her.

"I love you."

He placed her on her feet and snorted an almost laugh. "Love you too. Let's find your mom."

"Charlie!"

That sounded like Lou. Charlie scanned the churning crowds of animals and onlookers before she spotted the waving woman, on her knees in a cluster of goats. "There she is!" Charlie waved back as she waded through the surging goats. Kieran followed, his hand still holding a fistful of the back of her shirt, as if to be ready in case the goats took her down again.

"Charlie!" Lou shouted excitedly when Charlie and Kieran drew close. "Look who we're sitting on!"

Charlie took a few steps closer, and the goats parted like a wiggly, fuzzy curtain, revealing Lou, Rory, Daisy, and Ellie—the entire Simpson Murder Club—all helping to keep a furious Jane pinned to the ground. Charlie grinned. "You guys give the *best* gifts."

Fifi and Bennett, having finally made it through the goats to Charlie's side, suddenly halted. "Is that Mom?"

"Kind of hard to tell under all the goat poo, isn't it?" Charlie laughed when Jane let out a frustrated roar at that. "Come on, Fifi. Our skip has a court date to make."

"I'm not the one you should be chasing," Jane insisted as they each grabbed one of her arms and hauled her to her feet. Fifi quickly pulled Jane's hands behind her back and cuffed her. "I don't have the necklace. Rhys or Bones must've lifted it off me. You can still catch them. They got out of the car at the same time I did, so they'll be on foot."

"Nah," Charlie said, her grip not loosening on Jane's arm. "They can keep it."

"Whaaat?" Jane's shriek held complete outrage. "That's *my* necklace! You can't just let them take it!"

"It's okay." Charlie made her voice as annoyingly soothing as possible, delighting when her mom gave an irritated huff in response. "After court, we can go to Target, and I'll pick up another necklace just like the one the fortune hunters have. We can even attach the nifty GPS tracker, if you like?"

"The…" Charlie saw the second realization hit Jane, and she took advantage of her mom's stunned silence to give Lou and her friends a wide grin.

"We owe you one, Murder Ladies. Thanks for all your help."

"Thank *you* for bringing some excitement to Simpson," Lou responded. "It's been so sleepy and boring lately. What's the point of having a murder club when there aren't any murders?"

The chirp of a siren interrupted the other women's chorus of goodbyes. Chris, Daisy's deputy husband, gave up trying to maneuver his squad car any closer and got out to wade through the goats.

"Everyone okay at the school?" Daisy called to him.

He nodded, looking annoyed. "False alarm." His sharp gaze landed on Jane. "Know anything about the bomb threat that was called in? Maybe to keep law enforcement out of the way while you were driving through town?"

Her mom's face was blank with innocent confusion—too

blank. Charlie knew that look. "Just let us get this court visit over, and then we'll bring her back to you for an interrogation," she promised Chris.

He gave a grim nod before looking around at the chaos. "All this to replace me?" he asked, looking a little proud of the fact.

"We'd better go if we're going to make it on time," Fifi said, and Charlie nodded. Flanked by Bennett and Kieran, they hauled their mom through the goat sea to Fifi's car and wedged Jane between them in the back seat. Bennett headed for the driver's seat, and although Kieran looked for a moment like he'd challenge the other man to a quick rock-paper-scissors game to determine the driver, he instead headed for the front passenger seat without saying a word.

With a final enthusiastic wave to the murder club ladies and all the early-rising residents of Simpson, Charlie turned back around and caught her sister's gaze across their still-quiet mother.

"We did it, Fifi."

"Of course. Never doubt our awesomeness, Charlie."

SEVENTEEN

"...SHOULD NEVER TREAT THEIR MOTHER the terrible way you've all treated me, especially you, Felicity. Putting *handcuffs* on your poor mother's wrists—and too tightly! You know I bruise easily. And you, Charlotte..." Jane shook her head sadly. "You used to be such a *sweet* girl. I don't know where I went wrong with all of you, to raise such vicious and ungrateful daughters."

"Mm-hmm," Charlie said absently, craning to look over Kieran's shoulder at the traffic in front of them—the very *slow* traffic. Jane had been going on in the same vipers-in-her-bosom way for *hours*, and her monologue had turned into white noise in Charlie's brain by the time they'd gotten ten minutes out of Simpson. "Is traffic stopped up there?"

Jane abruptly broke off, a tiny smile touching her lips. "Oh dear," she said with patently false concern. "We only have fifteen minutes. There's no way we'll make it in time."

Rolling her eyes, Charlie yanked open her door as soon as the car came to a complete stop. "We have eighteen minutes, and that's plenty of time if we run there." She hoped. They were six blocks from the courthouse. "C'mon, Fifi. Let's put our cardiovascular fitness to the test. You too, Kieran."

She scooted out, pulling Jane with her, and Fifi helped by pushing from the other side.

Jane squawked. "There's no way I can *run* the whole way. I have asthma."

"No, you don't." Charlie barely waited for Fifi and Kieran to join them on the sidewalk before taking off at a fast jog. "Norah has asthma. You're just lazy unless there's something sparkly at the finish line. Let's go. Pretend cops are chasing you."

She and Fifi bracketed their mom, each holding an upper arm and sweeping her along with them despite her reluctance. Without even checking, Charlie knew Kieran was close behind, guarding her back as usual. She felt the same spreading warmth in her chest, a sensation that was getting more and more familiar the longer she knew Kieran.

They dodged around slower pedestrians and strollers, crossing the street against the light and getting honked at. Charlie gave the irritated motorist an apologetic wave but didn't slow down. A small dog on a leash darted toward them, yapping excitedly, and Charlie jumped the furry hurdle easily. Her lungs were starting to heave with the effort of keeping up her speed, but she ignored the discomfort and ran even faster. Jane tried to lag behind, but she couldn't slow down without being dragged along, so she ran between them with a sour look on her face.

"Aren't you grateful for all the sprints I made you do?" Fifi asked, not even sounding winded.

"I'm always…grateful for you…Fifi." Charlie couldn't hide the way she was sucking air, and Fifi tsked.

"Sounds like we need to up our training—maybe sprints while carrying each other?" Fifi mused like the evil torturer she was. "That'd be handy in an emergency."

"I can teach you some of our firefighter training drills," Kieran offered.

If she hadn't been so preoccupied with running and not crashing into any innocent bystanders, Charlie would've shot him a glare. He'd *promised* to keep his mouth shut about that. Fifi didn't need any encouragement or new torture methods.

Apparently, Fifi didn't agree, since she literally squealed with excitement. "That would be wonderful! Thank you, Kieran!"

Charlie scowled, but she couldn't hold it, since she was trying very hard to breathe *and* because they'd actually reached the courthouse steps. "Time?"

"We have thirteen and a half minutes," Kieran reported as they ran toward the doors.

"Hang on a sec," Charlie gasped as she grabbed a handcuff key from her pocket. She unlocked Jane's cuffs, and then they were moving again, towing her through the doors and into line for the metal detector. The security guards didn't bat an eye at their red faces or labored breathing—well, *Charlie's* labored breathing—so she assumed they had a lot of people hurrying to make it on time to court. She dumped the cuffs into a tray before dashing through the metal detector, dragging Jane after her.

Jane glanced over her shoulder, her expression set in the sedate lines that Charlie recognized right away. Jane was plotting something, and that was never good.

"Do not," Charlie bit out. "You have used up all my patience—every single drop. If you try any kind of nonsense, I'm going to let security drag you into court, and then you're on your own. Or you can come quietly, behave, and things might just work out better than you expect."

Jane flashed her a resentful glare but stepped quietly through the detector, with Fifi and Kieran right behind.

"You found her!" Molly crowed from where she stood next to one of the courtroom doors, waving them toward her. Cara and Norah waved as well, jumping up and down as if greeting them at the airport after a long absence.

"When have we ever failed you?" Charlie asked.

"Well, there was that time—"

"Zip it." Charlie gave her sister a fake glare, too happy to see her to make a real attempt at it. "Or we won't show you the present we brought you."

"Mom's not enough of a present?"

"Nope." Charlie couldn't hold back a grin. "We're that good. Kieran?"

He grabbed the back of his sweatshirt and yanked it off. "Is *he* the present?" Molly asked. "Because although I appreciate the thought, Carmondy might have feelings about—*ohhh!*" She broke off as Cara and Norah gasped out loud.

Jane swore under her breath.

As Kieran posed like a surly model, the diamond necklace

around his neck caught the florescent light and reflected it back a thousand times brighter. Reaching up, he undid the clasp and let it slide off his neck.

Charlie couldn't stop grinning. "Think the judge will give Jane a deal if she returns the necklace and says that Zach Fridley forced her to help him steal it?"

"But—" Jane started protesting as she reached toward the necklace.

Fifi smacked her hand. "Nope. Not yours. Never was. Get in that courtroom and get our house back. And you're going to be signing the title over to us."

When Jane's lip curled, Norah stepped forward. "No. You're going to do it, or we won't offer to take responsibility for you. Sign over the house that *we* paid for and get cushy house arrest, or get sent to a dirty, crowded prison. You pick."

"You go, Norah," Charlie crowed.

"Fine," Jane snarled.

"Great." Molly smiled broadly. "Then let's get in there. It's time for court."

EPILOGUE

A MONTH LATER, AT THAT same courthouse, Charlotte Calamity Pax married Kieran Sullivan Byrne. The happy couple went out for dinner afterward with all of Charlie's sisters and their various and assorted men. Due to her court-ordered ankle bracelet, Jane wasn't able to leave the house to join them, which everyone except for Jane appreciated.

"A toast!" Molly announced in a voice loud enough to cut through all of the laughter and chatter. "To Charlie and Kieran— may they bring in all the skips and fight all the fires—respectively— but, most importantly, may they be very happy together."

Everyone's cheers almost—but not quite—drowned out Molly's tiny sniffle, but Charlie was relieved to see Cara hop up to pull their oldest sister into a consoling hug. Even though it was her wedding and her fault that Molly was overtaken by happy tears, Charlie was never a fan of hugs, and she'd already been bombarded by too many of them by her sisters since she'd married Kieran.

Fifi stood next, a wicked grin on her face, and Charlie knew the next toast would be as brutal as one of her little sister's workouts.

"Nope," Charlie said, standing up. "My turn to make a toast." When Fifi opened her mouth to object, Charlie pulled her trump card. "My day, my rules."

With a mutter of "Bridezilla," Fifi sat down.

Charlie blinked, realizing that she had to actually make a toast now that she'd foiled Fifi's plan of embarrassing her. "Okay, so here's to keeping Dad's house and having it officially belong to all of us." Everyone toasted, and Charlie was tempted to call it good and sit again, but it felt…incomplete. Other things needed to be said. "It's been an awful few months, but I knew we'd win in the end. That's what we Pax sisters do. So here's to my wonderful and annoying sisters, and all the men who make them happy. You're like the brothers I never wanted."

Everyone laughed as John, Henry, Bennett, and Dash lifted their glasses to Charlie. Molly and Cara were full-on bawling, and Charlie sat quickly before anyone could hug her. A heavy arm dropped over her shoulder, and a warm little shiver tripped up her spine as Kieran whispered in her ear, "Don't I get a toast?"

"You know, the longer I'm standing, the higher the likelihood of a long, drawn-out group hug, right?" When he just smirked at her—her third favorite expression of his—she heaved a huge sigh. "Fine. But if you get tackle-hugged by one or more of my siblings, it's on you."

This time, he left his hand on her lower back as she stood, and she reveled in the feeling. Even in this, he was watching her back.

"Finally, since he won't shut up about it…" Charlie peeked at Kieran and saw that he was grinning at her. She rolled her eyes even as her insides turned to warm goo. "To my husband. That first time I met you, when you screeched your truck to a stop so a fluffy squirrel could safely cross the street, I knew I'd eventually marry you. In this, like so many other things, I was right."

There were a few uncertain toasts to Kieran but more confused looks from everyone except her new husband.

"Of course I wouldn't run over a squirrel," he said, his brows furrowed at the thought. His scowl smoothed into a smile as he looked up at her. "And you are right about *almost* everything."

"Yeah, I am."

"It's one of the things I love about you."

Charlie felt her stomach dive and soar as, to her horror, her eyes started to prickle with tears. "Okay, okay. I love you too. Now let's shut up about it." She went to plop down in her chair before she started all-out bawling, but Kieran grabbed her hips and directed her to land in his lap instead. She was perfectly happy with this new plan.

Their food arrived before anyone could make any more toasts or declarations of love, to Charlie's relief. She forked up a bit of pasta, but before she could get it into her mouth, Fifi jabbed her in the side. The bite of food almost went flying from the force of Fifi's elbow poke, and Charlie glared at her sister.

Fifi was staring across the room, so she didn't even notice. "Isn't that Jim Jabsen?"

Norah turned around and peered at the man in question. "Yes. That's him." She turned back around and started eating again.

With an excited chortle, Fifi slipped out of her seat. "Well, don't just sit there," she said to Charlie. "Let's go get him."

"He's a skip?" Charlie felt a bit miffed she was out of the loop. She'd been a little preoccupied with Kieran for the past month, but she hadn't been *that* oblivious. Had she? She automatically got up with Fifi, trying to spot who her sister was looking at.

"Here." Norah held up her phone, showing the mug shot of an average-looking middle-aged man with pale-blue eyes and a snub nose. "He skipped out on a five-hundred-thousand-dollar bond."

"What'd he do?"

"Domestic assault."

Taking a mental picture of the mug shot, she turned to Kieran, who was calmly eating. "Go ahead," he said with a smile, making a shooing motion with his fork. "Be safe. Have fun. I love you."

Since that was pretty much word-for-word what she told him when he was went out on calls for his new job with the Langston Fire Department, she grinned back at him. "Love you too. And you know this'll be fun." Bending down, she smacked a kiss on his cheek and then scanned the room, spotting Jabsen at a table in the corner.

"Give us a holler if you need help," Molly said, taking a sip of wine.

"We'll be fine. The smug ones never expect us," Fifi assured her before looking at Charlie and grinning her anticipatory shark's grin. "Ready?"

"Always."

ABOUT THE AUTHOR

A fan of anything that makes her feel like a badass, Katie Ruggle has trained in Krav Maga, boxing, and gymnastics; has lived in an off-grid, solar-and-wind-powered house in the Rocky Mountains; rides horses; trains her three dogs; and travels to warm places to scuba dive. She has received multiple Best Books of the Month and a Best Book of the Year. Katie now lives in Minnesota with her family.

Website: katieruggle.com
Instagram: @katieruggle
Threads: @katieruggle

ALSO BY KATIE RUGGLE

Fish Out of Water

ROCKY MOUNTAIN SEARCH & RESCUE
Hold Your Breath
Fan the Flames
Gone Too Deep
In Safe Hands

ROCKY MOUNTAIN K9 UNIT
Run to Ground
On the Chase
Survive the Night
Through the Fire

ROCKY MOUNTAIN COWBOYS
Rocky Mountain Cowboy Christmas

ROCKY MOUNTAIN BOUNTY HUNTERS
In Her Sights
Risk It All

BENEATH THE WILD SKY
The Scenic Route
Crossing Paths